ALSO BY BRITTAINY CHERRY

THE ELEMENTS SERIES
The Air He Breathes
The Fire Between High & Lo
The Silent Waters
The Gravity of Us

if
you
stayed

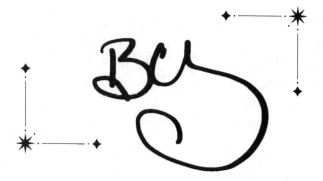

BCJ

BRITTAINY CHERRY

sourcebooks
casablanca

Published by Sourcebooks Casablanca, an imprint of Sourcebooks
P.O. Box 4410, Naperville, Illinois 60567-4410
(630) 961-3900
sourcebooks.com

Cataloging-in-Publication Data is on file with the Library of Congress.

Printed and bound in the United States of America.
LSC 10 9 8 7 6 5 4 3 2 1

For the hurting souls.

Grief is just love with no place to go.

—*Jamie Anderson,*
All My Loose Ends:
Nourish Your Roots (blog)

AUTHOR'S NOTE

This novel came from a place of compassion for women who have gone through very dark times and struggled to find the light after their hardships. I wanted to write a truthful story that dealt with tough subject matter to help anyone going through the same struggles as the heroine in this novel so they can know that there can be light at the end of the tunnel of darkness.

For those reasons, I'd like to note that parts of this story may be sensitive to a few readers due to the subject matter, which includes spousal abuse (verbal and physical), adultery, attempted sexual assault, loss of a child, and sizeism.

If you or anyone you love has been a victim of domestic abuse, please call 1.800.799.SAFE (7233) or text START to 88788. Or visit www.thehotline.org for help.

With love and nothing less than
every ounce of compassion,
BCherry

PROLOGUE

Kierra

NINETEEN YEARS OLD

Blood trickled down my forehead, landing on my slightly parted lips. I licked it from my mouth as I stared at Gabriel's mom, Amma, searching for any sign of forgiveness in her brown eyes. For any sign of understanding. I hunted for any evidence that she didn't blame me. That she could still see me as me and not as the monster who destroyed her family's life. That it wasn't my fault, even though I knew it was.

It was all my fault.

I kept searching Amma's expression for understanding, yet no sign of hope existed.

I saw the truth in her eyes. The moment she began to blame me. The second she let go of any form of love she had for me. I shivered from my soaked clothes as she stood still in front of me.

My body trembled in fear of her next words or actions as I stepped toward her. I felt as if I'd forgotten how to breathe, how to move air in and out of my lungs. Everything felt heavy and hard and confusing and…

What have I done?

"Amma…" I stopped as she held a hand up in front of me. With one shake of her head she told me everything she felt without uttering a sound.

She wanted me to stay away. She wanted me to drown in my misery while she suffered in her own.

"Are they…are they okay?" I asked her. "Are Elijah and Gabriel okay?"

"They're in surgery. They…" She shut her eyes and let out a pained cry.

Oh my goodness.

They weren't okay.

I was going to be sick.

The hospital lights flickered overhead as the aching of my heart intensified. Tears mixed with the dripping blood, blurring my vision. A whimpered sob broke from me as I shook my head and rushed over to her, tugging on her work uniform. Begging, pleading, praying for her forgiveness, for an update, for any evidence that somehow Elijah and Gabriel were all right. "I'm sorry, I'm sorry. Please, Amma." I sobbed uncontrollably. I wrapped my fingers tightly around the fabric of her shirt, tugging as if I were holding on for dear life.

"Let go, Kierra," she whispered. Tears rolled down her cheeks as she shook her head. "Let go."

"No," I whimpered, holding on tighter. Because I knew once I let go, the reality of the situation would sink in. I knew when I let go, I'd be letting go forever.

"Don't let me go, Amma," I begged. I wanted to bury

myself against her and search for comfort that I didn't deserve. I wanted to go back to yesterday, when everything was okay. When everything was filled with joy. When every breath wasn't so damn painful.

When she still loved me like the daughter she never had.

Before she could reply, her husband, Frank, came around the corner. He brushed his thumb against his nose and sniffled. "I just spoke with the doctor...and Eli... He didn't... He..." Before he could finish, Frank broke into sobs.

Amma let out a cry that pierced my ears as her knees began to buckle.

Elijah.

He didn't make it.

Elijah was Frank's son. Gabriel was his stepson.

Amma and Frank had met a few years ago at a group therapy for individuals who'd lost their former partners. Through the grief of those losses, they found comfort in each other and fell in love. From that love came Elijah, Gabriel's half brother.

Gabriel...

How was *he*?

What was the update on him? I needed an update on Gabriel.

Oh my goodness, Elijah didn't make it.

My chest felt on fire as Amma fell to the floor, howling in pain. Frank hurried over and wrapped her in his arms as they shattered together.

My breath caught in my throat as the panic of the situation hit me. I stepped toward Amma and Frank in an attempt to comfort them both, but Amma shook her hand toward me. "No!" she shouted. "Get away from us, Kierra! You did this! You killed him. *You did this!*"

I stumbled backward. When I looked into her eyes, I saw it. I saw all the heartbreak bleeding out of her. Frank raked his hand through his messy hair as the tears kept falling faster and faster. "Fuck!" he shouted, his rage mixing with his sorrow. A rage that wouldn't have existed if it weren't for me.

Elijah was dead. Gone. Once living, now gone. And he was gone because of me. All because of me.

Frank muttered the cussword one last time as he placed the palms of his hands over his eyes. This time, the word was filled with a kind of aching that I wasn't certain hearts could ever heal from—with a pain so deep that it seemed as if he'd be trapped within that heartache forever. It was quiet. A whisper of sorts. An ending. A final goodbye. "*Fuck.*"

"Leave," Amma ordered me. "Now."

I didn't know what else to do or what else to say, so I walked away. I walked out of the hospital, back into the snowstorm, and I paused in the middle of the parking lot. As I stood there, a car pulled up. The headlights shone on me, reminding me that I was still alive, but barely living. I should've been gone, not Elijah. It wasn't fair. It wasn't right.

Oh, Elijah…I'm sorry. I'm so, so sorry…

My parents flew out of the passenger's and driver's seats, looking straight at me.

"Kierra!" Mom shouted as she and my father rushed over to me.

"Are you all right?" Dad asked with a concerned tone.

The headlights kept shining, reflecting off the falling snow.

My parents didn't wait for a reply. The moment their arms wrapped around me, my knees gave out, and I crashed to the cement as uncontrollable sobs rippled through me. They held me tight as I kept saying the same words over and over. "I'm sorry, I'm sorry, I'm sorry," I whimpered, choking on each chilled inhalation.

"I'm sorry, I'm sorry, I'm sorry," I echoed as my parents tried their hardest to comfort and collect the breaking fragments of my soul.

Each breath grew more difficult, and each cry grew more intense.

Fuck.

1

Kierra

PRESENT DAY

Claire Dune was having a bad day. Or a bad string of days. She was convinced hers was a bad life. She'd sat across from me in my comfy chairs three times a week over the past few months to inform me just how bad a life she'd been living.

My notebook stayed in my grip as I listened attentively to each syllable that fell from her mouth. I studied not only her word choices, but also the way she moved when she expressed them. I had noticed over the past few months that her story seemed to grow ever more intense. I'd also noticed that if I didn't solely agree with her, she'd say I was acting just like her mother.

"You just don't get me," she complained as she flopped backward in her chair. "No one gets me."

"I get you, Claire. I see you, and I am learning more and more each time. I know I am still new to you, but I think we've had a few breakthroughs. I'm really proud of your progression over the last few weeks. Unfortunately, we are out of time for today."

She glanced up at the clock, grimaced, and then turned to me. "But I need to tell you more."

"Yes, and I am excited to hear more during our next scheduled appointment." I stood. "But these next few days, remember to make a list each day. Every time you have a negative thought, think of what the opposite thought would be, and try to sit in that for a while. To feel the opposite of—"

"*Dread?*"

I smiled. "Of whatever the emotion is. Then tackle it from there and see what steps you could take to get closer to that feeling."

"Fine. But if it doesn't work, I'm not paying my bill," she warned.

"Yes, well, that's not how this works. For now, though, enjoy your weekend. I'll see you next week."

She stood and dragged her feet. "If I make it that long," she muttered.

"You have to make it that long. Rumor has it that Kehlani is coming out with a new song next week."

She perked up slightly. "She is?"

"Yup. Just saw a post online. Plus, that new movie with Zendaya is around the corner. You haven't missed one of her movies yet, and it would be a shame if you started now."

Her thick brown brows knit, and she pushed out her bottom lip. She scratched the back of her neck. "Well, it wouldn't be very girls' girl of me if I checked out before supporting both of them."

"That's very true. And we are all about being a girls' girl,"

I said as I slightly nudged her. "Three things before you go, other than Kehlani and Zendaya."

"Ugh. Can't they count?"

"Nope. Three things that made you smile this week." At the end of every session, I have patients tell me three things that make them smile. It can be big things or small things. Just to help them see that there isn't only darkness around them. That there is still something good to seek in life.

She grumbled and pushed her fingers against her brows. "Fine," she said. "Well, my garden is all dug up. My neighbor helped me and he picked up some seeds for me to plant."

I raised my eyebrows. "Peter?"

"Yeah, Peter." Her cheeks slightly blushed. "It's just a nice gesture. Don't read into it."

I tossed my hands up. "Not reading into anything." Except that I was completely reading into it. Claire had told me she had a crush on her neighbor Peter for the past two years, but never had the courage to speak to him. This was a much bigger step than she realized. We'd revisit that next week.

"Oh! And I got a raise at work. Only a dollar more an hour, but that was good," she added with a small curve to her lips.

"Claire! That's remarkable and a big achievement. I know you were nervous to ask for the raise, but it worked out."

"Yeah. I guess people do need to speak up for themselves sometimes… Oh! I know my third thing." She was almost full-blown smiling as the memory came back to her. "My niece said her first word and it was 'Claire.'"

There was a flutter in my stomach at the mention of the little girl. "Oh my goodness. That's something worthy of making top three. She must love you so much."

"She does," Claire agreed. "She's a good kid."

"Who *loves* you," I added. "There are so many people who love you, Claire. And each of their worlds is better with you in it."

She grew slightly bashful and shrugged. "You're not that shitty at your job."

I laughed. "I guess that's why you keep coming back."

"Yes, I suppose so. But your free candy helps," she half-joked as she grabbed a piece from my desk. As she did, she paused and studied the photograph of my daughter, Ava. Her smile faded. "Is that your daughter?"

"She is."

"Is she one of your good things?"

I nodded. "She's the best thing."

"She doesn't really look like you," she observed as she tilted her head. "Does she look like her dad?"

I didn't reply, even though the answer was yes. My daughter looked more like her father than she'd ever look like me. Having Claire mention that fact made me sadder than I thought it would.

I smiled, not wanting to dive deeper into my private life. Ava was my daughter through my marriage to Henry. I'd known her since she was five years old. She'd just turned fourteen and was hands down the greatest thing that had ever happened to me. Still, I didn't want to overshare with Claire.

It was important to keep things professional. The more my clients knew about me, the worse off it could be.

Claire frowned. That wasn't uncommon for her, and I hated that it was that way. She had a remarkable smile whenever it appeared. "I always wanted kids."

"That's still an option."

"I don't know. I just don't see it sometimes for me." She shifted and nodded toward the photograph. "Is her dad like you?" she asked, her voice cracking slightly.

I raised an eyebrow. "Like me?"

"You know…" She crossed her arms over her chest and shrugged her left shoulder. "*Good.*"

I pushed out another grin, though this one didn't feel as great as the ones prior. "He loves his daughter." Her frown deepened, yet before she could reply, I said, "I'll see you next week."

"Yeah, right. Okay. See you next week, Kierra."

She left my office seemingly just as sad—if not sadder— than when she came in, which was hard for me to see. Yet I understood that breakthroughs looked different for everyone after a therapy session. Sometimes, people left in tears and feeling worse than when they came in. That was part of healing, though. Sometimes things seemed to be getting worse before they got better.

My mom always said resolving issues was like decluttering a house. You emptied all the closet spaces into the living room, making a big mess before organizing and clearing out the junk that was dragging you down. It was an important part of the process.

"Let go of what's dragging you, baby girl. Then you can walk more freely," Mom would always say when giving me advice.

It was solid advice that I revisited often.

Just as Claire had, I would remind myself of three good things that had kept me going over the past week:

1. Ava and I were going to eat a good amount of leftover birthday cake.

2. During lunchtime, I got free extra guacamole at my favorite Mexican restaurant.

3. We had officially moved into our new home a few months ago after buying a large plot of land, and the official build of our larger forever home was about to start there. We were currently living in an older house on the property until our home would be finished.

As I gathered my things to head home, there was a knock at my door. I looked up to see Joseph, one of the other therapists in our private practice, standing there. Joseph was the one who had opened Healing Waters Therapy Center.

Healing Waters used all different types of therapy to help our clients heal. Joseph's specialty was music and water therapy, which seemed to be remarkably helpful to many individuals. He was a genius at his job, and over the years he'd become one of my closest friends. Joseph was the definition of positivity, always able to put a spin of light on any situation. Plus, he was remarkably educated and easily one of the most intelligent individuals I'd ever known. We'd celebrated his sixtieth birthday at the office a few weeks ago, but with the way that man searched for adventure, one would've thought he was in his early twenties. Just last month he'd spent a week climbing a freaking mountain for fun. That was how I knew Joseph's idea of fun was different than my own. A week of fun for me included binge watching *Below Deck* in pajamas with take-out food.

"Are you off to finish prepping for your dinner party?" he asked.

"I am. I wish you were coming. Henry's friends and colleagues are boring," I half-joked. The parties my husband hosted weren't just mellow dinners. They were full-blown celebrations. I was pretty sure we've had dinner parties that were fancier than our own wedding a few years before. Fireworks and all. This one was even more exciting for Henry since it was the first gathering on our new land. Unfortunately, the parties always included Henry's friends and colleagues and not my own. Our groups were like oil and water: we didn't mix well. Where my friends were welcoming and inclusive, Henry's friends were, well, not. My best friend, Rosie, called Henry's dinner parties a pissing match for rich snobs to talk about who had the bigger yacht.

She wasn't that far off.

If I had things my way, dinner parties would include a *Below Deck* viewing party, in pajamas with Chinese food. Obviously. Toss in *Vanderpump Rules*, and we'd be staying up past midnight.

Joseph grinned, knowing how much I dreaded the parties.

"I would be there if I could. I'll make the next dinner party when I'm back in town."

I smiled. "Where are you off to this weekend?"

"Austin," he said. "I'm seeing an old friend who just had a baby. But trust me, I'd rather be at one of Henry Hughes's parties. Rumor has it, you have the best champagne."

"Only the best for my husband," I teased.

"That's why he has you," Joseph replied, nudging me in the arm before saying goodbye.

After he left, I took a few minutes to mentally prepare for the amount of socializing I would have to do that evening. Some people were gifted at entertaining big groups for hours while keeping their spirits high. Me, on the other hand? I always worked best one-on-one with individuals. It was one of the reasons I dived into my career. I loved to zoom in on individuals and learn how they ticked. With the big parties that Henry threw, there was a lot of drinking and many blunt personalities that I found hard to connect with on a deeper level.

I loved to go deep with people, yet those parties made that next to impossible. I found it hard to really get to know a person when there was so much chaos around. Still, I'd do what I did best: I'd pretend that I was happy and having a good time.

Otherwise, I'd end up arguing with Henry when the night came to an end. And by arguing, I meant he'd point out all the ways I was a flawed wife.

I was very careful about picking my martial battles.

Dinner parties were a battle I was willing to lose.

2

Kierra

Some people daydreamed about dinner parties. The perfect space with elegant floral arrangements. Gold silverware and plate settings. Classical music playing in the background. Guests dressed to the nines with wine and champagne poured at a ridiculous pace. There was such an elegance to dinner parties with wealthy individuals, yet the one thing that always seemed to be missing was the heart of it all.

My husband, Henry, was a perfectionist. He also happened to be one of the most brilliant minds in Maine, if not the world. But when my husband wasn't being a super genius, he was busy becoming my greatest heartbreak.

I met Henry Hughes during the hardest chapter of my life.

I had many regrets in life. Choosing Henry as my husband might've been among my top three worst decisions. I didn't love Henry anymore. Most days, I debated if I even liked him. I'd seen his red flags from the beginning, yet I'd chosen to quietly ignore them. A part of me at the time probably thought that was the love I deserved. A part of me believed I was lucky that anyone would want me—scars and all.

That was the problem with falling in love when you were out of love with yourself: even monsters looked appealing then. Some say that during the lowest moments of life a person can come across someone who will bring them their warmest summers or their coldest winters. Henry was my cold front, the chilling punishment during my season of despair.

We weren't in love; we were imprisoned in a loveless marriage. At least I had been. For the longest time, I'd figured he was my karma for the mistakes of my past.

Sometimes I wondered why I even bothered staying in a marriage as harsh as my own, but then I'd see her face—Ava Hughes. The greatest gift Henry had ever brought into my world. I feared deep down that if I left Henry, he would never let me see her again—and that was always enough to get me to stay.

Our daughter, Ava, was a professional at hiding out in her bedroom to read whenever a party was going on. I wished so deeply that I could hide away with her. With a book in my hand, of course. I'd choose fictional realms with dragons over reality with Henry and his friends any day of the week.

"Shouldn't you be getting ready to entertain your guests?" Ava asked as I walked into her bedroom with two slices of three-day-old birthday cake. We had just celebrated her birthday, and I was blown away by the fact that I had a fourteen-year-old.

"I needed a moment of solitude before everyone arrives. Cake?" I offered, plopping down on the edge of her bed.

"Always," she replied, taking her slice and diving right in. "You know, you could always tell Dad that you don't like dinner parties," she stated matter-of-factly. As if going against Henry's plans was ever an option. If he didn't get his way, he'd be a nightmare to deal with. I had to pick and choose my battles with him, which resulted in dinner parties and fake smiles at people who I could hardly stand.

"The dinner parties are fun," I lied.

"Liar," she replied.

Ava was a professional at reading me like an open book. Some days, I swore she knew me better than my husband did.

"It's a very important dinner, I guess," I explained.

"All of Dad's parties are important," Ava commented as she shoved a forkful of Funfetti cake into her mouth. "Because *he's* important."

She wasn't wrong. In addition to being brilliant, Henry was extremely important in his industry. He didn't think like other people, which was so refreshing when we'd first met. His business, Sweet, was a high-tech company that was taking home technology to a whole new place. It covered everything, and I mean everything. The latest technology used artificial intelligence to learn humans within their home, so it would know exactly when a person wanted a cup of coffee—before the thought even crossed their mind. They were also working on a system that used light to brighten people's moods in an instant.

While what he'd accomplished was impressive, I was kind of scared of how little control his technology seemed to give people. If artificial intelligence could be used to brighten a person's mood, it could probably be used for darkening a person's personality, too. I didn't like the idea of that, yet Henry simply told me that I wasn't informed enough to understand what he was doing.

Henry not only spoke to Ava and me about his technology. Often, his work also came home with him. And of course, my home was the laboratory to test everything out. I lived in a fully operating smart house that knew me better than I knew myself.

Though, sometimes I wondered about the coffee system. It felt very "which came first, the chicken or the egg" to me. Did the AI know I craved a coffee, or did I smell the coffee after it was brewed and then I craved it?

Either way, Sweet lived up to its tagline. *Let us take care of the small tasks so we can make your life Sweet.*

You couldn't go a week without seeing his name in the headlines. He was basically the next Steve Jobs when it came to innovation. He even went through a black turtleneck and blue jeans era when he started out.

Like I said, Henry Hughes was a brilliant businessman. He was a good father, too, when he wasn't traveling the world for business meetings. And when it came to his friendships? Top tier. That man was loved by so many that I was somewhat jealous of the version of him that the world received. I was jealous of every being that crossed his path. When my husband spoke to anyone, he spoke as if they were the center of his world. He revolved around them solely. And when I was present in front of others, I'd get flickers of that light. In front of others, I was his everything. I was the love of his life, his sun, his galaxy. Yet when those doors closed, I became his shadow.

It wasn't always like that. At one point, I thought he really loved me. Cherished me. Yet, those days seemed few and far between. Still, I put on a brave face as if I were happy with him because I cared more about keeping my relationship with Ava as strong as it could be. You see, Ava wasn't my biological daughter. I met her and Henry when Ava was five years old. She was the brightest light and had been the greatest gift to my life I'd ever received. Though, when Henry and I first went through a rough patch, he told me we could divorce but I'd never see Ava again.

That threat alone was enough to make me stay. A life without Ava was no life at all, to my mind. Even if that meant staying in a loveless marriage. I never complained around Ava about living in Henry's shadow because I knew how much she loved her father.

To be fair, I often wished I felt the same way about Henry that Ava did. Maybe I would've liked him and his dinner parties a lot more.

"How's the book?" I asked, shifting the conversation. "What page are you on?"

"Two hundred and ninety-five. Oh my gosh, Mom! You won't believe what Fania does."

"No spoilers!" I said, swatting her arm. "And how did you surpass me already? Maybe I should skip the dinner party and play catch-up..."

She laughed. "Your introvert ways are showing, Mom."

"Is it that obvious?"

"It is," she said. "You haven't even changed out of your pajamas yet. And people are arriving—"

The doorbell rang.

I glanced at my watch.

"Oh shoot!" I yipped, leaping up from the bed. "I have to go get my dress on."

"You're lucky that Dad picks out all your clothes for you," Ava said. "Otherwise, it would take you years to get ready."

I kissed her forehead. "I'll see you after dinner. I'll have Lena send you up a plate."

Lena was the chef that we'd used every weekday for the past few months. She was brilliant in the kitchen, and the one thing that wasn't run by some high-tech program. Though, sometimes Lena seemed a little *too* perfect. I wouldn't have been surprised if there was a battery pack attached to her spine. Still, I was thankful for Lena during the dinner parties. Most of the time, I snuck into the kitchen to talk to her instead of Henry's snobby friends.

Lena wasn't only an amazing chef, but she'd also grown to becoming one of my closest friends. Her bubbly personality made her feel like sunbeams on a chilled evening. My favorite pastime was gossiping to her about how ridiculous the dinner guests always were.

"Can you tell her to add extra spaghetti sauce to my pasta?" Ava asked.

"Will do, but I'm sure she's already aware."

Ava Hughes was always an extra-sauce-and-dip girl.

A woman after my own heart.

———————

"Where have you been?" Henry whispered as I walked down the steps to the grand dining room. He wrapped his arm around my waist and pulled me in for a gentle kiss to the cheek. He smelled like bourbon and cinnamon. The scent of the cologne wafted from his expensive gray suit. The apple-red dress he'd picked out for me paired perfectly with it. Though I would've loved to wear one of my original pieces. I'd spent much of my youth in the fashion industry, yet it had been a long time since I'd made pieces for myself and my husband. Henry said it was too on the nose to wear my own clothing line. Then he followed it up with saying he preferred well-known luxury designers.

What a charmer.

I couldn't remember the last time I used a sewing machine, let alone sketched a design. I missed that part of me a little.

"I had to get changed into the dress." I smiled at him, feeling his fingers dig a little too deeply into my side. He was irritated with my late arrival, but he wouldn't complain in front of an audience. "How do I look?" I asked, pulling away from him.

"Late," he replied with a cocky smile. He then gestured toward the room. "Go ahead and mingle. Freddrick's wife, Wendy, was asking about you."

I glanced around the room and put on a brave face. A robotic machine holding a tray filled with champagne flutes scooted over to Henry and me, pausing right in front of us. "Mrs. Hughes, can I offer you champagne?" the robot asked.

"Thank you, Jacob," I replied. I chose the champagne flute filled the highest. If I was going to make it through the night, I'd need to find a glass of champagne any chance I could get. I smoothed my hand over my slicked-back ponytail that had taken me way too long to straighten. My hair was normally tightly coiled and set at my shoulders, yet when I straightened it, it swept against my bra line. Mom always said my hair was drenched in our Black heritage, and each tight coil held the love of my ancestors who came before me.

When I was a kid, I couldn't stand my hair, though the older I grew, the more I learned to love it. It defined me and my personality. When I looked in the mirror, I saw my mother and grandmother staring back at me. I only straightened my hair for the dinner parties because Henry requested it straight. He thought it looked more sophisticated that way. I argued with him once about it, but he never let me win a fight. Somehow, I always ended up being the one to apologize after his clever word-game skills.

Henry caught my hand and reeled me back in for a kiss. "You look remarkably beautiful, Kierra."

His words dripped with sincerity in a way I didn't expect. I tilted my head, a bit dazed and confused by the gentleness in his voice. For a split second, the butterflies that used to gather for him when we were younger came back in full swing. His eyes were full of such care that I almost teared up from the sensation they sent throughout my system.

My lips parted slightly, and I hesitated for a moment, wondering if he was speaking to me. "Thank you, Henry," I replied, completely confused by the private compliment. I'd probably seemed as if I'd just witnessed a ghost. The ghost of my husband's past when he truly used to love me.

That was until someone behind me cleared their throat and said, "It's always nice to witness a man who cherishes his wife."

My pounding heart? It slowed its pace. There had been nothing private about that sweet moment. Shame on me for getting big feelings from something that was nothing more than an act.

"Oh, you made it," Henry exclaimed, shifting his stare to the person behind me. He then moved in closer to me and placed his hand back around my waist. He began to turn my body around as if I were one of his robots and gestured in front of me. "This is my brilliant wife, Kierra, and Kierra, this is Gabriel Sinclair, the outstanding man I was telling you about earlier."

Did he say Gabriel *Sinclair*?

As my gaze rose to meet the guy in front of me, my heart malfunctioned. My mind turned into a puddle of mush as I stared into his eyes. Eyes that I'd known a little *too* well once upon a time.

Brown eyes, beautiful dark-brown skin, and a full, thick beard paired with a remarkable smile.

A smile that I also once knew all too well.

There was no way…

Without any thought from me, the glass in my hand slipped through my fingers, shattering instantly as it hit the floor.

Everyone in the room turned to face me. Funny how a once-solid thing could fall apart so quickly. While all eyes were on me, my eyes were still on him. Gabriel Sinclair. *The* Gabriel Sinclair. *My* Gabriel Sinclair.

For a few seconds, I couldn't recall how to breathe. My chest tightened even more as his deep-brown eyes stayed on me. Every thought possible began to swirl through me. We held eye contact for mere seconds, but that was long enough to know he saw me. Yet at the same time, he didn't *see* me. He didn't remember me at all. He stared at me as everyone else had—as if I were nothing more than Henry Hughes's wife.

"Sorry," I blurted out to the room filled with fancy people in fancy suits who were all looking at me as if I were the clumsiest person in the world. I hurriedly shook my attention away from Gabriel, bent down, and began trying to gather the broken pieces. Within seconds, I felt a hand wrap around mine.

"It's fine, leave it," Henry stated, gripping my arm.

"No, I'm sorry. I didn't mean to make a commotion," I said with a shaky voice that mimicked my shaky soul. What was Gabriel doing in this room? What was he doing standing in front of me? What in the world was happening?

"Kierra," Henry growled through gritted teeth. "You're embarrassing me. I have Jacob on it. Don't worry. You should head upstairs and get changed." Of course, he said it with a smile. Henry always kept a smile around others. Though I knew I'd hear about my clumsiness later that evening after everyone headed off to their own homes.

I looked down at my wet dress and then back toward Gabriel. He had a look of pity packed in his stare, as if he felt embarrassment for me.

Just then, a beautiful woman with red hair walked over and stood extremely close to Gabriel. "Is everything okay?" she asked.

I was going to be sick.

Who was that?

Were they in love?

Did he love her?

Why did I check so quickly to see if they were wearing wedding rings?

They weren't.

But why, oh why, did I even look when there was a heavy ring resting on my own finger?

What was happening?

"Kierra," Henry urged as Jacob rolled over and began to vacuum up the mess. "Go change," he repeated.

I pushed out a smile toward Gabriel and the woman who seemed superglued to his side. "I'm sorry. How embarrassing. I swear I'm not always this clumsy," I explained.

Gabriel grinned. It was such a comforting smile. He rubbed the back of his neck and shrugged. "I'm probably the clumsiest person in the world. If my head wasn't attached to my shoulders, I'd probably lose that, too."

The woman laughed. A little *too* hard, if you asked me. She threw her head back and poked her chest out as she smacked Gabriel's chest with her palm. Henry laughed, too, but the tone of his chuckles was more a warning for me to get a move on.

I shook off my nerves the best I could. Which wasn't saying much. "I'll be back after I change, and I'll make a better second impression," I swore, before hurrying up the stairs to my bedroom.

After reaching my room, I shut the door behind me and held my hand to my stomach. The swirling taking place within me made me hesitate for a second. I swallowed deeply, but before I could finish, I was darting for the bathroom, throwing up the birthday cake I'd shoved into my system not that long ago.

I felt weak and dizzy in that moment.

I fell backward onto the black-and-white-tiled floor and wiped my hand against my mouth.

It was as if my past and present were merging.

Gabriel Ayodele Sinclair.

As I lived and breathed.

Within moments, every single flashback of that man and me came rushing back. Every laugh and tear that we'd shared hit me like a ton of bricks. He looked so different in so many ways, yet very much the same.

He looked so much like his father when we were young. Gabriel's mother was a beautiful Nigerian woman, and his father was an extremely handsome Frenchman. Gabriel was named after his father, and his middle name, Ayodele, was a Yoruba name that meant "joy has come home."

Joy has come home.

Gabriel looked like the perfect blend of his parents. His once slim frame had been replaced with quite an impressive build. He looked as if he'd spent the past two decades lifting automobiles for a fun pastime. His hair was longer, too. His midnight hair was shaved on the sides but longer on top and showcased a few of his curls. He wore thick-framed black glasses, and even though he was dressed in a stunning suit, I couldn't help but notice the neck tattoos that crawled up from his slightly exposed chest. It was clear he hadn't given up his love for ink since I'd last seen him.

We were only sixteen when I watched him get his first tattoo in the creepy basement of a friend's house. The stupid things kids did in their youth. I wondered if he still had the tattoos he'd gotten for me, or if he knew the meaning behind them.

He wore gold necklaces, one with a cross and another with an eagle symbol. The same necklaces that he wore when we were younger. They were his father's and he began wearing them after Mr. Sinclair passed away.

Gabriel was dressed in black from head to toe, but his eyes held so much light. A light I used to be so desperately in love with. A light that saved me time and time again. Still, those eyes hadn't held even a moment of recollection when they looked at me. It was as if to him I were nothing more than the wife of Henry Hughes.

Why did that make me feel so ashamed?

I unzipped the back of my dress and stepped out of it, still feeling lightheaded. After quickly brushing my teeth, I headed over to my closet to find something else to slip into. I grabbed a navy-blue fitted gown and switched into a pair of cream heels.

After touching up a little bit with makeup, I stared at myself in the mirror. "Just act normal, Kierra," I told myself with a slight headshake. "Don't be weird."

I said those words even though I knew the situation was going to be uncomfortable for me no matter what, because once I returned downstairs, I'd be placed in front of my husband and the first man I'd ever loved.

A first love who didn't even remember my name.

3

Gabriel

EIGHT YEARS OLD

She kept tapping.

Tap, tap, tap, her fingernails went against the wooden panels as she stared at me.

Tap, tap, tap, stare.

It was freaking annoying.

"Will you knock it off already?" I barked at the stupid girl who wouldn't stop gawking at me like a freak. She sat there with her big, brown bug eyes staring at me, as if she had no clue that I couldn't stand her. The only reason she was anywhere near me was because a year ago, the stupid new neighbors told my mom that Kierra was having trouble making friends. Mom, of course, thought I'd be the perfect person for that girl to be friends with, so she forced me to be friendly to Kierra.

I hated how parents always did what they wanted without caring what us kids wanted. The last thing I wanted to do was hang out with the weird kid with some kind of wire helmet on her head that connected to her braces.

A few kids in our class called her Brace Face. I didn't call her that. I figured that was *too* mean. But I really wished she'd stop staring at me like she was in love with me. A part of me wanted to tell her that I was forced to hang out with her after school, but Dad told me not to be a dick about it.

I didn't even know what being a dick meant. Mom yelled at him and smacked the back of his head for saying that. Then she told me to never say it, and that my dad was a bad influence. I didn't think he was a bad influence, though. I thought he was the coolest guy ever. I wanted to be just like him when I grew up. I wanted to take over his architect business someday, too, if I could, and I wanted to use the same kind of words he used all the time. So I'd spent the next day at school calling everyone a dick every chance I got.

"I mean it," I huffed at Kierra. "Stop it!"

"Stop what?" she hummed, curling her hair with her finger as she lay on her stomach in my tree house, kicking her feet back and forth in the air.

"*That,*" I urged, gesturing toward her. "Stop staring at me like you're in love with me or something."

"*I'm not in love with you!*" she spat out, seeming disturbed by the idea. She didn't have to sound *that* bothered by it.

"You don't have to be a dick about it," I muttered.

She pushed herself up to a sitting position. "I'm not a dick!"

"You sure do act like one."

"No, I don't!" She narrowed her eyes and crossed her arms as she huffed. "What's a dick?"

"*You,*" I said, only 'cuz I didn't exactly know how to explain it to her 'cuz I didn't exactly know what it was, either. All I knew was I didn't want to be stuck in my tree house with her for the next forever hours and always minutes.

"Well, you're a bigger dick!"

I leaped to my feet and marched over to her. "No, I'm not!"

"Yes, you are! You're the dickest dick that's ever dicked!"

"You don't even know what that means!"

"I don't care. I just know it's true. That's why you dress like a toad."

I gasped. "I don't dress like a toad!"

She nodded her head as she stood, standing a few inches away from me. "Uh-huh. You dress like the ugliest toad out there. If you had any common sense, you'd let me dress you, because I'm the best fashion person ever, but you must just like looking ugly!"

"Well at least I don't walk like a penguin!"

"I don't walk like a penguin!"

"Yes, you do! The other day I saw you get out of your pool and you waddled like a freaking penguin!"

"Well, jokes on you because I love penguins!"

"Good, Penguin!"

"Don't call me 'Penguin'! Just because I like them doesn't mean you can call me that."

"I can call you whatever I want! Now get out of my tree house, *Penguin!*" I ordered.

"I'll leave when I want to, Toad!"

"Shut up, why don't you? I didn't even want you to come into my tree house."

"Yes, you did."

"No," I hissed, "I didn't."

She stuck out her neck and waved a finger in my face. "Then why did you invite me over in the first place?"

"Because my parents made me, you bonehead! Your mom told my mom that you were a loser and had no friends, so my mom forced me to hang out with you!"

She gasped. "I'm not a loser!"

"You are. That's why you have no friends!"

"I don't want friends," she said. "I like being alone. People are annoying, like you!"

"Yeah, well, how about you go back to being alone!"

"I will!"

"Good!"

"Great!"

"Greater great!"

"Greater great, great!"

"Whatever, loser. Just go," I said, rolling my eyes. I was sick of her being in my space, breathing in my tree-house air. I hated that a girl like her was able to breathe the same air as me. I hated everything about Kierra Hughes, and I wanted her out of my life as soon as possible. "That's why you're weird with your brace face," I shouted to drive my point home that I wanted nothing to do with her.

I saw her eyes flash with tears, and I felt bad right away.

I was no better than the other kids.

I was such a dick.

Before I could apologize, Kierra puffed out her chest, made

a fist, and shoved it straight into my gut, making me fall to the floor.

"Ouch!" I blurted out, rubbing the elbow that had slammed into the wooden floor. "That hurt."

"That's what you get, you stupid boy! I never want to talk to you again."

Before I could reply, I heard Mom shouting from outside of the tree house. "Gabriel! Gabriel, get down here, will you? Kierra, you come down, too."

My stomach knotted up, knowing she was probably going to yell at us both for fighting. I pushed myself up. "See what you did? You got us in trouble."

"I didn't do anything wrong," Kierra stated as she climbed down the tree-house ladder. I followed her, ready to defend myself.

"It was her fault, Mom! She—" After I hit the last step of the ladder, I turned around to face my mom and stopped talking when I saw her eyes. She was sobbing uncontrollably as she shook her head back and forth. "What's wrong?" I asked. I'd never seen Mom cry, except for when she laughed so hard that tears fell down her cheeks. But this wasn't that kind of crying. This was the kind of crying that scared me.

She combed her hair behind her ears and hurried over to me. "We have to get to the hospital, Gabriel, okay? We have to go now. Kierra, I tried to call your parents, but they didn't answer, so you must come with us."

"Why are we going to the hospital?" I asked, confused.

"It's..." Mom's voice cracked. She sniffled and started

crying more. "It's your father, Gabriel. There was an accident. We have to go. *Now.*"

Kierra

Gabriel and I sat in the hospital waiting room with his mom. We hadn't said anything to each other, and as we waited, his mom paced back and forth. She kept glancing at the clock on the wall, then she'd move to the receptionist desk, ask for an update on Gabriel's dad, and then argue that she wasn't getting enough answers.

Then she'd pace again.

A few others waited in the same area as us. I'd never been in a hospital waiting room. I felt a little sick and scared.

I might not have liked Gabriel, but I liked his dad a lot. Mr. Sinclair was always sneaking me money whenever I'd come over to visit, since he couldn't give me candy because of my braces. "Save it up for some Sour Patch Kids and Skittles when you get your braces off. Then come share with me. Those are my two favorite candies," he told me.

I already had fifty bucks for candy thanks to him.

And whenever I'd get off the school bus, he'd ask me how my day was going and ask me about my designing and how softball was going for me. Those were two of my favorite things, fashion and softball. Gabriel played baseball, too, but I was actually good at it, unlike him.

Mr. Sinclair always made sure that I knew I was good, too. He even showed up to my games with my parents whenever he had free time.

I wanted him to be okay.

I *needed* him to be okay. If not for me, then for the toad sitting next to me.

Gabriel looked sad. Sadder than I'd ever seen anyone look. His head was lowered as he fiddled with his fingers in his lap. His legs kept bouncing up and down, and he hadn't said a word since we got to the hospital. I didn't say anything, either. I didn't know what to say.

I wondered what Mom would say if she were there. She was really good at making people feel better when they were sad, and even though I hated Gabriel, I didn't want him to be sad.

When the doctor finally came out to speak to Mrs. Sinclair, Gabriel and I looked up. We couldn't hear them from where we were, but I knew it was nothing good. The doctor's eyes looked sad and he shook his head.

"I'm sorry," I heard him say before Mrs. Sinclair dropped to her knees and broke into a howling cry. Gabriel darted over to her side and wrapped his arms around her. He held on to his mother tightly as she fell apart. He began to cry, too, and fell apart with her, so I did the only thing I could think to do.

I went to hold him because he had no one to hold *him* through the sad part. Everyone should have somebody to hold them during the sad parts.

As I listened to him cry, I started to cry, too.

It was a heart attack.

Mr. Sinclair's heart just gave out without warning. The doctors all tried their best to bring him back, but it didn't work. Mom said it was one of the saddest things that ever happened. Daddy didn't say much. He and Mr. Sinclair were good friends, and when Daddy found out about his death, he went into his study and didn't come out for hours.

A week later was the funeral for Mr. Sinclair. I sat between Mom and Daddy in the church pew, two rows behind Gabriel and his mom. The two of them sat in the front row. Mom said the front row was for the people closest to the person who passed away, which meant to me that it was the hardest row to sit in. I hoped I'd never have to sit in the front row… I hoped Gabriel would never have to do it again, either.

I couldn't stop staring in the Sinclairs' direction as I sat in the pew. Gabriel hadn't been to school over the past week. I didn't blame him. I wouldn't ever wanna go back to school if I'd lost my dad. I wouldn't want to do anything.

"You okay, sport?" Daddy asked as he leaned in to whisper to me.

I nodded.

He took my hand in his and squeezed it lightly. Mom took my other hand and did the same thing.

I could only see the back of Gabriel's head with his dark hair. He wore an all-black suit, like everyone else, and didn't raise his head to acknowledge all the adults who kept walking up to try to engage with him. At one point, his uncle tried to get him to go up to the open casket to say goodbye, but he refused to do it.

I was too scared to go up there, too.

The pastor did a speech, and some people shared stories about Mr. Sinclair. There was music, and after the service, they moved the casket to a car. Gabriel and his mother had to walk behind the casket, and I thought that was kind of evil to make them do. I thought at any second they both would've fallen down from being so heartbroken.

At one point, Gabriel looked over to me, and his eyes were so red and flooded with tears that I started to weep, too. I didn't know why, but over the past week, whenever I saw Gabriel cry, I'd start crying. It was like his tears sparked something in me that made my chest hurt so much that I was forced to cry, too. Before that, I didn't know my tears could match another's.

At the end of the burial, everyone tossed a rose on top of the casket, and they lowered it into the ground.

"*No, no, no,*" Mrs. Sinclair wailed as that happened. She dropped to her knees and reached out for her husband, and it broke my heart that Mr. Sinclair wasn't there to reach back out toward her.

I didn't understand death. How could it be so cruel?

Gabriel stepped up and took her hand, though.

"It's okay, Mom. It's okay," he told her, even though I wasn't sure he believed that himself. How could he believe that it was okay? He no longer had a dad. But still, he tried his best to make sure his mom was all right.

Maybe that was when I started to hate him a little less.

Maybe that was when I started to wonder who was making sure he was all right if he was in charge of making sure his mom was all right.

I didn't mean anything against Mrs. Sinclair when I thought that, but it seemed she was hardly able to keep herself together, let alone her son who was being forced to grow up a lot faster than he should've been. I had a feeling Mrs. Sinclair would never be the same after that. Maybe that's what death did to the people who were still stuck being alive—changed them forever. I didn't know if that was a good or bad thing.

Gabriel

"Gabriel Sinclair! Get back in here. And you will stop slamming these doors, young man. Do you understand me?" Mom yelled as she followed me out to the backyard. I didn't say another word to her. I was sick of it all. I was sick of her telling me to do my homework. I was sick of her trying to do the stuff with me that Dad always did. I was sick of her asking if I wanted to play catch with her. I was sick of it all! I was mostly sick of Dad being dead, though.

How could he do that?

How could he die?

I hated him for that! I hated him so much that it made me want to explode.

I glanced to my left and saw Kierra sitting in her backyard on her tire swing, and for some reason, that made me mad, too. I hated how she looked at me lately. As if she felt bad for me. I much preferred it when she was busy calling me a toad. I didn't want her to feel bad for me. I didn't want her to feel *anything* for me because I *hated* her. I hated how she had two parents. It wasn't *fair*. Nothing was fair anymore.

I shot her a dirty look before stomping my feet to my tree house. The tree house that Dad had built for me. I climbed the ladder and ignored Mom the whole way up. When I reached the tree house, I felt as if I was going to cry. Or shout. Or shout and cry. I felt so much and I didn't know what any of it meant, which made me even angrier.

When I heard someone climbing the ladder, I was certain it was Mom coming to tell me to head back inside and finish my homework. But instead there was Kierra and her stupid face storming into my space.

"You can't be mean to her!" Kierra yelled at me as she stepped into the tree house. "You can't talk to your mom like that!"

"It's none of your business," I said as my chest rose and fell.

"You're making her really sad, Gabriel. You need to knock it off now."

"Who are you to tell me what to do?" I grumbled, annoyed with her stupid face that for some reason made my stomach feel weird whenever she looked at me. I kicked the baseball on the floor across the tree house because I was so annoyed. The baseball wasn't even supposed to be in the tree house. It was supposed to be in Dad's glove in the backyard, so we could play catch together.

Kierra stood tall, even though she was short. "I'm me! And I get to tell you when you're acting like a stupid boy."

"Whatever, Kierra. Leave," I huffed, feeling my eyes start to water up. I wished that would stop happening so much. But whenever I felt anger lately, I'd feel like crying, too. And I always felt angry, which meant I always cried, too.

Kierra must've noticed because she got quiet. I didn't even know she had the kind of mouth that could shut up. Most of the time, she was just yap-yap-yapping about nothing.

Now, she was quiet.

Freakishly quiet.

Next, she did something I didn't expect her to do.

She hugged me.

Then, I did something I didn't expect to do.

I hugged her back.

I didn't understand why, but something about Kierra's hugs made me feel safe. I hadn't known I felt unsafe until her arms wrapped around me, just like when we were in the hospital the day Dad died. Most of the time, I didn't want anyone to talk to me, let alone hold me. But when Kierra hugged me, I felt like I could breathe again. It was like her hugs reminded my heart to continue to beat.

She held on for a long time, and I didn't try to pull away. I wanted to stay there with my arms wrapped around her for five more minutes. For ten more minutes. For sixty more minutes.

As long as she'd hold me, I wanted to hold her back.

"Gabriel?" she whispered as we kept embracing.

"What?"

"Want to play catch?"

I stepped back and wiped my eyes with the back of my hand. "Are you any good at catch?"

She shook her head. "Nope."

"*Fine.*" I grumbled and rolled my eyes as I picked up Dad's baseball. "I'll show you, but if you suck, I'll tell you."

"If you tell me I suck, I'll tell you that you have a big nose, Toad."

I smiled. Maybe for the first time in weeks because for a moment everything felt normal again. "Deal. Come on, dick."

4

Kierra

PRESENT DAY

"What took you so long?" Henry whispered as I emerged back at the dinner party. He eyed me up and down once before grimacing. It was clear he wasn't a fan of my outfit change, but he couldn't say that in a crowded room with his associates and friends.

"Sorry. I had to find something different to wear." I smoothed my slightly shaky hands over my gown as my eyes glanced around the room, searching for Gabriel. When my stare returned to Henry's, I allowed a small fake smile to slip out. "How do I look?"

"Like you aren't even trying," he whispered before linking my arm with his. "Let's try this one more time. And I'd prefer if you didn't make such a scene this go-around."

"Yes, dear," I sarcastically remarked. "I'll be your perfect little robot."

Henry pinched my arm slightly in response to my remark, and I yipped quietly, but I didn't say another word. He led us over to where Gabriel and his redhead were situated. My stomach instantly began to twist once more as we stood in front of the two.

"Let's try this introduction again," Henry smiled, nodding toward Gabriel. It was unsettling how quickly my husband could seemingly shift his whole mood when others were around. It was as if his perfect mask was always in place except when he and I were alone together.

"Sweetheart, this is Gabriel Sinclair of GS Architecture, and Ramona, his associate," Henry said.

Associate?

Not his girlfriend?

The way my stomach slightly unknotted from that news should've been a big warning sign.

"And this is my beautiful, brilliant, successful wife, Kierra," Henry continued.

"I could get used to that kind of introduction," I half-joked. If Henry always treated me the way he did in front of others, I would've been head over heels for the man. It was the private conversations that made me despise him. The hardest thing about my husband was how he looked at me in front of others compared to how he acted toward me in the privacy of our lives. I'd never met another man who acted like heaven in public but in the shadows felt so painfully like hell. He was the definition of a handsome devil.

I held my hand out toward Ramona first. "It's nice to meet you both."

"The pleasure is all ours," Gabriel said as he reached his

hand for me. As his palm linked with mine, a pool of heat gathered in my stomach and I worked like heck to keep tears from falling from my eyes. I probably held on to his grip too long. I probably left his hand moist from how much my own had been sweating. I'd probably appeared like a deer in headlights as our eyes locked together. Still, I couldn't look away.

He dropped my hand.

I instantly missed his warmth.

I rubbed my sweaty palm against the side of my dress and forced another smile. "And how do you three know one another?"

"I told you," Henry said. "He's the head architect on the build."

My jaw slackened. "You mean he's *the* Gabriel?" I asked, stunned. I turned back to Gabriel. "Henry says you're one of the top three greatest architects in the whole world."

Gabriel laughed the kind of laugh that made his left dimple deepen as if it had been carved out by Michelangelo himself. "I'd hate to know who the other two are. I'm a jealous man and would turn it into a competition to be first."

"My wife didn't mean any harm by the comment," Henry urged. "Sometimes she speaks without thinking."

Oh, screw you, Henry.

I smiled. "Yes. I didn't mean anything bad by it. It's very impressive."

Gabriel's hand brushed against his slight beard. "I took no offense. I'm not that sensitive. And thank you. That means a lot to me. I'm surprised we haven't met yet. Henry has spoken so highly of you."

I wasn't surprised that we hadn't met. Henry left me out of many things. I didn't even know the building plan for the new property was ready to go until a week ago. A construction team showed up to clear the land of trees, rocks, and debris. I had to force Ava to stay out of the way because she was so intrigued by construction and architecture. Buildings fascinated her even more than novels—which was saying a lot.

Gosh, Gabriel looked remarkable. So grown up. I'd never envisioned him with facial hair when I was younger, but it worked well for him. He looked so…adult. A handsome adult with a full beard. I bet someone was in love with him. How could they not fall in love with a face and stature like that? He was tall, dark, and handsome. And he definitely no longer dressed like a toad.

Armani now, it appeared.

"An architect," I muttered, amazed. "You always wanted to be an architect." The three looked at me confused. I shook my head. "Sorry. I meant that as a question. Did you always want to be an architect?"

I knew the answer because I knew him.

The answer was yes.

Just like his father.

"Yeah, for a long time. My father was an architect. He passed when I was young, and unfortunately I don't remember much of him. I was in an accident as a teen and suffered from memory loss."

"Oh?" I breathed out, pretending I didn't know every freaking detail, which I did because I was there the night it happened.

"Yeah." He smiled, but it felt a bit sadder. "But from the stories my mother told me, I looked up to my father quite a bit. It only seemed right to take after him. I studied his blueprints for a long time. They're framed in my office. He was a genius. I just hope I'm making him proud. Even though I don't remember much about him, there's still something in me that wants to make him damn proud."

"He loved you so much," I blurted out.

Again, strange looks from the three.

Luckily for me, Lena appeared from the kitchen and said, "Sorry to interrupt, but dinner is ready if you'd all like to take your seats in the dining hall."

Saved by the roasted chicken, creamy pasta, and mashed potatoes.

Henry gestured for Gabriel and Ramona to head in the direction of the dining room, guiding me behind them. He leaned in and whispered, "What the hell is wrong with you?"

I managed a tiny smile and shook my head. "Sorry. Tired."

"Well, wake up. You're embarrassing me."

Henry, Ava, and I lived on more than fifty acres of land. When we bought the property, there was only the smaller house on it. Living in that house had been fine, especially after all the issues we'd had with people stalking my husband. After those scary moments, I'd rather only a few people knew where we lived. I'd never forget the night I went outside and found a hooded woman dumpster-diving in my trash bins. She ran before I could see her, and our cameras didn't have a good angle on her face, but it wasn't the first time we'd found people lurking. The downside of being married to a visionary like Henry was that he came with both enemies and fanatic fans.

I felt comfortable knowing our safety was intact. Sometimes, I argued with Henry about how hosting such extraordinary dinner parties put our solitude in jeopardy. With how his parties went, I was certain it wouldn't take long for people to find our new location.

He told me I was being too dramatic and that the security cameras on the property were the best of the best, since he'd created them. He believed we just needed more space to improve our safety, not fewer drunken parties.

Even in our current house, we had been able to host gatherings with twenty individuals for dinner, so I supposed "smaller house" was in the eye of the beholder.

Based on Henry's vision for the new home, we'd easily be hosting hundreds at our parties. I worried living in such a large house would lead to a cold, lonely feeling when the parties weren't taking place, but Henry didn't much care about my thoughts on that. I'd tried to convince him that bigger didn't always mean better, but he'd told me I didn't have much say on the subject because he had a vision.

His vision was of building the largest high-tech smart

home known to mankind. He'd worked on finding the right architect for the build, and lo and behold he'd found Gabriel.

My Gabriel.

My once-upon-a-time Gabriel, that was.

All through dinner, I'd forced myself to not stare too long at Gabriel, looking his way just enough to make it seem as if I wasn't completely avoiding eye contact. It was hands down the most uncomfortable dinner party of my life, and I'd once had dinner with a group of surgeons who loved to tell gruesome stories over a casserole.

After dinner, the crowd would converse for a few more hours over music. Henry had hired a jazz musician for after-dinner entertainment, and I was almost certain there would be a fireworks display. There were always fireworks at Henry Hughes parties.

I hated fireworks. They always made my skin crawl.

The house was ringing with laughter, yet I felt so thrown off and sad.

So achingly sad.

After one too many surface-level conversations, I excused myself to take a walk outside. I was in desperate need of fresh air to clear my clogged thoughts. There was such a big part of me that had left Gabriel Sinclair in my past. I'd buried him away in my mind after his mother forbade me to ever see him again.

And now here he was.

The late-spring air brushed against my skin as I stood outside, breathing in the scents of the trees surrounding me.

The sun had set a few hours prior, and the only light was streaming from the house. The louder the laughter grew in the distance, the more bourbon was being poured. Henry was probably wasted by now and about to start playing the piano. I was sure he'd delivered one of his speeches, too—a speech that usually went on too long.

I liked the stillness of the land whenever I explored it alone. I liked the calmness of it all after living in the city for so long. There was something so peaceful about the quietness of the earth when no one else was around. I liked waking up and enjoying my coffee as the sun was just beginning to yawn awake, and the birds quietly sang their morning songs.

Henry joked that we lived on so much land that if we screamed, no one would hear us. I believed that to be true.

"You're currently standing in the kitchen," a voice boomed, shaking me from my stillness. I turned around to find Gabriel standing there. He smiled a little and gestured to the ground. "And if you take a few steps to the left, that will be the butler's pantry."

My confused heartbeat began to slow slightly. I stepped to my left. "Here?"

He walked over, placed his hands against my shoulders, and moved me two more steps to my left. "Here."

I smiled. "It's very nice butler's pantry."

"Very nice indeed." He slipped off his suit jacket and placed it over my shoulders. The breeze was chilly for the late-spring night, and he must've noticed my slight shiver.

He then rolled up the sleeves on his button-down shirt.

That wasn't surprising. Gabriel always ran hot-blooded. I swore he could go outside in the middle of a blizzard and complain that the snow felt warm.

He brushed a finger against his nose before pointing out into the distance. "Right there will be the primary bedroom with his-and-hers closets."

"I won't tell on you if you make my closet a *little* bigger than his," I joked.

He leaned in toward me and whispered, "It's already bigger."

"I knew I liked you."

He smiled, that dimple returning, and my body tingled all over. Gosh, I'd missed his smiles. I didn't know how much I'd missed them until they returned to me that evening. Gabriel's smiles were warm and lazy at the same time. As if smiles were just something he so easily crafted. His smiles felt like stable, expected love—so sure and effortless.

Though his proximity did bring me a whirl of emotions. Our closeness only made me want to lean in toward him more. I wanted to feel the warmth that radiated from his mere existence. He seemed so…happy. Confident too. That pleased me, because the last time I saw him, it was the opposite of that. Gabriel had grown into his own happiness. I couldn't think of a soul who deserved that more.

Who did he share that joy with? Who currently received the ghost of my past love?

"And what about here?" I asked, darting away from him and shaking off the butterflies that had no right to be forming in my gut. I placed my feet against solid ground.

He slid his hands into his pockets and arched an eyebrow. "That's the family room."

"And here?" I asked, moving to the right.

"The meditation space."

"Do you meditate?"

"Every morning before yoga."

I arched an eyebrow. "You do yoga?"

"It's good for my body and soul. Without it, I'd probably be as stiff as a board."

I laughed. "I tried to get Henry into yoga. He said that was a woman's fluff thing."

"Henry mentioned the meditation room was for you and your yoga."

"Yes, it was my only request. He took over the rest of the planning process, but I was determined to have a room just for me."

"Good for you, Kierra. You deserve that."

I didn't know why, but hearing my name roll off his tongue made me want to cry. So I moved again.

"Oh, oh, and here?" I asked, taking large strides across the empty plot of land.

"That is…" His brows knit and he tilted his head as if trying to recall his master plans for the property.

"It's okay if you don't know. I know it's almost impossible to remember it—"

I stopped speaking because he held up a hand. "No, I know this," he stated. He scrunched up his nose. "The only problem is I think you're standing in two places at once. Your left foot is in the family room, while your right is in the dining hall."

"I always wanted to be in two places at once."

"That's very *A Walk to Remember* of you," he joked.

I arched an eyebrow. "You know the movie?"

Of course, he did. I'd made him watch it a dozen times with me when we were young. He hated it, but he always watched with me. Did he remember it, though? Did he remember me? Is that why he'd brought it up? As a sign that he knew who I'd been and he was quietly trying to tell me? Is that why he came outside to find me? To tell me that he—

"My last ex was in love with it," he said.

The slight hope I'd had deflated instantly.

Why did I feel like crying again?

I wanted to shoot a million and one questions toward him that I knew he couldn't answer. Trillions of thoughts bombarded my mind as I stared into the eyes of a man who once knew me. How did he handle losing his brother? What was it like when his mother told him what happened to Elijah? I wanted to ask him everything, but I didn't know what lines were mine to cross. The last time I saw his mother, Amma made it clear that she wanted me to have nothing to do with her son. She made me promise all those years back that I'd stay away. It was the hardest promise I'd ever had to keep, but it was the least I could do after the harm I'd caused. I felt as if I didn't deserve Gabriel, not his love and not his friendship.

Yet there he was, standing right in front of me, reminding me of every memory we've ever made. An avalanche of emotions rushed through my system as the memories were unlocked, and he didn't seem to remember a single one. A million questions fluttered through my mind about him and who he'd become while he stared at me as if I were nothing more than a stranger.

Are you currently in love with someone? Who last broke your heart? Do you still brush your teeth with your nondominant hand? Did your mother open her bakery? Do you still think you dream in color? What's your favorite dinner spot nowadays? Do you have any pets? Do you still play baseball for fun? What's your best memory from the past twenty years? How do you deal with failure? When was the last time you cried? Do you remember anything from your past? Did any memories come back? How much did it hurt to learn about Elijah's passing? Is your heart okay? Has it healed? Do you remember me somewhere in your subconscious? Even small, minuscule details of us? Are there fragments of me lingering within your thoughts? When you look at me now, does your heart unwaveringly skip a few beats?

Gabriel took a step toward me, with his hands still in his pockets. His strides were direct and his eyes were packed with intent as he moved in closer. "I have an odd question for you."

I swallowed hard. "Okay. Shoot."

"Do we…" His voice faltered. He shook his head slightly. "Do we—"

"Gabriel," was called from the direction of the house. I turned to see Ramona walking toward us with jackets in her hands. Gabriel took a step away from me. He shook off the thought as he turned toward Ramona and gave her a smile.

She moved in closer, slightly out of breath. "I got our coats. We can head out." Her blue eyes moved over to me and she glanced around. "Was Gabriel telling you about his plans?"

"Yes, he was. It's going to be amazing."

"Trust me, you have no clue. He's a master," she urged, nudging his arm.

Oh.

She was in love with him.

I wondered if Gabriel knew it.

Ramona stayed close to his side. "But we should get going, since you have a big day in the office tomorrow."

"You work on the weekend?" I asked, somewhat surprised.

"It's busy season," he replied.

"Every season is busy season," Ramona countered. "Gabriel is a bit of a workaholic. I try to get him to take vacations but his mind doesn't shut off." She held her hand out toward me. "It was wonderful meeting you, Kierra. Thank you for letting us come to one of *the* Henry Hughes dinner parties. They are as legendary as I've heard them claimed to be."

I shook her hand. "I'm glad you enjoyed yourself."

"That's the understatement of the year. It was remarkable. Can I ask... What is it like being married to the future of technology? I can hardly process how incredibly wise Henry is. And handsome, too. It must be a gift to have such a man to call your husband."

I chuckled quietly. "It's interesting to say the least. Henry is very gifted. There's no getting around that fact."

"And handsome," Ramona insisted once more.

Gabriel frowned and took his coat from Ramona. "Thanks again for having us, Kierra." He held his hand toward me, and I shook it. "I'm positive we'll be seeing a lot more of each other over these next few months."

"I look forward to it," I said. "I hope you both have a great evening."

They thanked me and began to walk away. I studied Gabriel the whole time until I went to rub my arms and felt his jacket against me.

"Oh, wait! Gabriel!" I called.

He looked over his shoulder and saw me waving his suit jacket in the air. He whispered something to Ramona, and she nodded before continuing toward the front of the house where their car was waiting. Gabriel walked over toward me.

"Sorry, I almost stole your jacket," I said, handing it over.

"Not a problem. And I do apologize for Ramona's comments on Henry. I blame it on one too many glasses of wine."

"No worries. Henry is handsome. I hear it all the time. Plus, our dinner parties do have quite an array of alcohol flowing. It's part of the Henry Hughes experience. Most of the time, guests arrive in their own cars and are sent off in taxis."

Gabriel didn't smile this time. I wasn't even certain he was completely taking in my words. He hesitated as if falling back into thought. His mouth parted and then he said, "This is going to sound crazy, but I swear I've seen you before?" He asked it as a question.

I swallowed hard. "I—"

He narrowed his eyes and shook his head. "Do you get coffee from Florence Bakery?"

My gut dropped. I nodded my head. "I do. Every morning before I go into work."

He snapped his fingers. "That's it. That's where I've seen you before. I go every morning, too."

We've crossed paths in Florence Bakery before? How many times? Have we bumped shoulders before? Has his arm grazed mine? How many months have we been in the same room, breathing the same air? How have I not noticed him? Sure, Florence is normally packed, but still… I can't believe that for months I may have been so close to him, but still so far away.

It pained me slightly, seeing that he'd only recognized me from the bakery. It was clear he didn't recall me completely. It was clear that Amma made sure to never share anything about me with her son. A part of me resented that, but a bigger part of me understood. I'd already taken so much from their lives. The least I could do was keep the promise I'd made to Gabriel's mother during the darkest season of her life. Especially when those dark days were caused by me.

Besides, Gabriel seemed good. He seemed happy. I feared if he learned about his and my connection, it would only add confusion to his life. I didn't want that for him. All I wanted, all I ever wanted, was for him to be happy. Even if that meant he'd never have any memories of me.

"They have great coffee," I said, uncertain of what else to express.

"And cinnamon muffins."

I smiled. "I always get their cinnamon muffins. I get there extra early to get one, because they always sell out. I've never *not* gotten a cinnamon muffin from them."

He gasped. "Never?"

"Never."

"I have cried for hours over losing out on the muffins," he teased. "And now I'm almost certain it's you who is getting the last one before me."

I shrugged with a smug look of pleasure. "That's on you for showing up too late. Step up your game."

"That sounds like a challenge."

"All I know is I'm never going without my muffin. I will throw elbows for that dang thing. It makes my mornings that much brighter."

"So you work in the city?"

"I do. I'm a therapist."

"Oh." He nodded. "That makes sense."

I chuckled. "Does it?"

"It does."

"Why do you say that?"

"Because I'm pretty good at reading people. I study people all the time. I'm a professional at two things—architecture and people watching."

"Is that so?"

"It is." He smirked. "And you give off therapist vibes."

I narrowed my eyes. "I don't know if that's a good thing or a bad thing."

"It's a good thing," he said. "A very good thing."

"What exactly are the therapist vibes I give off?"

"Well…" He rubbed his cheek. "When you talk to people, you *really* talk to people and listen as if it's a late-breaking news story. You look at them as if the most important conversation ever is taking place. I saw you inside earlier talking to Marc Christian about rocks for a solid fifteen minutes, and you looked so intrigued."

"It was a very interesting conversation. I love to talk about a grown man's rock collection," I joked.

"It wasn't interesting at all, and Marc has a very monotone voice. I fell asleep eavesdropping."

"I thought I heard someone snoring."

"It was when he spoke about his rock polish. He said that, and away I went." He made snoring sounds, making me break into laughter.

Gosh, in the past few minutes, he'd made me laugh more than Henry had in the past three years. "What can I say? I like to know what people are thinking. Even if they are thinking about rocks," I said.

"Sounds about right, Mrs. Therapist."

Before I could reply, the sky was lit with fireworks. Our eyes instantly drifted up, and the lazy smile on Gabriel's face returned. As he studied the sky, I studied him.

"Don't read me, Mrs. Therapist," Gabriel whispered, feeling my stare on him. "My thoughts are a little messy and jumbled in my head."

"That's my favorite type of novel."

"Oh my gosh, Gabriel! Look! Fireworks!" Ramona said,

reappearing out of nowhere and pointing at the sky. She'd somehow returned with another glass of champagne.

Gabriel gave Ramona a thumbs-up as she swung around, her dress swirling, and stared as if the sky had just exposed a new dimension. So many *ooh*s and *ahh*s.

"I better get her home," Gabriel murmured. "I hope you have a good night, Kierra."

He began to turn away from me, but before he was too far gone, I called out to him. "Gabriel?"

He turned back in my direction, and my stomach fluttered as I rediscovered his gentle eyes. "Yes?"

"Are you happy?"

"Happy?"

"Yes. Sorry, I know it's a super-random question, but I'm just curious. Are you happy with your life?"

He raked his hand through his hair. "Life has its ups and downs, but I lean toward happy."

My troubled heart found comfort in that response. "Keep leaning that way, okay?"

The warm, lazy smile returned to his full lips. "I'll do my best. Have a great weekend. Maybe on Monday I'll beat you to the last cinnamon muffin."

"Don't threaten my life like that, Gabriel."

"'May the odds be ever in your favor,'" he said as he bowed slightly, delighting me with the surprise Hunger Games reference.

He began to walk away. And for a moment, I considered showing up at Florence Bakery and waiting all morning solely to fight Gabriel over the last cinnamon muffin.

5

Gabriel

"Gosh, that was amazing! Can you believe that we were at one of *the* Henry Hughes parties? Those things are legendary! And we were there!" Ramona exclaimed as she collapsed into my passenger seat. She raked her hand through her wild red hair, shaking her head in disbelief. "I bet that's what parties were like in *The Great Gatsby*. Oh my goodness. And he's so intelligent. It was like talking to Einstein."

I studied the darkened road ahead as Ramona went into overdrive from excitement. The party was impressive, I'd give her that, but our goal wasn't to be as social as Ramona had been that evening. If anything, she'd crossed one too many lines.

"I thought we agreed to a three-drink maximum," I said as my hand stayed glued to the leather steering wheel. Personally, I'd only had one drink, but that was because I knew I was still in work mode. If people weren't my family or friends, then they were my work colleagues or clients, and I had a strong belief that my work colleagues or clients should never see me intoxicated. It would make me too human for them, and that was never a good thing.

People respected you more if there was a bit of mystery to you. If they saw you off-kilter, they'd work like hell to remember you in that flawed state as a way to have power over you. I'd learned that fact the hard way.

"Oh, don't be ridiculous. Everyone was drunk," she said.

"I wasn't."

"That's because you're a buzzkill." She reached into her small clutch and pulled out two pieces of gum. She popped them into her mouth and chewed them like a camel. "So... what should we do now?" she asked, taking a piece of her hair and twirling it around her finger.

Remember how I'd learned that fact the hard way?

Ramona was my hard way.

One too many late nights in the office led to one too many hookups.

We'd only hooked up once, but like I said, it was one too many.

Now, she thought it was appropriate to call me a buzzkill and wonder what we'd do after a party.

"We aren't doing anything. I'm taking you home, and then I'll see you at work."

"*Or*," she offered, "you could stay at my place."

"Ramona," I said sternly.

She pouted. "Gabriel."

"We've talked about this. What happened between us was—"

"Fucking fantastic," she drunkenly sang. "I really appreciated that thing you did with your tongue when you licked my as—"

"*Ramona.*"

"*Gabriel.*"

"You're drunk."

"I am." She spread her legs and moved her hand between them. "And horny."

I ignored her, which made her huff and puff. "You're so boring sometimes. I liked you better when you drank."

"Of course, you did. I wasn't myself when I drank."

"I could learn to like you sober, too, you know."

I already knew where the conversation would begin in the morning. She'd come into work and state how she didn't remember anything from the night prior. Even though she probably did. It had happened a few times before. After holiday parties. During work celebrations. Ramona was a professional at hitting on me while she was drunk and then pretending like it never happened.

Ramona wasn't an awful hookup. She was beautiful and gifted in the bedroom, but that wasn't the issue. The issue was that ever since then, she'd looked at me with hopeful eyes. As if I'd someday give her more than that one night. That was a big issue because I didn't give myself away to anyone.

I was what my mother called the ultimate playboy. I didn't have the willingness to settle down with one woman. I'd never had that pull. I loved women—I did. In all shapes, sizes, and flavors. Still, I had a solid rule when it came to my hookups.

The moment their eyes looked hopeful was the moment I'd have to cut them loose. It was for their own good. Nothing good came from falling for a man like me. my career *was* my life.. There wasn't much room for anything else to exist within my realm.

Which was why it was odd how much Kierra remained on my mind after the evening came to an end. Most of the time, I kept to myself, but for some reason I'd felt a magnetic pull toward her all evening. I'd found myself searching for her out of the corner of my eye time and time again. Why was that? Hell if I knew. All I knew was there was something about her that just felt…right. I wasn't a people person. I was never one to seek out connections, but something about Kierra Hughes made me oddly want to wake up early to get a damn muffin.

Kierra was beautiful. As stunning as a person could've ever been. Beautiful smooth brown skin, entrancing dark-chocolate eyes, and full lips painted red. She wore gold jewelry and her dress hugged every curve of her body. She smelled like gardenias, too. Gardenias and honeysuckle.

Fuck, why did I know that? Why did her scent linger in my nostrils every time after we'd crossed paths tonight?

"Do you think they have a good sex life?" Ramona asked, breaking me from my thoughts.

"What?"

"Henry and his wife."

"Why the hell would you ask me that?"

"I'm just saying, he's brilliant and I'm curious if he's brilliant in all areas of his life."

"Maybe you shouldn't be thinking about our clients' sex lives," I muttered.

"I wonder if he uses sex toys that he's invented on her. To test out prototypes. Henry told me he was coming out with a line of robotic toys."

For the love of…

Did she really speak to Henry Hughes about sex toys?

That rubbed me wrong in every way possible. How unprofessional could Ramona get? She was too grown-up to be acting so inappropriately.

I gripped the steering wheel. "Perhaps we should hold off on conversations about sex toys with clients," I said, echoing my previous words.

I saw her smug smirk out of the corner of my eye. "Why? Are you jealous?"

I didn't say another word.

She grumbled to herself and turned her back toward me. It was clear that she was irritated that I was back to being her grumpy ol' boss man again, but I didn't mind. Honestly, I couldn't have been happier when I pulled up to her apartment building. She climbed out of the car, still not looking back at me.

"Drink some water," I told her.

She turned around on her heels and flipped me off. "Bite me, Gabriel."

I'd rather not. Biting her was exactly what led us to this uncomfortable exchange.

"See you in the morning at the office," I said.

"I'm going to be late," she promised.

I had no doubt she'd keep that promise, too.

After driving off from her place, I headed back home with my mind spinning with images of Kierra. I didn't know why I still hadn't been able to kick the idea of her from my mind. I could still see her smile lines and full, plump lips at the forefront of my thoughts.

As I walked into my house, I was greeted by my German shepherd, Bentley, who always welcomed me home with the utmost excitement. Then he followed me around like a shadow. I headed straight for my office and pulled out my sketchbook, then sat down with only the dim glow of my desk lamp lighting the paper in front of me. Bentley lay right at my feet.

Whenever my mind was too busy with images, I'd sketch them out. I'd been doing it for as long as I could remember. Sketching was an outlet for me. Most of the framed drawings in my home were made from snapshots of moments in my mind.

Therefore, instead of sleeping, I sketched Kierra Hughes from memory.

Her long, toned legs.

Her high cheekbones.

Her slicked-black ponytail.

I drew her laughing because that was how she seemed to live within my mind. She radiated a kind of beauty that I'd thought only existed within my dreams. She seemed so damn nice, too. Sincere. As if she truly wanted to make sure everyone was enjoying their time. Henry seemed to be the opposite of his wife. Where he'd loved to show off his own talents, Kierra preferred to hear about others.

I stayed up way too late drawing Kierra Hughes in my book of sketches. When I headed to bed, it was almost three in the morning. That wasn't shocking, though. I didn't sleep much. I was equal parts a night owl and a morning person. Which meant more than half the time I was running on coffee and prayers.

As I lay in bed, all I could think about was that I couldn't wait until Monday. For better or worse, I'd be at Florence Bakery, waiting for a cinnamon muffin and Kierra Hughes.

The following Monday, I waited at the bakery. Kierra never arrived. I did my best to keep busy. Ramona was still giving me the cold shoulder, but I didn't mind. If she got her work done, I couldn't care less about how cold her shoulder was. At least that would've been true if Ramona wasn't half human, half pain in my ass.

"I made you an afternoon tea," Ramona mentioned, walking into my office. As she set it down, she spilled it over my desk, making me leap up from my chair. I hurriedly gathered the paperwork in front of me, trying to save all I could from the spill.

"Shit, Ramona!" I yipped, snatching up my phone, which was now dripping in tea. "What are you doing? I don't even drink tea."

"Oh? You don't?" she sarcastically asked. "I guess it turns out that I don't know who you are at all, Mr. Sinclair."

I groaned.

Well, well, well, will you look at that.

The consequences of my own actions.

"Ramona," I started.

"Yes, Mr. Sinclair?"

"Why are you calling me Mr. Sinclair?"

"Because I figured calling you 'dick' would inappropriate. Almost as inappropriate as you tongue fucking me one weekend and ghosting me the next."

I blinked at her a few times before nodding. "All right. Mr. Sinclair it is."

"Oh, fuck off, Gabriel." She huffed as she turned on her heels and stomped out of my office.

I stared down at the mess on my desk and couldn't help but blame myself. I was somewhat shocked that Ramona didn't go with her normal "I was so wasted I can't remember anything from the night before" routine, but then again if she had gone that route, she wouldn't have been able to gloat to all the other employees about attending one of Henry Hughes's parties. It was like she'd tossed a coin on which one mattered more in the moment, and the party of a century was where she'd landed. Which meant I'd receive spilled tea and Ramona's attitude.

After heading to the kitchen, I grabbed some paper towels and went back to my office to clean up the results of that woman's scorn.

"Maybe you'll learn to listen to your mother when she tells

you not to mix work with pleasure," I heard as I wiped up the last of the spill. I looked up to find my mother standing there with a wicked I-told-you-so smirk on her face. Despite her petite figure, she still made me feel like a damn kid when she looked at me like that.

Mom worked for me at GS Architecture. She had been our office manager for the past five years. I told her she should enjoy retirement since she'd been working her whole life. I also told her that she'd never again have to worry about money, seeing how lucky I'd been with my business. The amount of success I'd found over the years was remarkable, and I knew I wouldn't have had said success without my mom standing in my corner through some of the darkest periods of my life.

If I was successful, she was successful. Easy as that.

Still, she was a hard worker. She wasn't one to take a handout, so when she said she still wanted to work, it seemed only right to create a position in my office for her. Office manager seemed fitting since how Mom was a professional at managing all things—including me.

"I have no clue what you're talking about," I said as I laid out my paperwork to dry. Luckily, none of my blueprints had been out for Ramona to ruin.

Mom shook her head. "You cannot think I'm that naive. I know you and Ramona hooked up."

"How would you know that?"

"Because Ramona has a terrible time hiding her emotions. I might be old, but I can still put two and two together." She took a seat across from my desk. "How was the event last night?"

"Interesting, to say the least. Henry Hughes is just what you would imagine him to be."

"Somewhat of a show-off?" she asked.

"Exactly. Everything's an event to him." I pulled out my phone. "He had us take photographs in front of the plot where we're building. He said it was a good way to manifest his ideal property. Then, he told me a story about how he'd once seen a polar bear while hiking in Alaska." I turned my phone to show Mom the pictures. The moment she saw them, the small smile on her face faded.

"Who's that beside him?" she asked. "She looks familiar, but I can't quite place it."

"I thought the same thing. It's his wife, Kierra. It turns out she frequents Florence Bakery. I bet you've crossed her path there, too."

She sat back, still staring at the photograph as if she'd just witnessed a ghost. Then she gave herself a slight shake. "Maybe that's it." She handed the phone back to me and smiled once more. "Henry Hughes always seemed like the type to lie about seeing polar bears. Everyone in my book club has at least one of his gadgets in their houses, too. They talk about him as if he's some kind of saint. When I told them you were designing his home and you'd be going to one of his parties, they all gasped as if they'd fallen into an orgasmic state."

"The idea of your friends falling into an orgasmic state is something I didn't need to picture."

"We're old but still human, Gabriel. We still love a good o—"

"Mom," I urged. "Please don't. It makes me wonder what kind of books you're reading in said book club."

"The ones that always end with happy endings. No cliff-hangers at all. All pleasure, no edging."

For fuck's sake, did my mother just use the word *edging*?

Was I somehow still sleeping and stuck in an awful nightmare?

"Okay, Mom. That's enough."

She leaned in toward me and whispered, "I'm talking about erotic books, Gabriel. With happily ever afters, of course. I like my smut with cuddles, if you know what I mean."

"I need us to never have this conversation again, please."

She laughed. "How much more work do you have? Do you want to grab an early dinner with me? I'm all done here and thought a nice dinner out might be wonderful." She always invited me to dinner after she finished work. I always declined.

"I'm actually planning to work late," I said, walking to sit back in my chair.

"Work, work, work." She shook her head as she stood. "One day, Gabriel, you'll join me for dinner. And one day, you'll have to actually live *life* instead of living *work*."

"My work is my life."

"I know." She frowned as she walked around toward me and kissed my forehead. "That's why I worry. Have a good night. And don't stay here too long. There's more outside to see than there is in here. Maybe you could get on one of those dating apps that those youngsters are talking about. Find yourself a nice girl of your own."

"Mom."

She tossed her hands up in defeat. "I'm just saying. It wouldn't hurt for me to have a daughter-in-law someday. One who doesn't work in our office."

I smirked. "Lesson learned. Don't screw at work."

"Good boy." Mom started for the door and turned around for a moment. "Gabriel?"

"Yes?"

"You mentioned what you thought of Henry Hughes, but what did you think of his wife when you met her? Other than her seeming familiar."

"Oh, well, I thought she was...kind."

Mom raised her eyebrows. "Kind? That's it? That's all you felt?"

"Yes," I replied. "She was kind."

And beautiful, and charming, and funny, and clever, and smart, and yes...

Kind.

6

Kierra

Sometimes I wondered if I hated marriage as a whole, or if I'd only hated the marriage I was in.

My husband didn't see me, even when I was standing right in front of him, begging for his attention. I didn't beg much anymore, of course. He seemed so disconnected that it felt pointless. But we always had weekend dinners together at home. Lena didn't cook over the weekends, so I loved to take on the task. Ava always requested her favorite meals for the weekends, and I'd spend hours cooking up a storm to make everything come together.

Henry often mentioned how he preferred Lena's cooking over mine, but Ava thought I was the greatest chef in the world. I doubted Ava truly believed that, but she acted like she did.

"This is amazing, Mom," she swore that Saturday evening as she shoved a forkful of meat loaf into her mouth. "The best you've ever made."

Smiling, I thanked her for the compliment—the same compliment she gave me each time I made anything for her.

I wondered what made that girl so sweet. She sure didn't take after her father in that respect.

I also wondered when my heart would stop tugging from bliss whenever she called me Mom. When I first met Henry and Ava, she was a five-year-old. The two were at dinner in an old diner where I used to work, and I couldn't take my eyes off sweet Ava. Everything about her seemed so adorably gentle.

And then she spilled her chocolate milk all over the table—and into Henry's lap.

"Whoa, buddy!" Henry remarked, leaping up and shaking off his pants.

With haste, I hurried over with rags to help clean up the mess. I began wiping down the table as Henry muttered an apology for the spill.

"Yeah, sowwy," Ava said, showcasing her two missing front teeth. She then frowned and picked up the cup that she'd knocked over.

"No worries. Spills happen in life. It's just a matter of how fast we can clean them up," I said before turning toward Henry. I held a clean rag out toward him.

He smiled, and it felt so safe and genuine. "Thank you... um—"

"Kierra," I said.

He nodded as he began to wipe down his pants. "Thank you, Kierra."

"I'm Ava!" the little girl remarked loudly. "And my dad doesn't have a girlfriend."

I laughed as Henry shot her a stern look. "Ava!"

"What?" She shrugged. "You told me to say that when she came back ova."

I placed a hand against my hip. "So, was the spilling of the chocolate milk all part of the plan? And she was playing your wingwoman?"

Henry laughed. "No, but I did mention that you were beautiful."

"Give her your numba, Dad," Ava said. What a good wingwoman she'd been.

For the next few years, she'd called me Kierra until the day Henry and I got married. As we ate dinner at the reception, Ava leaned over and asked if she could call me Mom now that we'd said "I do."

I cried as I pulled her into my arms.

That was officially the best day of my life.

And ever since, every time she said, "Mom," I melted a little more into the promise of being her forever.

I often wondered if I would've stayed so long if it weren't for Ava. I wondered if I would've said yes to Henry when he proposed. I wondered if I would've felt pulled toward Henry at all. I wondered if I would've left when he first raised his voice at me. I wondered if I would've packed my bags when he cussed me out and grabbed my wrist too tightly. Heck, I wondered if I would've left after the first date when I didn't feel butterflies. But none of those wonders mattered because I didn't only fall in love with Henry; I fell in love with his daughter. I knew if I let go of Henry, I'd have to let go of Ava, too. That was too much of a risk for me.

Besides, if Henry's cruelty was directed at me and not Ava, I would be fine with his harsh words and critiques. I'd rather it be me than my daughter any day. I could handle Henry's bad mood and cutting remarks if that meant Ava didn't have to.

And besides, even though Henry wasn't good to me, he did love his daughter, and Ava loved her father, too. She looked up to Henry as if he were the greatest man in the world. I never wanted that to change for her.

"It's a little dry," Henry mentioned as he cut into his slice of meat loaf.

I passed him the gravy.

He thanked me and poured more than enough over his slice.

After dinner, I hung out with Ava as Henry went off to work in his office. We lay in bed looking over a few of the architecture books she'd received as a gift for her birthday. Ava was in love with the world of architecture and was certain she'd be the greatest architect the world had ever seen. She would've been thrilled to meet Gabriel. I loved escaping into her visions and dreams of her future. I loved how much she shared with me, too. For a while, I worried about her becoming a teenager and blocking me out, but if anything, we were closer than ever. She even opened up about how she'd been bullied before for her weight. I offered to help her and set her up with a therapist. Yet knowing I was a safe place for her meant more than anything to me. I'd always be in her corner.

After she headed to bed, I went to my room to get ready to sleep. I found Henry in bed already, with a dozen books scattered around. If my husband was going to do just one thing, that would be researching technology to help with his business. Half the time, his books took up more space in our bed than I did.

I washed my face and slipped into my pajamas before crawling into my side of the bed. We shared a California king. Sometimes when I was in that bed, I felt so far away from him, but we weren't a cuddly couple. I'd be shocked if our feet even touched beneath the comforter.

I clicked off my nightstand lamp and fluffed my pillow a little before melting into a comfortable sleeping position.

"I'll have the light off soon," Henry said as he flipped a page in his book. "Maybe another hour."

"That's fine." I turned to face him. My heart was scattered in a few places that evening. A part of it went to bed with Ava, another part was left thinking about Gabriel, and the rest remained hovering over Henry's and my room. "Henry?"

"Hmm?"

"Are we happy?"

He glanced my way and lowered his reading glasses for a moment before turning back to his novel. "Let's not do this tonight, Kierra."

"What does that mean?"

"Ask these stupid questions. Of course we're happy. We have everything we could ever need."

"Like?"

"Money," he said. "Success, and Ava. I have everything I need."

"Is there anything I could do to make you happier?"

He leaned over and smiled before kissing my head. "You could go to sleep and stop overthinking."

"Okay." I shifted slightly before turning away from him. "Good night."

"Night."

I fell asleep for a little while before I was awakened by Henry shaking my arm. "Hey, Kierra. Wake up."

I grumbled a little and rubbed my eyes. "Yeah?"

"I was thinking about your question. About how you could make me happier."

I turned, somewhat surprised. "You woke me up to tell me that?"

"Yeah. I figured if I didn't, I'd forget."

"Okay." I yawned. "What can I do?"

"Drink differently."

I sat up. "What?"

"During the dinner parties. You always wear your red lipstick, then you sip out of your glass all around the rim, getting lipstick all over. It would make me happy if you drank from the same spot. It's embarrassing having others see how you drink."

I laughed, shaking my head. "Yeah, okay, Henry." His intense stare gave me a bit of a shock. I sat up straighter. "You're serious."

"I am. It's ridiculous. No grown woman should leave three different lipstick stains on one glass."

Oh.

Wow.

"I'll try to do better," I muttered as I lay back down.

"Don't try, just do. You're not weak. You can avoid getting lipstick everywhere. Even Ava does better than you with that," he said before shutting off his lamp. "Night."

———

When Monday came, I decided to skip my morning muffin and head straight into the office. I wasn't ready to face having a seemingly innocent run-in with Gabriel. Even though such a big part of me craved crashing into him again. Instead, I needed input on my current situation from those whose opinions I'd valued the most.

"On a scale of one to ten, how bad would it be for me to reengage with a person from my past who happened to be my best friend and first love? Who has no recollection of me at all because he lost his memory?" I blurted out to Joseph as he stood in the office relaxation room, brewing a cup of coffee.

He turned to face me and arched an eyebrow. "Happy Monday to you, too."

"Oh, right. Sorry. Happy Monday. How was your trip? I hope it was amazing and just out of curiosity…" I walked over to the countertop where the coffee machine was, hopped on top of it, and kicked my feet back and forth. "On a scale of one to ten, how bad would it be for me to reengage with a person from my past who completely lost his memory of me, even though he was the biggest part of my life until I was almost twenty years old? And then he randomly showed up to my husband's dinner party as the architect building our new house? And he felt like we knew each other, but he didn't *remember*, even though a big part of me wishes he remembered, but I don't want him to remember *everything* because everything wasn't *good*, but it also wasn't all *bad*."

Joseph snickered, added too much sweetener to his coffee, and lifted his mug. "This sounds like a telenovela. Have you been watching *Jane the Virgin* again?"

"I wish this were a show. A show wouldn't leave my stomach in knots."

He arched an eyebrow. "This really happened?"

"One hundred percent."

"Wow," he breathed out. "I feel as if you've been spiraling over this for a while now."

"A little over fiftysome hours."

"And where are you landing on your decision to engage?"

I bit my bottom lip. "I don't know. That's why I'm asking the older, wiser man in the coffee room."

Joseph laughed. "Age has nothing to do with wisdom."

"Yes, but you seem to be full of both."

He narrowed his eyes, glanced at his watch, and then said, "I have thirty minutes before my first client. What happened?"

I told him the story. The whole story about Gabriel and me and our past together. I told him about the good days and the worst nights. He listened to me intently, not breaking his stare.

His attention to every word always made me feel safe around him. I was certain that was how all his clients felt, too.

"I see." He brushed his palm against his chin. "Now I ask you, are you looking for a friendship response or a therapist response?"

"Friendship," I said. "I know what you charge per hour, and you're out of my budget," I half-joked.

"Well, as a friend, I say this… My advice doesn't matter."

My eyebrows shot up. "What? Why not?"

"Because it's not my life, and I haven't lived through the string of struggles and joys attached to your situation. Therefore, my input would be from a place that lacks the emotional depth and understanding that your heart needs to make this decision. You could ask a million people what their advice would be, and their words wouldn't matter because it's your situation, not theirs."

I sighed. "That *is* therapist advice. Good advice, but therapist."

He shrugged. "My friendship and therapist advice intertwine at times."

I scrunched my nose and grumbled before slapping my hand against my face. "Okay, but if you were just to humor me with your thoughts on what you would do in the fictional world where you were walking in my shoes?"

"First, I have a few questions."

"Shoot."

"Do you miss your friendship with him?"

"It was ages ago."

"Time doesn't determine whether a friendship can be missed."

I nodded. "I do miss the friendship."

"And if you didn't connect with him, would you regret it?"

"I think so, yes. For the rest of my life."

"Then, if I were in your shoes…" He paused and sipped his coffee. "I'd be saying hello again to my old best friend."

A wave of chills raced over me as the words left his mouth, because that was exactly what I thought, too. I thought if I didn't take the chance to connect with Gabriel and see if he really didn't recall everything that went down between us, I'd regret it for the rest of my life. Because if I had the chance to see him, to see the old version of him that I'd missed for so long, I'd take it.

"Thanks, Joseph," I said, hopping off the countertop.

"Mm-hmm, but you know what I'd also do?" he asked.

"What's that?"

"I'd tell my husband all about the situation and make sure you both were on the same page."

I grumbled. "Yeah. I figured you'd say that."

Good advice—I just wasn't certain I was ready to talk to Henry about it.

During my lunch break, just to make sure I had all sides covered, I called my best friend, Rosie, to update her on the situation. Getting her point of view would be very helpful, since she'd known both Gabriel and me since high school. Plus, Rosie seemed to live in a state of delusion that I sometimes needed instead of Joseph's realistic mind.

Rosie and I met at a restaurant between both of our jobs. Unlike Joseph's, Rosie's reaction was a bit more animated.

"Oh my gosh, you're kidding me!" she gasped as I sat across from her in our booth. She slammed her hands down on the wooden table and her blue eyes all but bugged out of her head. Her strawberry-blond hair danced across her shoulder blades as she remained in complete and utter shock.

She'd changed her hair since I'd last seen her. Which was only last Tuesday. We'd been meeting up each week for the past two months to plan her upcoming wedding to her fiancé, Wesley—the one individual who made my fiercely independent friend who didn't believe in relationships believe in love and marriage.

The older Rosie grew, the more she looked like her mother, a very beautiful Asian woman who had straight black hair. Ever since Rosie had been a kid, she'd liked to dye her hair to look less like her parents. It drove them wild.

"Like, *your* Gabriel?" she questioned.

"He's not exactly mine, but yes. Him."

"Oh my goodness." She sat back in the booth, flabbergasted. "And he still doesn't have his memories?"

"Nope."

"So…he doesn't recall you two falling in love?"

"Nope."

"He doesn't recall you at *all*?"

"Not at all."

"But…everything you shared together…" Her hands fell to her chest, over her heart. "You were everything to him, Kierra. You and Elijah."

Just hearing Elijah's name out loud made my eyes fill with tears.

I glanced down at the tattoo sitting on my wrist. A trail of penguin, toad, and bear footprints trailing up my arm. A daily reminder of my past with Gabriel and little Elijah. A daily reminder of what used to be, and what would never return again.

I blinked and my mind took me back there. I blinked and I could feel the chill of that cold December night.

"Don't worry, boys," I shouted. "I'll drive."

"Kierra…" Rosie reached across the table and placed a hand against my forearm, bringing me back to reality. "This is a lot." She was teary-eyed as she held my arm. If anyone knew how deep the cuts of the accident were, it was Rosie. She was the one who was there for me throughout that whole period. She was the one who held me as I wailed into the night. She was the one who told me everything would be okay, even when I knew for a fact that that would never be true again.

"It is a lot. And I don't know what to do. Tell me what to do. Give me any kind of advice."

"I don't even know. This sounds like a twisted *Black Mirror* episode."

"Joseph said *Jane the Virgin*."

"That's a very Joseph choice."

I sighed and picked up my water for a sip. My mouth felt dry as I sat heavily in my emotions. "It's so messy."

"You have to keep seeing him," she stated. "No question about it. Not only is he building your home, but he's Gabriel."

"I know." He was Gabriel. My once-upon-a-time love story. "Joseph said I should tell Henry all about Gabriel."

Rosie worked her hardest not to roll her eyes. It was no secret that Henry and Rosie didn't get along. She didn't complain much about him anymore now that years have passed, but she didn't go out of her way to pretend she could stand him.

"Joseph would be one to tell you to be a responsible wife. Stupid Joseph." She huffed. "Being an adult sucks."

"Tell me about it."

"So, when do I get to see him?"

"What?"

"Gabriel. Sure, he was your everything, but he was my friend, too. Plus, I'd kill to see how you act with him around."

I laughed. "That's not happening."

"What? Come on! You know I thrive off uncomfortable situations. I'd be the comic relief in your tragedy of errors."

"It's a strong negative."

"Just host another dinner party. I love Henry's dinner parties."

"You *hate* Henry's dinner parties."

"It's true." She nodded. "Too highbrow for me and not enough mozzarella sticks. But I would one hundred percent show up if it meant I'd get to see you act super awkward and clumsy around Gabriel Sinclair."

"What makes you think I'd be super awkward and clumsy around Gabriel?"

She shook her head and patted my hand. "Oh, sweet, sweet Kierra. Because I know you so well. I bet you spilled something when you saw him."

I rolled my eyes. "Let's change the subject."

She pointed a stern finger my way. "You totally spilled something."

"All over myself, yes."

"I knew it." She reached to my plate and stole a few of my fries. "It is kind of exciting, though, isn't it?"

"What's that?"

"You and Gabriel being reunited after all this time. And for the record, you don't have to take Joseph's advice. I hardly ever listen to my therapist. It's more of an optional thing, really."

I laughed. "I fear a lot of my clients feel the same way."

———————

When I returned to the office, I was thrown off as I walked into the lobby to find a person I was not expecting to see sitting in a chair. My head tilted sideways as I stared at the familiar stranger. That saying felt like the biggest oxymoron known to mankind. A familiar stranger. Someone you once upon a time knew yet who had shifted into nothing more than a sad memory.

"Amma," I whispered, stunned by the sight of Gabriel's mother sitting in front of me. The moment I spoke her name, she rose from the chair. She held her purse close to her chest and released a sigh as she stared my way.

"Hello, Kierra."

I narrowed my eyes as my heartbeat began to rise. "What are you doing—"

"You had a run-in with my son over the weekend," she said, her voice as stern as the last time we'd spoke. Well, truthfully, the last time we spoke, her sternness was bathed in heartbreak and despair. The heartbreak and despair that I'd caused. I was almost certain back then would've been the last time I'd ever see her, but for some strange reason my past was sprinting straight into my present day.

My mind was still reeling from seeing Gabriel over the weekend. Seeing Amma made my brain want to simply explode. Not only because our parting was so traumatic for the both of us, but also because seeing her standing there sent my mind straight back to that day. There were many things in life I tried to avoid, but at the top of the list were memories around Amma and the day of the accident.

"Yes," I said, glancing around the lobby. "Would you like to speak in my office?"

"No, I don't need much time. I just want to say one thing and one thing only." She took a step toward me. "Stay away from him, Kierra."

I shook my head slightly. "What do you mean?"

"I mean exactly what I said just now and years ago. I want you to stay away from my son."

"Amma, I didn't seek Gabriel out. I had no clue he was going to be the architect on the build."

She rolled her eyes. "Oh, please. As if I'd believe that. It just so happened you had no clue who was working on your home building?"

"It's exactly like that," I said. "My husband planned it all.

I was shocked to see Gabriel at my house this weekend. I can swear to you that I had nothing to do with it."

She moved her hand to her earlobe and began to rub it, something she used to do whenever she was uncomfortable and uncertain of a situation. I knew this because I knew her. For a long while, Amma was like a second mother to me. She was in the list of my top five favorite humans back then. Unfortunately, favorite human lists could change over time, and people could be X-ed off said lists.

She X-ed me out years ago, and I knew I'd never make it back on that list.

Amma crossed her arms over her chest. "Well, my stance is the same. Stay away from him."

"I…can't do that. Especially since he'll be at our property a lot of the time and I might have to help go over the plans. Listen, I get why this is awkward, especially since Gabriel clearly doesn't have any memories of me, but I won't do anything to hurt him."

She huffed as if she didn't believe me.

That hurt my heart more than she'd ever know. Gabriel was the one person, apart from Ava, that I would never want to hurt. If I could've suffered all the pain in the world to make sure he didn't suffer any, I would've. Which was exactly why I walked away all those years ago—for his and his mother's well-being. Amma swore to me that my staying would've made Gabriel's life worse, and I believed her. So I did the hardest thing I'd ever had to do—said goodbye to my very best friend. To the other half of my heartbeats.

"Well, do your best not to bring up anything about your past together. It would be detrimental to his well-being. Especially when it comes to Elijah. You will not speak of him," she ordered.

A knot formed in my stomach.

Elijah.

It was the first time I'd heard another, outside of Rosie, say his name in years. Even though I wrote it down in my journal every single day for years. There wasn't a moment that Elijah didn't cross my mind. Yet I felt sick hearing Amma bring him up in such a way.

"Why can't I talk about him? What if he brings up Elijah in casual conversation?"

"Trust me, he won't."

"Why wouldn't he?" I questioned, fearful of the answer she might give me—the answer I knew was true based on the amount of fear that flashed across her brown eyes. My chest tightened as tears burned at the back of my eyes. *Oh my goodness...* "You didn't tell him," I whispered, stunned.

"That's none of your business."

My breath was knocked out of my lungs.

She never told Gabriel about Elijah.

"Amma." My mind was fighting the urge to go straight into therapist mode with the reveal of that information. "There's no way you've gone this long without telling Gabriel about Elijah." My mind struggled to wrap around that concept. Because how could she keep a whole brother hidden from Gabriel? There was no way that was possible.

She stood tall, her shoulders rolled back and a look of dismay plastered on her face. "You have no clue what it's been like for me. Frank left me after Elijah passed away. He told me he couldn't stick around with me and Gabriel when his son passed away. He couldn't handle the grief and being with me. I was alone with Gabriel, trying my best. You don't know what I've been through. What you've put me through, so how dare you judge any choice I've made between my son and myself. You don't know what it's been like. You weren't there."

"That's because I was trying to respect your wishes. I would've been there if you'd allowed it. I would've been able to help you tell Gabriel. I would've helped you figure it all out."

"*Help?*" She huffed with a slight shake of her head. "You would've helped me figure it all out? Really, Kierra?"

"Yes, really. I would've been there for you. I would've—"

"*You killed my son!*" she shouted, tears flooding her eyes. Her voice cracked as she pointed a finger toward me. "You caused all of this! You're the reason that I had to figure anything out to begin with. You're the reason I've been living this daily nightmare for all these years. So, how dare you say you would've helped. How dare you judge me for not telling Gabriel about, about…" She took a deep breath, stilling herself to keep from falling apart. If there was one thing Amma never did, it was fall apart. At least in public. She stilled herself long enough before shaking the tears from her eyes.

She took a deep breath and released it slowly before saying, "Just don't say anything that relates to before the accident, okay?"

I didn't know what to say, so I agreed with her request. "Okay. But Amma…you have to tell him about Elijah. You have to." It wasn't fair to keep such a big part of Gabriel's history from him. It was one thing to blot out my storyline in his world, but Elijah? No. Elijah deserved to be remembered. Gabriel deserved to know every single detail about his beautiful little brother.

"Don't tell me what I have to do. You get to live with your demons. Let me live with mine."

"Amma—"

She grimaced as she glanced around the lobby, shifting the conversation. "A therapist, huh?"

Even though I was uncomfortable with the shift, I allowed it. Sometimes, certain topics were too hard to stay within for a long period of time. "Yes."

"Do you have a PhD?"

"I do."

"So you're a doctor."

"I am."

Her scowl deepened as her smile lines turned into frown lines. "So you help people."

"I try my best to, yes." The tension in the space was thick, and I knew the conversation wasn't going anywhere positive. Amma's emotions were on high alert, and I could tell by the look in her eyes that she was ready to turn me into her punching bag.

She shook her head in disapproval. "Do you try to help people to make up for some of the karma you've built up over the years?" Amma hissed, her voice dripping with disdain and resentment. "Is it how you try to make peace with what you've done in your past? With how you killed my Elijah?"

Instead of instantly responding, I paused for a moment.

Mom taught me that whenever things were heated in the kitchen, it worked best to turn down the temperature on the stove instead of allowing things to boil over and make a bigger mess. I'd learned over time to speak slowly and with care. Just because Amma's pot was boiling over didn't mean that mine had to, too.

I could've matched her energy. I could've swung my words at her because she was coming after me and my character. I could've allowed her words to break me into a million pieces right then and there. I could've called her all types of names because she seemed to have no problem attacking me.

Instead, I stood still and said only a few words. Words that were loaded with truth and sorrow. "I'm so sorry you're still hurting, Amma."

Her eyes flashed with sadness, and that broke a little part of me.

Then I turned away and removed myself from the situation.

I walked into my office and shut the door behind me. My back fell against the closed door, and I took a few deep breaths with my eyes shut. My body began to shut down with the overwhelming feelings of the past few days. I always told my clients that if you didn't deal with the internal issues, they would manifest on the outside. Be it your body getting sick, injured, or sliding down the back of a door and falling into an eruption of tears.

Amma's words stung me so deeply because they held a heavy amount of truth within them. I did kill her son.

And I'd spend the rest of my life trying my hardest to forgive myself for a momentary mistake that cost Amma everything.

Because I *killed* her *son*.

When I closed my eyes, I was back there.

New Year's Eve.

It was Elijah's birthday, our little New Year's Eve baby.

We celebrated at Amma and Frank's house before Amma had to go into work for a night shift. Gabriel wanted us to stay in and stuff our faces with junk food and watch the ball drop on television, but I wanted to take a trip to Sky Hill—where snow tubing was taking place into the night. It was supposed to be a huge deal, with fireworks going off at midnight over the hillside.

"Or we can just keep eating birthday cake and play board games," Gabriel offered for the hundredth time.

"Or we can go tubing!" I countered for the hundredth-and-first time.

"Snow tubing!" Elijah exclaimed.

There was a knock on my office door, forcing me back to reality.

"Kierra? Are you okay?" Joseph asked through the shut door. "That seemed like an intense exchange I overhead."

"I'm fine," I said, shaking myself out of my jolted memories. "Everything's fine."

7

Kierra

The next morning, I tried to dismiss all the anxiety that had built up within me over the past few days. I felt beyond exhausted, due to a lack of sleep. The problem with being a parent was that when you were in the middle of anxiety attacks, you still had to take care of someone beside yourself. So, while my body wanted to fully shut down and curl up into a ball and sob for seventy-two hours straight, I had a whole human to keep alive and fed, and a job to attend where people poured their struggles out on me.

Therefore, my own problems had to take a back seat for a good while. I'd just keep pushing said breakdown deeper into my system. That seemed healthy enough. That was until Tuesday morning when the smallest inconvenience made me crack.

"Sorry, Kierra, we're all out of cinnamon muffins," Claire said as I stood at the front of the line of Florence Bakery the morning after Amma reminded me of the worst moment of my life. The last thing I needed was a punch to my spirit that there were no more cinnamon muffins. I knew it was ridiculous, but I almost broke down into tears from the mere idea that a freaking pastry was out of stock.

"We're actually out of dark roast, too," Claire stated, "But I can get you a light roast."

When it rains, it pours.

"Yeah, okay. That's fine," I said, feeling defeated. After she rang me up and handed me my coffee, I turned around to run straight into a body, spilling my coffee all over the hardened chest that I hit.

"*Fuck!*" he shouted, hopping backward.

I looked up to find Gabriel standing there with a brown paper bag in his hands and scalding coffee covering his cashmere chesterfield coat.

"Oh my goodness, I'm so sorry," I blurted out as I began to rub his coat.

"You did say you weren't always clumsy, but I'm starting to think that was a lie."

"Oh gosh, yeah, I know, I'm sorry. I'm so sorry." The tears that were sitting at the back of my eyes pushed their way to the forefront and began to fall down my cheeks as I kept swiping at his coat. "I'm so, so sorry and—"

Gabriel grabbed my arm and paused my excessive wiping. "Kierra. It's fine. I was just teasing." I raised my head to meet his stare. The moment our eyes locked, true concern appeared in his eyes. He placed a hand against my shoulder. "Are you crying? Are you okay?"

"No," I said, then I shook my head. "I mean yes, I'm okay, and no I'm not crying."

He arched an eyebrow. "I see the tears streaming down your face."

"It's allergies," I lied.

"It's not allergies."

"It's totally allergies."

"Kierra."

"Yes?"

"You're a bad liar."

I burst into more tears and covered my face in embarrassment. The buildup of the past few days was finally catching up to me, and I didn't know how to handle it. "I ruined your coat!" I blabbered, having a full breakdown in the middle of the bakery.

"Oh, no. No. Hey, it's okay." Gabriel wrapped his arm around my shoulders and pulled me to the side of the bakery. "It's fine. Actually, I hate this jacket. I've been waiting days, *weeks*, for someone to spill scalding-hot coffee all over it just to give me a reason to get rid of it," he joked.

I cried even harder because he was being so nice to me. Because that's who Gabriel had always been—so freaking nice. He began rubbing my back to try to get me to calm down. I felt so embarrassed by my whole meltdown, but Gabriel seemed more than okay handling it.

"I'm so sorry," I muttered, wiping away my tears. "This is humiliating."

"Actually, I know what the real issue here is. I know what's going on."

I raised an eyebrow as my heart dropped to my stomach. He knew? Did Amma tell him? "You do?"

"Yeah." He grimaced. "I do."

Oh my goodness. "Gabriel—"

"I bought all six cinnamon muffins, just so you'd feel how I suffered in the past." He held up the paper bag and shook it. "Though I didn't think it would make you sob like that. I didn't know how much these muffins meant to you."

He didn't know.

I didn't know if that made me relieved or depressed.

I pushed out a chuckle. "You're right. That's exactly the cause of my breakdown." I tried my best to shake off my nerves.

Gabriel held the bag out toward me. He frowned slightly. "I feel like shit that I made you cry. I was just hoping to tease you with the full intent of giving you the muffins."

"Yeah, well, you should feel awful," I joked.

He frowned.

I slugged his arm. "I was kidding, but you do owe me those muffins. I'm willing to share one with you, too, if you buy me a new coffee."

"Only if you take fifteen minutes to drink said coffee with me and help me look over the blueprint that I'm going to send to your husband later today."

I smiled. "Deal. Grab a table and I'll run to the bathroom to freshen up so I don't look like a hot mess."

"You look remarkable."

Oh, Gabriel.

Why did you have to grow up to be so…great?

The flutters in my stomach shook me slightly as I tried not to appear too flustered. "I'll only be a second."

"Sounds good. How do you like your coffee? Other than scalding hot on my coat."

I smiled again. He made it so easy to smile. "Preferably dark roast, but they only have light. So light roast with heavy cream and two sugars."

"You got it. I'll be at the table in the corner waiting."

I hurried off to the bathroom and stared at myself in the mirror. "Everything's fine, and you're okay, Kierra," I told myself. Most of my life was spent inspiring others to be their best selves. Every now and again, I had to give myself a pep talk or two. "You are strong, you are smart, and you can deal with hard situations."

I fixed my makeup and shook off the discomfort I felt. I could handle the situation before me. Gabriel didn't remember me. I could sit with him, eat a muffin, and go about my day as if everything was perfectly fine.

After I refreshed myself, I headed back to the table where Gabriel was sitting. I slid into the chair across from him and smiled as I looked at the coffee and muffin sitting in front of me. "This makes things a lot better," I said.

"I'm glad." His lazy smile was back, and I couldn't help but realize how much I'd missed that smile. "How are you?"

"Oh, I'm good. Thanks for asking." I smoothed my moist hands against my thighs. "How are you?"

He rubbed his hand against the back of his neck. "Do you always do that?"

"Do what?"

"Lie about being good."

I bit the corner of my lip. "I don't know what you mean."

"I doubt you were really crying over a cinnamon muffin, Kierra. Listen, I get it. I'm nothing more than a stranger to you, but you don't have to lie about being good if you're not good. I won't tell anyone the truth. Our little secret."

I let out a nervous laugh. "Are you the therapist, or am I?"

He held his hands up in surrender. "I'm just a guy asking how you are. But forget it. Cheers," he offered. He lifted his muffin into the air. "To the blueprint changes being approved by Henry tonight."

"Cheers," I said, bumping his muffin with my own before taking a bite of it. And just like that, life didn't seem as bad as before. All thanks to cinnamon muffins and Gabriel Sinclair. The rest of the interaction went to Gabriel pulling out the blueprints and showed them to me. He talked in architect talk that I didn't understand, and it was a lot of me just nodding and agreeing with his plans.

"I'm sure you've already seen all of this, but it helps to pick your brain," Gabriel mentioned as he rolled up the plans and placed them back into his briefcase.

"Actually, I haven't. Henry likes to keep all this stuff to himself, since it's more of his dream than my own."

"You haven't had involvement in the planning? I was under the impression that Henry was coming to me on behalf of you both."

"Yes, and he was. That's why my meditation room is

included. I told him that's all I really cared about. I wanted that and a sewing room, but he said he'd only go with one. Everything else was his choice. Between you and me, I don't really care about a big mansion or things like that. I just want comfort and my family under a warm roof."

Gabriel's mouth parted as if he was going to make a comment, but instead he pressed out a grin. It didn't seem genuine, so it made me wonder what thoughts were in his head.

"Well, talking to you helped me realize a few changes I'd like to make. So, I appreciate your time."

"I'm glad. I'm sure Henry will love all of this. Our daughter, Ava, will love it, too. She dreams of being an architect someday."

"No way," Gabriel replied with a raised brow. "It's not every day you hear about someone wanting to go into architecture."

"Well, she's been of that mindset ever since we bought her first Lego set when she was a kid."

"How old is she now?"

"Fourteen going on forty," I joked.

"No way… You have a fourteen-year-old?" he questioned, amazed.

"Yes. Henry's about nine years older than me. When I met him, he had a five-year-old. I instantly fell in love with Ava, and well, she's my daughter. Maybe not by blood but—"

"By heart," he finished. "That's the kind of love that matters most. I love that you have her, and that she has you."

"Me too. She's special."

"Well." He tossed his last piece of muffin into his mouth.

"If she's ever interested, I'm more than willing to have her shadow me at the office this summer if she wants to take on an internship of sorts."

"Are you serious? She would lose her mind over that opportunity."

"Yeah, for sure. We can even set up a payroll to pay her to get the experience and she can help around the office."

"Wow, Gabriel. That's…more than kind. Thank you."

He pulled out his wallet and handed me one of his business cards. "You can call me to set it up. Then you have a direct line to me, outside of Henry."

"Thank you. I'll reach out later this week to set something up."

"Wonderful." He glanced down at his watch and nodded. "I guess our time is up, and I should get to work." He stood. "But I actually really enjoyed this, Kierra."

"Me too," I confessed. Guilt hit me from the realization that I'd enjoyed his company. Guilt attached to enjoying another man's company when I was a married woman, and guilt for going against Amma's request. A wave of discomfort washed over me as I rose from the table.

"Have a great day," he said as he turned to exit the bakery.

"Gabriel," I called out.

He looked over his shoulder, his brown eyes piercing my heart. "Yes?"

"Can you ask me again? Ask me how I am."

He turned completely toward me. "How are you, Kierra?"

"Overwhelmed and a little sad."

He slid his hands into his stained coat pockets. "I'm sorry to hear that."

"Thank you."

He took a step toward me. "Is there anything I can do to help?"

"No," I whispered and shrugged, feeling the tears building back up in my eyes. I didn't know the last time I'd told someone the truth about how I was feeling. I was so used to being the strong one. To being the one who was always good, that I didn't even know I was allowed to say out loud that I wasn't okay. Until Gabriel gave me that freedom. "I just needed to say that out loud."

"I understand." He stepped closer. His brows lowered. "Is it okay if I hug you?"

My mouth parted and I wanted to say yes. I wanted to wrap myself in his embrace and hold on to him tightly as he told me everything would be okay someday. Because I knew who Gabriel had been in the past, and I was quickly learning who he was in the present: comfort. He was and always would be comfort to me.

But I wasn't the same girl I'd been when I met Gabriel. Holding on to another man when I had a husband of my own felt wrong. I even felt bad for the coffee and muffin.

"It's okay. I'll be fine. Thank you, though. Thank you for asking me again."

He brushed a thumb against his chin. "Thank you for being honest. It takes a lot of guts to be that honest."

8

Gabriel

Is it okay if I hug you?

What in the absolute fuck was I thinking asking Kierra such a question? It was beyond bizarre and out-of-the-world inappropriate. It was even inappropriate for me to ask her to eat a damn cinnamon muffin with me.

I should've been a bit embarrassed, too, seeing how I waited around the bakery for her the day prior, but she never showed up. That had felt like a gut punch for some reason. I stood there like a goofy fool, holding a bag of muffins, hoping a married woman client would walked through the doors in search of said muffin.

What was even more humiliating was the fact that I did it again that morning. When she arrived, I felt even more batshit because a pool of giddiness hit the pit of my stomach. That was until I saw her break down into tears.

I wouldn't blame myself for the tears she shed, but they still broke my heart as I watched her fall apart. And I did want to fucking hug her, okay? I wanted to hug her for so long and not let go, if she was crying or not. My mind still couldn't make sense of why I felt that way.

There was just something about her that felt so familiar. I haven't had something feel familiar to me in what felt like two decades. Since my accident, truthfully. Other than my mother, everything and everyone felt distant. Most days, it felt as if I was walking through a fog. Passing by people and places that felt so black and white. But Kierra felt like color. Not just any color, either. The most vibrant of tones, which made my heart pound wildly in my chest.

That was *not* okay.

I came down hard on Ramona for drunkenly talking to Henry about sex toys, and there I was, soberly daydreaming about Kierra.

I wondered what was overwhelming her and making her sad.

I bet it was that fucker Henry.

Okay, maybe he wasn't a fucker toward me, but he was a fucker toward her, which made him a fucker to me. What kind of man went ahead and made all the choices on a home, giving his wife a meditation room to shut her up, instead of adding her input? How did he not involve her in the plans? How had she not seen the blueprints when we were about to break ground? And why, oh why, did it rub me the wrong way?

I wasn't one for relationships, but if I had been and I had a wife, I'd want her involved. If I was married to Kierra, I'd want to know all her thoughts on it. Heck, I currently wanted to know all her thoughts.

Why did I want to know all her thoughts?

"Hey, Boss Man. More cinnamon muffins?" the front doorman, Eddie, asked as I walked up to the GS Architecture building.

I smirked and handed him the three extra muffins I had, just as I had done the day before. "There's only three this time. I got greedy and ate some."

Eddie smiled big and shook his head. "I don't care. I took these bad boys home to the missus, and I'm pretty sure they have some kind of drugs in them, because she devoured them within five seconds."

"I'm pretty sure they are drugged," I agreed. "I haven't been able to stop eating them since I had my first one."

"The missus told me if I didn't bring her more, she'd divorce me. But I know that's just her hunger hormones acting up with the baby."

I arched an eyebrow. "Baby?"

Eddie stood tall and nodded with pride. "She gave me the okay to start telling people. We're three months in. I'm going to finally get my linebacker football son or my ballerina daughter. Or vice versa. The kids can be whatever the hell they want, as long as they're healthy."

I patted Eddie's shoulder, genuinely overjoyed for him. Eddie had been working for me for over three years now, and I knew he and his wife, Sarah, had been trying for years to get pregnant. Even through the ups and downs, Eddie held on to his faith that what's meant to be would always find its way. He said his and Sarah's baby was out there in the universe; he or she just had to find their way home.

It felt good to know that some stories received happy endings.

"Congratulations, Eddie. You both will make great parents. That's a lucky kid."

"I'm a lucky man," he countered. "With muffins. What more could a person want? Have a good day, Boss Man."

"You too, buddy."

One of the projects I was most proud of working on was the GS Architecture building. The building itself looked like a piece of contemporary art with an oval shape from the outside that had over six floors. The outside was all white, with large windows that were a pain in the ass to have cleaned, but worth every second. We worked with a fantastic crew who handled that task. I knew it wouldn't look as good if I had to clean them myself.

Inside, the building felt fresh and modern with an avant-garde structure. Each floor held an open-plan interior that was flooded with natural light from all the windows. The use of geometric shapes and innovative materials was one of my favorite elements to explore.

Speaking of elements, each level had a focus on a certain element. The first floor was covered in earth tones. It was designed to make you feel as if you'd walked straight into a Zen garden. The colors were very muted greens and browns. The front desk was made with rustic stone that had a welcoming nature, and the sign resting on the wall behind the entrance desk was made of bamboo and read GS ARCHITECTURE. From there, the floors built up around the other elements.

Though the best floor was the fifth floor—the gaming lunch hall where one could go to decompress. I learned early on that my job could be very stressful. The same was true for my employees, who worked harder than most. I thought it was important to have a place where they could go escape during the workday for a short time to breathe. Whether it be taking advantage of the candy bar, playing video or arcade games, or taking a stroll to the meditation room—also known as the nap room. That was what the fifth floor was for, and it went over amazingly.

After I took the elevator to that floor to get water, I nodded once toward Bobby, who was one of the best architects at the firm. Not only was he a genius at his craft and a million times more talented than I'd ever been, but he was also my best friend, who handled my crazy ideas and spur-of-the-moment actions.

"Morning, dickhead," Bobby joked as he poured creamer into his coffee.

"Morning, asshole," I replied as I walked to the fridge and pulled out a water.

"I've been a bit out of the loop since I just got back into town last night. How was that party with the Hughes client? Ramona hasn't stopped going on and on about it since I got in this morning."

"It was weird but good. Do you know that he has a robot that brings everyone drinks and cleans up messes? It's very Disney Channel *Smart House* style."

"I just think you showed your age there, old man," Bobby joked. "But to be fair, that's a fantastic damn movie."

"The cream of the crop." I actually rewatched the film a few years back. When I was searching to recall my old memories, I would rewatch the popular ones from when I was a kid. I'd hoped it would jog some memories. It didn't. "But the party was fine. Ramona loved every second of it."

"I bet she did. She loves luxury more than anything. And champagne."

"So much champagne."

"Rumor has it she talked sex toys with the client."

My gut tightened up at that reminder. "I'm trying to forget that."

Bobby smirked and patted me on the back. "I'm sure there's a lot of things you're trying to forget when it comes to Ramona."

I'd never talked to Bobby about what went down between Ramona and me, but he wasn't an idiot. Plus, I wouldn't have been shocked if Ramona herself told him every little detail about the night we'd hooked up. If there was one thing about Ramona, it was the fact that she loved to talk about her private life. It was my fault that I'd put myself in that situation.

Not wanting to dive deeper into that topic, I shifted the conversation. "I'm getting ready to launch our internship mentoring program."

Bobby cocked an eyebrow. "Our what with the what-what?"

"Our mentoring program."

"We don't have a mentoring program."

"Yeah, that's true, but I need to come up with one."

"Why do you need to come up with a mentoring program?"

"Because I might have told Henry Hughes's wife that we have a mentoring program for their daughter."

His cocked eyebrows knit together. "Why would you tell Henry Hughes's wife that we have a mentoring program for their daughter?"

"I actually don't know why I told her that."

"*Ohh*," he sang. "She's hot."

"What? No."

"She's not hot?"

"Well, no. I mean, she's beautiful. I mean, she's my client's wife, Bobby. I don't see her like that."

"Then why are you offering her daughter a job?"

"I don't know. To help a kid chase their dream or something." Shit, why did I offer up a mentorship? Now I had to come up with some things for Ava to actually do.

"Don't worry, buddy. I think it's cool. It would be good to have a kid here. I love kicking kids' asses at Mario Kart during my lunch break."

I smirked. "That's a bit childish, don't you think?"

He grabbed a banana from our fruit basket and shook it in the air as he walked off. "Never grow up. It's a trap."

———

A week after I offered Ava a mentoring position, my whole team was on board. Each day, she'd study on a different floor and see how everything was run. She'd also travel with us to appointments and run tasks so she could get a real feel for the environment. I felt extremely grateful for how on board everyone was with me randomly bringing in a kid to follow us around for the summer.

Another week passed, and when Monday came around, Kierra showed up with her daughter, who seemed very timid and shy. I met them in the lobby, where Ava hid slightly behind her mother.

"Hey, you made it. Welcome," I said.

Kierra smiled, and I felt that shit in my gut. And chest. And all over my body. "Good morning, Gabriel. This is my daughter, Ava."

Ava stepped out a little and gave a timid grin and waved. "Hi."

"Hey, welcome to the team. We're so happy that you're here," I informed her.

She just kept nervously smiling.

Kierra leaned in toward me. "She's a little shy at first but warms up quickly."

"We can handle shy. Shy isn't a problem. But I'd love for my receptionist, Jackie here, to take Ava up to the wellness floor so she can make herself comfortable. A few of my employees are there to greet her and show her around."

"What's a wellness floor?" Ava quietly asked as Jackie walked over from behind the reception desk.

"It's a cool way to say video game and candy bar floor," Jackie whispered, nudging Ava in the side.

Ava's eyes lit up. "You have a video game and candy floor?"

I slid my hands into my slacks and rocked back and forth. "Sure do."

"I want to see!" She started to hurry off with Jackie to the fifth floor. "Come on, Mom."

"I'll be right there, Ava. I'm just going to speak with Gabriel for a second."

Ava was already pushing the elevator button as she told her mom okay. If she could've, she would've flown to the fifth floor faster. I didn't blame her. It was a damn cool floor.

Kierra nodded once toward me as she crossed her arms. "Thank you so much for doing this for her, Gabriel. This is truly remarkable. She hasn't stopped talking about it since I informed her about the mentorship. Henry and I are both truly grateful for the opportunity."

"Not a problem at all. It will be nice to have a young mind around. It will keep us on our toes."

"She's a tad bit shy at first, but I think being around other people besides her classmates will be good for her self-esteem. She dealt with a bit of bullying this past year at school, which was really hard to watch. It broke her down a bit, but I truly think this is an opportunity that will make her feel confident again."

"Don't worry. She's in good hands."

"I have no doubt about that." Her words felt so genuine and kind that it made me want to be even more protective over Ava than I had already planned to be. The last thing I wanted to do was let Kierra down.

Oh, and Henry.

I kept forgetting about that guy.

"I'll be picking her up after the day's done. Normally, Henry will be the one dropping her off. If there's any other issues, by all means, let me know," Kierra stated.

"Of course."

As we were speaking, the elevator opened and my mother and Bobby emerged from it. They looked our way before heading over.

Kierra stood taller as I went to introduce her.

"Mom, Bobby, this is Kierra. Her daughter, Ava, is the one interning here."

Mom raised an eyebrow. "Is that so?"

"It seems that way," Kierra shyly replied with a chuckle. Maybe her daughter got the touch of shyness from her. It slipped out every now and again.

Mom held her hand toward Kierra. "I'm Amma. I'm the office manager here. It's nice to meet you."

"You too," Kierra replied, shaking her hand.

Bobby shook her hand next. "I'm Bobby, one of the architects. I just want you to know I plan to destroy your kid in a game of Mario Kart."

Kierra laughed. "Don't be shocked if she makes you cry when you lose. She's really good at those kinds of things. She's pretty great at everything, really. If she gives any trouble here, though, please let me know."

"I doubt you're the type of person who brings trouble into people's lives, Kierra Hughes," Mom said. Which seemed like an odd-as-fuck thing to say, but then again my mom was odd when she didn't get enough coffee in the morning.

"I'm going to take Kierra up to meet with Ava and give them a proper tour of the office space," I told them both, and off Kierra and I went.

When we finished the tour, I said goodbye to Kierra and headed back to my office to get to work. Right as I sat down, Bobby popped his head around my doorframe and smiled from ear to ear.

"You lied," he said, matter-of-factly. "She *is* hot."

9

Gabriel

It only took a few days of Ava mentoring at my office to realize that she was shy up until the point she got excited about architecture. Everyone who worked for me was the best of the best, and I'd often find Ava getting them to talk their heads off about what they were each working on. The cool thing about it was that my employees loved to nerd out when speaking about their passions, so it made Ava's day whenever they'd go into deep detail on topics for her.

She was wise beyond her years, and watching her open up more and more each day, seeing her grow comfortable with being at GS Architecture, made me happy. She was a good kid with a good head on her shoulders. I was glad I was able to give her an opportunity to break out of her shell a bit.

"I heard rumors about you," Ava said one afternoon as we walked off the elevator to the fifth floor for our lunch break.

"That's never a good intro to a conversation," I joked.

"It's nothing bad," she argued, "Just weird. Is it true that you lost your memory?"

"That's true."

"Like *all* your memories."

"Most of them, yes. Anything before I was twenty."

"So, you're telling me your whole memory is gone from when you were nineteen and younger? Like, nothing?"

"Yup. Nothing."

"How is that even possible? You had to relearn everything?"

"A lot." I nodded. "Some things were just instinct, I believe. But for a long time, it was hard."

"And then you built all of this?"

"Uh-huh. I became highly focused on my career because even though everything else outside of me felt out of control, at least I had this thing that I could control. This building, my job, is my life."

"What about your friends from back then?" she asked as we walked over to the buffet for the afternoon. A Mexican food spread from a local restaurant was laid out in front of us, and the smells were enough to make my stomach rumble. Ava seemed less interested in the meal and more interested in asking me a million questions about my memory loss. "Or girlfriends. Did you have a girlfriend? Did you lose your friends?"

"A few people reached out, but it felt very hard to connect. I ghosted a lot of the people because I struggled with being what they expected me to be. Others ghosted me. I didn't blame them. It was a very dark period." I handed her a plate. "Why so many questions on this?"

"No reason," she said, taking the plate. "I've just never met a rich person who forgot half their life."

I laughed. "What makes you think I'm rich?"

She glanced around and waved her hands at everything. "Dude. You have an arcade room at your workplace, a whole room with candy, lunch catered every single day, a meditation room, *and* a Ping-Pong table. Only rich people do that."

"Touché."

"Plus," she started, "I googled your net worth."

"Those numbers are always extra extreme."

"You built properties for A-list celebrities and royalty in England. I doubt the numbers are fluffed."

Turns out Ava must've read my résumé.

She grabbed a few soft taco shells and began to fill them up with chicken and fajita peppers. "So, you didn't have a girlfriend before you lost your memory?"

"Not that I know of. If I did, she never showed up," I joked.

"But you didn't have some kind of feeling in you…as if there *was* a person?"

I did. Often. I figured that was why I dated around so much and met up with so many different types of women. For a long time, I felt as if I was searching for something, but the older I grew, the more I realized the woman in my head only existed there. She was a figment of my imagination. I didn't tell Ava all of that, though. It seemed too bizarre to mention to a fourteen-year-old.

"Sometimes, I get nudges," I explained. "Hunches, I suppose."

"Nudges and hunches?"

"Yes. As if something is familiar…but they don't always lead anywhere."

Ava frowned a little as she added toppings to the fajitas. "That kind of sounds like hell."

"Language," I scolded her.

"My mom said hell is a place, not a curse word. Anyway, I'm fourteen, Gabriel."

"Oh, well, all right then." Heck, I didn't know what words fourteen-year-olds were allowed to say.

"Do you have a girlfriend now or are you single?" she asked as she continued to build her tacos.

"Single."

"Do you like women?"

I smiled. "Love them. Quite a fan."

"Do you want to get married someday? Have kids?"

"Yeah. Maybe."

"*Tick- tock, tick-tock*," she said, tapping the invisible watch on her wrist. "You're kind of old to be single, and you're not getting any younger."

Once this kid's shyness wore off, she didn't pull her punches. "I'm only forty."

"'Only' and 'forty' don't belong in the same sentence. That's like five hundred and four in dinosaur years." She narrowed her eyes as she looked at me. "You have gray hairs in your beard."

"Trust me, kid. Time flies faster than you think."

"You're just saying that because you blacked out and missed twenty-one years of time."

"Again, touché." I chuckled. Ava was a smart-ass and I appreciated it. "What about you, kid? Are you dating someone?"

"Gosh, no. Guys my age are just so…gross. That's why I read my books. Fictional men will always do better by me than real boys. Men written by women are just better."

I laughed. "I have absolutely no clue what that means."

"It means the idea of boys is actually better than the reality of them." She shrugged. "Plus, a lot of boys in the real world don't like girls like me."

I arched an eyebrow. "Girls like you?"

"You know." She grew a bit somber as she looked down at herself. "*Fat* and *ugly*."

My jaw dropped. I froze in my tracks as I held a spoon of crema in the air. "Who the fuck told you that lie?" I barked, feeling a newfound rage shoot through my body.

"Language," Ava echoed.

"I'm forty years old. I can say 'fuck.' So again, who the fuck told you that lie?" I repeated, still beyond livid that this poor girl was told such bold-faced lies.

"Cory and James Harrison."

"Who the fuck are Cory and James Harrison?!"

"Twin brothers from my school. They told me that on the last day of school. The whole school year, they'd moo behind me, too, and make pig noises and call me Porky Pig."

"Where do they live?" I asked, dropping the spoon back into the container. "I'll kick their fucking asses."

"I'm pretty sure that's a crime," she said.

Then put me in prison.

Or at least let me beat up the assholes' parents.

"It's really okay," Ava said, continuing her way down the assembly line. "I'm fine with it."

I took her plate out of her hand and set it down on the buffet table. I placed mine down next. Then I placed my hands on her shoulders as I lowered myself to look her in the eyes. "Ava Hughes."

"Yes?"

"I need you to know a thing. 'Fat' isn't a bad word, but the way those boys used it was as an insult, and that shit's not okay. And the names they called you are not okay. And them calling you ugly is not okay. Because you are none of those things. Okay? You are not a cow, you are not a pig, and you are the furthest thing from ugly."

Her eyes watered and she nodded slightly. "Okay."

"Now say it to me. Say, 'My name is Ava Hughes, and I'm fucking beautiful.'"

She laughed. "I'm fourteen. I can say 'hell,' but not that word."

"Right now you can. It will be our secret. Say it."

"My name is Ava Hughes, and I'm fucking beautiful," she whispered.

"Again. But louder."

She giggled slightly, feeling silly, but she said it. "My name is Ava Hughes, and I am fucking beautiful!"

"Louder!" I said, tossing my hands into the air. "Louder! Like you mean it."

She took a deep breath and covered her face for a moment

before tossing her hands up like mine. "My name is Ava Hughes, and I'm fucking beautiful!" she shouted.

"Hell yeah you are, queen!" Erika from accounting shouted from the drink station.

I almost wanted to start jumping up and down with excitement, seeing Ava's confidence building from Erika cheering her on. I didn't even have to tell her to repeat the words, because she did that on her own.

"*MY NAME IS AVA HUGHES, AND I'M FUCKING BEAUTIFUL!*" she screamed at the top of her lungs, hopping up and down, waving her hands as if she believed every single word. As she should've. Because it was true.

Her name was Ava Hughes, and she was fucking beautiful.

"That's right, kid," I said, slightly shoving her shoulder. "And if those fuckboys ever say that kind of shit to you again, kick them in their balls."

She laughed and combed her hair away from her face. I knew she was Kierra's stepdaughter so the two of them didn't share DNA, but I swore they had the same smile and laugh—the same spark of light. "Can I eat my fajitas now?" She chuckled.

"Yeah, yeah. Go for it."

We grabbed our plates and walked over to join Erika to eat our lunch.

"I guess I don't have to do what Dad said I had to do in order to get them to stop making fun of me," Ava said as we took a seat.

"And what's that?"

"Lose weight. He said if I lost weight, they'd like me more."

Well. Now I wanted to kick her *father* in his fucking balls. What kind of advice was that? Losing weight would be one thing if it was for her overall health, but to tell her to lose weight so some dumbass, closed-minded boys would like her? Parenting fail.

"But now I know I can be fat and beautiful," she continued, taking her fajita and biting into it.

"Sure can. But also, never change yourself to fit into another person's box. Create your own life and ignore the opinions of others. You got that?"

"Yeah." She nodded. "And when all else fails, kick them in the balls."

Damn straight.

The problem with giving kids advice was that it often came back quickly to bite one in the ass.

On a Thursday morning, Ramona, Ava, and I ran errands all morning. I figured it was a good way to show Ava the miscellaneous tasks that popped up throughout the week. Our final stop was at a Home Depot. Ramona stayed in the car to make a few business calls, leaving me and Ava to head inside to get the supplies I needed.

"So you are busy all the time," Ava noted as she grabbed a cart for me to push.

"All the time," I echoed. "But it's a good busy. I like being busy."

"Me too. Plus, it's kind of cool to see how things start in architecture and then seeing the finished product."

"Exactly. The reward is great."

"Do you have a favorite project you've built?"

"There's a couple—"

"Oh my gosh, look, Cory! It's lard ass," a person said as Ava and I rounded a corner. There stood a pair of twin teenage boys, and I knew instantly from the comment who the dickheads were. Beavis and Butt-Head.

Ava's vibrant personality almost completely dissipated instantly, and that reaction broke my damn heart. It was like watching a shining star be burned out in an instant. Now I was angry.

The twins started snickering and making oinking noises. Ava stepped slightly behind me, trying to hide herself.

"Hey, what the hell is wrong with you two? Knock it off, assholes," I blurted out. Was I allowed to call teenage boys assholes? Who knew? Didn't care. All I cared about was making Ava feel safe and protected.

Before they could respond, a man rounded the corner. A big, big man. A man who was probably twice my size.

"Did you just call my boys assholes?" the beast from *Beauty and the Beast* asked as he puffed out his chest and walked toward me.

I could've shriveled up and said no like a little punk, but Ava was still hidden behind me, and I wasn't going to allow those teens to get away with the disrespect toward her.

I puffed out my own chest and nodded. "Yeah, I did.

Because your boys are being beyond disrespectful toward this nice young lady. I don't like bullies."

The grown ogre looked at his two boneheads. "Were you bullying her?"

"No, Dad! We weren't!" one of them stated.

"Yeah! We were just saying hi," the other lied.

Ogre looked at me and tilted his head. "You hear that? They were just saying hi to a friend."

"By oinking at her and calling her lard ass?" I bit back, getting even more annoyed as the words fell from my mouth.

Ogre looked at his sons, a small smirk on his face. "You oinked at her?"

The boys didn't respond, but snickered to themselves, shoving each other.

"Was it like this?" Ogre asked. "*Oink-oink-oink?*" he said, looking in Ava's direction.

I stepped in front of Ava to shield her from his eye contact. "All right, that's enough."

"I'm just making a joke." He laughed, patting my shoulder. "But maybe little Miss Piggy should avoid a cookie every now and again." He then shoved a finger to his nose, pressed it down, and made more oinking noises toward Ava.

And.

I.

Blacked.

Out.

At least for a solid five seconds, and somewhere within that five seconds, my fist slammed into the jerk's face. When I came back to reality, my face was being smashed in by his rock-hard fist. I went flying back against the shelf and caught Ava out of the corner of my eye kicking both twins between their legs and shouting, "You stupid fuck faces!"

The staff came and broke up the fight, kicking us all out of the store. As Ava and I walked back to the truck, Ramona jumped out to see me with one eye shut, and Ava hopping up and down.

"Did you see, Gabriel? Did you see me kick their asses! They didn't even touch me! They fell over to the ground like little wimps! I bet they never make fun of me again!"

"What in the world happened?" Ramona cried with the most perplexed look. "Geez, are you okay?"

"He's super! You should've seen him take a swing at that guy! Sure, maybe the guy swung *more* and *harder*, but boy oh boy, did Gabriel get one hit in! Sure, he didn't get *more* than *one* hit in, but—"

I swung the door open for Ava. "Get in the car, kid."

"Okay, Boss Man," she said, calling me the name that everyone else called me at work. If my head wasn't pounding from my pounding, I would've found that real fucking cute.

Okay, even with the headache, I found that *really* fucking cute.

After Ava climbed into the car, I shut the door for her. I then walked past Ramona and tossed her the truck keys. "It might be best that you drive. Seeing how I can't see."

The whole drive back to the office, I sat there grumbling to myself, thinking about how I'd have to tell Kierra about what happened when she picked up Ava later that day.

"Wait a second. Let me get this straight. You told her to kick them in the balls?" Kierra asked, alarmed, as I sat in my office with my head down in full-blown embarrassment. I had sunglasses on, too, hoping to avoid Kierra seeing the damage that Cory and James's father got in.

"I might've told her that. But in my defense, I didn't think we'd have an actual run-in with them and that she'd kick them in their damn balls."

"If there's one thing you should know about my daughter, it's that she takes everything literally. If you tell her to fly to the moon by tomorrow, she'll have the whole spaceship built tonight," she joked. "Can I ask you something, though?"

"Sure."

"Why are you wearing sunglasses and staring at the floor instead of looking at me?"

"Oh, it's just part of my creative process," I lied.

"Gabriel."

I groaned. "Yes?"

"Did you get into a fight at Home Depot, too?"

"I might've fallen into an altercation."

"Gabriel."

"Yes?"

"Look up."

I tilted my head up slowly.

She stood from her chair and walked over to me. She sat on the edge of my desk, facing me, and then removed my sunglasses. "Gabriel!" she gasped, her hand flying over her mouth.

"If you think this is bad, you should see the other guy," I joked.

"You beat up two kids?" she spat out, stunned.

"What? No! Of course not! I'm not some kind of madman." I flicked my thumb against my nose. "I beat up their father."

"Gabriel!"

"I know, I know, okay. Violence is never the answer. But those fuckers..." I grumbled as I struggled to open my left eye. "They were oinking at her, and it pissed me off. So I tried to get them to apologize, and then the dad made a few inappropriate jokes about Ava's weight, and next thing I knew, I was swinging and Ava was karate-kicking the boys' private parts."

Kierra's eyes flashed with a look I wasn't certain how to decipher. She touched my face slightly and I tensed up from the pain. I had a splitting headache. She then frowned and stood. She headed for the front door, and I felt an ache of sadness, realizing I'd pissed her off.

"Kierra—"

"Don't," she ordered, holding up a hand toward me.

She walked out of the room, and I slumped in my chair. What the hell was I thinking? Getting into a fight like that in front of a kid? Telling her to kick her bullies' asses? I knew better than that. I was better than that. But for some reason, watching that grown man talk down to Ava sent a rage through me that I wasn't certain I could hold in. It was one thing for teenage boys to be idiots, but to watch a grown man look at Ava and make those disgusting noises…

I sat for a few minutes, debating what I could text Kierra to show the depth of my apology. As I sat with my phone in my hands, I paused when I saw Kierra reentering my office with an ice pack wrapped with paper towel. I didn't say a word, and neither did she. She walked over and sat back down on my desk, leaned toward me, and placed the ice pack against my face.

I cringed slightly from the chill, but I took a deep breath as she held it in place.

"You're better than this," she whispered. "You're too mature to go around punching grown men."

"I know," I agreed. "It was idiotic."

"It was," she echoed. "But also…thoughtful. And heroic."

I sighed. "I don't want you or Ava to think less of me for this, Kierra. It was an impulse thing, and I hate that it happened. You don't beat bullies by attacking them. I'm sorry I even gave Ava that shitty advice."

"Yes. Maybe we should just stick with blueprints with her."

I huffed, feeling like complete dog shit. "Yeah, of course. Sorry. I just have a solid three rules when it comes to violence, I suppose."

"What are those rules?"

"Rule number one, never lay a hand on children. Number two, never lay a hand on women. And number three, knock out any man who breaks my first two rules." Kierra's fingers slightly brushed against my cheek as a small laugh escaped her. "What's funny?" I asked.

"Nothing, nothing. This just reminded me of someone I once knew. He used to be like you. He'd do anything to defend my honor."

"What happened with him?" I asked.

"Well." She pulled the ice pack away and gently touched the edges of my eye. Her eyes locked with mine and her lips quivered into a hesitant smile. "I fell in love with him."

"And then you married him?"

"Oh, gosh, no. He wasn't Henry."

That didn't surprise me in the slightest.

She placed the ice pack back on my eye.

"How many times have you been in love before?" I asked. It was probably too personal, but I couldn't help but wonder how many men caught the heart of Kierra and lost it before she settled in with Henry.

"Just twice."

"What happened to the first love? Did he break your heart?"

"No," she quickly stated, shaking her head. "I don't think he could break anyone's heart if he wanted to. He was one of the good ones. One of the best."

"So, you broke his heart?"

"In a way, maybe. But really, life broke both of our hearts. It has a way of taking great things and ruining them." She shifted slightly on the desk. "What about you? Have you ever been in love?"

"Well." My eyebrows drew together in a perplexed frown. "I'm still trying to figure out what that is."

"What *what* is?"

"Love."

She retracted the ice pack from my face, her fingers lingering against my skin with an unintentional caress, which made me wheel my chair in closer against my own will, as if she had a magnetic pull on me that I was unable to resist. The warmth of her touch ignited a longing in me that inexplicably made me want to grow closer and closer to her.

I'd be willing to endure endless black eyes just for the short-lived touches of her hand against my skin.

Her lips parted ever so slightly, yet the silence remained unbroken by words. I was at a loss for words, too. All I could do was gaze into her deep-brown eyes, lost in visions of what might've been if she wasn't a married woman and what touches I could've given to her if she wasn't another man's.

Yet, she was married. She was forever beyond my reach. Still, those fleeting moments, those tender touches fueled dreams I dared not confess.

My body gravitated closer to hers, drawn by an irresistible force that alarmed me as much as it enticed me. "Kierra..." I whispered, the word tumbling abruptly from my lips as my heartbeat quickened.

"Yes?" she responded, her voice quivering with uncertainty at our closeness. Yet, she leaned in, too. *She leaned in.* She felt it—the pull between the two of us. Each time I saw her, the magnetic pull felt stronger, more intense. More real. At first I thought I was making it up, but she leaned in, too.

"Are you happy with him?" I ventured, knowing I shouldn't have asked her such a question but needing to know the answer.

"Happy?" she echoed, her head tilting slightly in bewilderment, puzzled by the weight of my question. "With Henry?"

"Yes."

She was close. So close that her breath fell against my mouth. So close that if she whispered, only my soul could hear her secrets.

Abruptly, she rose from my desk. She shot back a few feet and cleared her throat. "You should ice your eye for a few hours tonight. And take Advil. And have someone check in on you to make sure you don't have a concussion."

I rose to my feet and walked toward her, not ready to leave the feeling that I felt—the feeling that she felt. "Kierra—"

"Does someone live with you?" she asked. "So they can check in on you?"

"No, they don't."

"Well, maybe someone should stay the night with you, to make sure. Or have someone call in to check."

"Kierra—"

"Can you not?" she asked, holding a hand up toward me. "I…" Her voice dropped and tears flooded her eyes. "Whatever you're going to say, can you just not say it?"

"I just want to know if you're happy."

"I know and I can't have you asking me that, Gabriel."

"Why not?"

"Because I can't force myself to lie to you about that, and if I told you the truth, it would be the first time I've said the words out loud, and I'm not ready to go there yet, okay?"

I nodded. "Okay."

"Okay." She sighed and shook herself slightly. "Keep icing your eye," she said, deflecting. The answer lay in her refusal to address my question; unhappiness was her unspoken truth. Had she been happy with Henry, affirmations of her love for him would've rolled off her tongue. Yet instead of declarations of love, she left me with advice for my eye.

"Keep icing," she repeated, a firm note in her voice. Maybe to silence my questions or maybe to steady herself and come back to reality.

I nodded and placed the ice pack back on my face. The coldness of it seeped into my skin, which was a strong contrast to how her warmth felt against my soul.

As the silence stretched between us, the sudden creak of the door shattered the moment. Ava peeked into the room, unaware of the tension she diffused with her simple presence.

"Mom, are you done yelling at Gabriel? I'm pretty sure he apologized like a billion times," she stated. Right then, reality snapped back, pulling us from the precipice of my forbidden emotions.

"Yes. I think he got the message," Kierra said, turning to her daughter. "And I'm happy to inform you that you'll be going to Cory and James's house to apologize in person with me later this week."

"What?" Ava gasped.

"Both of you," Kierra said, turning her stare to me.

What? I silently remarked.

"Oh, come on. Those guys deserved..." Ava started, but the stern look Kierra gave her made her words stop. "*Fine,*" she grumbled, then looked over at me. "Thanks anyway, Gabriel. I know you were just trying to look out for me."

"There are better ways than using fists, kid. Your mom made sure to remind me of that."

Kierra smiled slightly before wrapping her arm around Ava's shoulders. "Let's get home."

"Okay. Bye, Gabriel! See you later," Ava said.

"Bye, you two," I said with a small wave.

"Mom?" Ava whispered as she and Kierra walked out of my office.

"Yes?"

"I know you're probably pissed about what happened, and I get it, but you should've seen how he backed me up. It was just like in those books. I think he was written by a woman."

A small chuckle escaped me as Kierra glanced over her shoulder to look my way. A tiny grin flashed over her face before she turned back forward and continued walking. "Me too, Ava. Me too."

10

Kierra

SIXTEEN YEARS OLD

"A party?" I asked with a cocked brow as Rosie set down her lunch tray across from me. "At Brett's house?"

Rosie swirled her straw around before sipping her chocolate milk. We had been friends for a while, even though we were quite different people. She was more of a partier than I was. Gabriel was, too, but he never tried his hardest to get me to go to parties with him. If anything, he told me time and time again to avoid said parties.

"Some things are for good people, and some things are for not-so-good people. House parties aren't for you, Penguin," he'd swear.

"Is that because I'm a good person or a not-so-good person?" I replied.

He'd smile and roll his eyes. "Don't play dumb. You're a good one."

Rosie, however, didn't think like Gabriel. Her thoughts were the complete opposite of his, if I was honest. She was so determined to get me to a house party that one would think her life depended on it. She stood on the firm foundation that everyone deserved to go to parties.

"Yes, Kierra. A party at Brett's house. Just imagine how great it would be. Booze. Boys. Boys and booze." She clapped her hands together as if that combination was the highest level of life's success. "We have to go."

"Or," I offered, "we could *not* go."

Rosie pouted as she sipped her chocolate milk and gave me puppy-dog eyes. "Kierra. Please."

"Don't you normally go to these things with Monica?"

"She's in Florida visiting her grandparents. Besides, I want to go with you."

"Why?"

"So you can stop being antisocial and actually talk to Brett Stevens."

My cheeks flushed. "Why would I want to talk to Brett Stevens?"

"Because you've been in love with the guy for years, and he doesn't even know you exist."

"Exactly. Crushes should never know that a person exists. It ruins the mystery of it all." Gabriel thought I was crazy for having a crush on Brett. Then again, Gabriel hated every guy that I ended up having a crush on. To be fair, I hated every girl he'd ever fallen for, too.

"Kierra." Rosie pouted. "Please. It's my birthday weekend, and I really want to go with you! It would be the best birthday ever."

I grumbled, feeling guilty. If that was her main birthday wish, I could make it come true. Besides, how bad could a party at Brett's be? "If we go—"

"We're going!"

"*If* we go," I continued, "we only stay for a while, and we leave together. No matter what."

"And you'll kiss Brett Stevens."

"I'm not kissing Brett Stevens."

"Why not? You've been crazy about him for years!"

"I know," I agreed. "That's exactly why I don't want to kiss him. You don't kiss the person you're crazy about. Then there's always room for a letdown. I've never even spoken to the guy. I prefer to keep my distance from him."

"Like a creeper lurker in the bushes."

"Exactly. Then he can't crush my crush on him due to not being interested."

"Why wouldn't he be interested in you? News flash, Kierra—you're hot. Yeah, sure you went through your weird brace-face phrase, but you came out stronger for it."

"I...don't know if that's a compliment."

"Doesn't matter. I'll pick you up at eight. This is going to be so much fun."

Why did I not have the heart to tell her I didn't want to go? Oh, because I was a sucker for wanting to please other people before myself. If I had it my way, I'd be home each night reading about fictional people who felt more alive than most real humans.

Later that night when Rosie showed up, I dreaded dragging

myself over to the party. I felt a mixture of nerves, panic, and excitement. What if I officially talked to Brett that night? What if we were able to interact with each other? What if he had a crush on me the same way I had a crush on him?

Clearly, I was in a full-blown delusional state as I walked up his front steps. The party was blasting with music, and a ton of people I knew but didn't really know were all over the place laughing and drinking.

It was funny how you could be around people all the time and realize not a single person knew anything about you.

"Drinks, drinks, we need drinks!" Rosie cheered. She placed her hands on my shoulders and locked her eyes with mine. "Don't move, okay? I'll grab drinks. Vodka or tequila?"

"Water."

Rosie smiled. "Vodka it is!"

She hurried away, and I leaned backward against the staircase. As my eyes darted around the room, I felt more and more out of place. The things we did for friends.

"Penguin, what the hell are you doing here?" was heard from my left.

I looked over to meet Gabriel's brown eyes and felt a wave of comfort. Someone I actually knew and loved. My eyes moved to the person Gabriel had his arm wrapped around. Ali Thomas.

Ugh.

They'd been dating for over a year, and I was almost certain I was her sworn enemy. I'd never even done anything to her, but I knew it was because Gabriel was my best friend. It wasn't shocking that the girls Gabriel dated had something against me. I probably would feel weird, too, if my boyfriend's best friend was another girl.

But there was nothing between Gabriel and me except the greatest of friendships. Ali had nothing to worry about. Still, I got her cold, harsh stares whenever we crossed paths.

I smiled. "Rosie wanted me to come to my first party in celebration of her birthday."

Gabriel's brow knit. "You could've just bought her a gift. You hate parties."

"Yeah, well. It's what she requested."

Ali smirked and shook her head. "What would you even do at a party? Read a book?"

"My hope is to find one hidden somewhere in the house," I joked. Well, half-joked. Because Rosie had made me leave my current read at home, I was certain she secretly hated me.

Gabriel's mouth curved up, and I loved how it looked on him. "Good luck finding a book here. I doubt Brett knows what reading is."

"Hey now, be nice," I ordered.

He rolled his eyes. "Oh right. Your stupid crush."

"It's not stupid," I argued, glancing around to see if Brett was anywhere to be found.

Ali began picking at her nails and looked around before pouting. "Gabriel, I need a drink."

His eyes darted back and forth between Ali and me before he nodded. "Sure. Okay."

"I doubt Kierra drinks, though. So just one for me," Ali demanded.

I stood taller. "For your information, I *am* drinking tonight." Ali's jabs were growing more and more annoying with each minute that passed. I knew how to let loose. I knew how to have a good time.

It just so happened that my good time didn't involve booze; it involved fiction. Still, I wanted to shove it in her face. Luckily for me, Rosie came over with my drink in her hand.

"Here you go, Kierra. Hey, Gabriel!" Rosie sang. Her eyes moved over to Ali, and she grimaced. "Alison."

"*Ali*," Ali corrected. "Nice to see you, Rosalina."

"*Rosie*," Rosie responded.

Gabriel chuckled slightly. If there was anyone Ali hated more than me, it was Rosie. Maybe because Rosie didn't back down from Ali's controlling nature. She stood ten toes down against Ali and her rudeness.

Gabriel nodded toward Rosie. "Happy birthday, Rose."

"Thanks, Gabriel. My gift is getting Kierra out to a party. Are you as shocked as I am?"

"Stunned," he said.

I took a sip of my drink and instantly wanted to spit it out, but I powered through because Ali thrived on witnessing others' weaknesses. For the life of me, I couldn't understand why Gabriel was obsessed with dating the rudest girl at our school. Then again, Ali was easy on the eyes, and Gabriel did have a bit of a bad-boy persona. On paper, they made sense. Except that Gabriel wasn't a complete monster. At least not with me.

He didn't showcase the soft side he shared with me in private very often, though. It was his best-kept secret.

Ali grumbled. "Gabriel. My drink."

"Oh, sorry, Ali. I didn't even notice that you don't have feet," Rosie said.

Ali cocked her left eyebrow. "What?"

"Well, seeing how you are ordering Gabriel to get your drink, I figured your own legs didn't work."

"Oh shut up, Rosie. I'm done here," Ali said, marching off to retrieve her drink on her own. "Hurry up, Gabriel!" she shouted over her shoulder.

Gabriel shook his head. "I'm going to get my ass chewed out for that. You know that, right, Rose?"

"Yeah, well, it might wake you up to the fact that you shouldn't date monsters. Speaking of... I'm going to go hurry off to see Jason." Rosie looked over at me. "You good?"

I nodded. "Yup. I'll be...here."

"Okay. I'll be back soon!"

Rosie scooted off, leaving Gabriel and me together. I leaned against the staircase, and he leaned right beside me. I took another sip from my cup and made a slight face.

"You do know you don't have to drink that, right?" he asked me.

"What? No. It's fine. I'm cool. I'm hip. I'm a party animal."

He laughed. "Penguin."

"I mean it. I'm sick of Ali hating me and calling me a good girl."

"So you feed into her bullshit by drinking?"

"If that will get her to shut up, yes."

His brows knit. "I can tell her to stop being rude to you. I have no problem doing that."

"Don't you dare," I ordered. "I'm not going to be the reason you end up single, because I run off everyone you date."

"You know why she hates you, right?"

"Because I'm ridiculously charming, likable, and beautiful?" I joked.

"Yeah."

He didn't follow it up with anything else. A strange butterfly sensation hit the pit of my stomach from his words. He looked down at the floor and flicked his thumb against his nose before looking back up. "You don't have to try to fit in here, Kierra. You weren't born to do that."

"To have fun?"

He laughed. "To fit in."

"Gabriel!" was hollered from the kitchen, and we both looked over to see Ali standing there, pouting.

"Duty calls." He nudged my arm. "I'll check on you later."

"You don't have to. Be a good boyfriend," I told him. "I'm good."

"I'll check on you later," he repeated before giving me a half grin as he walked away to his whiny princess.

I stayed glued to the staircase, studying everyone around me as I sipped the disgusting drink in my hand. Rosie seemed to be having the time of her life, finding her social butterfly skills hitting an all-time high. Her birthday dreams were coming true, and I was fine taking a back seat to be a side character to her story. I knew if I asked Rosie to spend the day reading with me in the library, she'd be right there, front and center. Even if that meant she'd have to be quiet. My dear friend struggled to not talk much.

"Do you always hang out against stairwells at parties?" a person said, making me stand straighter.

I glanced up to find Brett Stevens in front of me. I looked over my shoulder to see if he was talking to someone else, but all I found was the stairwell. Obviously.

As I tried to choke down my bursting spike of panic, I just smiled.

No words were anywhere to be found, which was expected. I had a way of freezing up when I was nervous, scared, happy—or, well, any emotion. I froze up instantly like a Popsicle.

Brett held another cup toward me. "I noticed you've been chewing on that cup for a while now. Figured you needed a new drink."

My eyes all but bugged out of my skull. He noticed me? *"You noticed me?"*

"How could I not? You're the most beautiful girl in this place." He leaned back against the stairwell beside me. "Want to screw?"

"Screw what?" I asked, taking a sip.

"Me."

I spat my drink out, stunned by his words.

That was not how I saw my first interaction with Brett Stevens going.

"What?" I laughed, feeling as if he was just joking. "No. Do you even know my name?"

"Yeah. Ali told me like five minutes ago. She told me you have the hots for me, so here you go." He rubbed his chest up and down. The level of disgust that hit me instantly was at an all-time high. That was exactly why one shouldn't ever interact with their crushes. They never live up to the hype.

A crush that was formed over three years was now *crushed* within two seconds of actual interaction. It was as if my sweet porcelain doll of Brett Stevens had shattered right in my face. Tragic.

"So…what is my name?"

"Naomi," he said with the utmost confidence.

Welp.

That was underwhelming.

I pushed out a smile. "I'm not interested, but thanks."

He gave me a stern look of disappointment. "You're a tease."

I then excused myself from the comfy stairwell that had been tainted by my ex-crush and started walking around, searching for Rosie or Gabriel to save me from my heart-shattering reality.

While I couldn't locate them, I felt an urgent need to use the restroom after my drinks of the evening. I felt a little dizzy, but I wasn't wasted. At least I didn't think I was. Was this what wasted felt like? It was hard to tell. I'd never been wasted before. All I knew was when I walked, sometimes I faltered, and when my stomach turned, I sometimes felt like throwing up.

After seeing a line for the bathroom downstairs, I headed upstairs in search of another one. When I opened a door, I found an emptied bedroom with an attached bathroom. I hurried inside, hoping to make a quick in-and-out.

Once I stepped out of the bathroom, I reentered the

bedroom to find Brett standing there in front of the bedroom door with his hands on his hips.

"Well, well, well. Funny meeting you here, Naomi."

Gabriel

"I can't believe Brett went for Kierra. I didn't know she partied like that," Ali said as she grabbed another drink from the fridge.

"What do you mean?" I asked Ali, completely confused.

"I told him she had the hots for him, and you know Brett. He's into anything with two legs. Rumor has it that Kierra was dragged off to Brett's bedroom. To be honest, I didn't think Ms. Goody Two-Shoes had it in her."

Dragged off?

If I knew anything about Kierra, it would be that she wouldn't want to be tossed alone in a room with some guy she had a crush on after their first night of talking. And last I saw her, she was pretty tipsy.

The sensation of jangling nerves filled my gut as my hands formed fists. "I'll be back."

Ali huffed. "You can't be serious. Let them be alone, Gabriel. If anything, this gets her to stop riding your dick so much. She's so annoyingly obsessed with you."

"We're done," I said without a second of hesitation.

Ali raised her brows. "Excuse me?"

"You and me—we're done." I didn't stay to hear her yelling

at me, calling me all kinds of names. I headed straight for Brett's room but before barging in, I waited a second. What if Kierra did want to be in there? What if I was being a massive cockblock? What if—

"Wait. Stop, Brett," was what I heard on the other side of the door.

That was enough to make me burst into the room. Kierra was pinned against a wall by her wrists, twisting and turning to try to get Brett off her. Without thought, I rushed over and yanked Brett away from her, tossing him across the room.

"Dude, what the fuck?" Brett blurted out as he crashed to the floor.

I ignored him as I placed my hands against Kierra's face. "You okay?"

She nodded nervously, her eyes packed with drunkenness, panic, and tears.

I wrapped my arm around her and asked if she was all right. She didn't respond. I hated that she didn't respond.

We walked out of the bedroom with people staring our way as we headed for the front door. Rosie saw us, and she hurried over.

"Is everything okay?" she asked, concern dripping from every word.

"I'm taking her home," I said. "You need a ride?"

"No, I'm walking. I'm only a few houses away. Kierra, are you okay?"

Kierra nodded slowly and forced out a smile. "I'm okay."

She was lying, and I knew it. I pulled her outside and

headed straight to my car. I placed her in the passenger seat, and the moment I slid into the driver's seat, I slammed my door shut.

I gripped the steering wheel and slowly released a breath before turning to her and asking, "Are you okay?"

"Yes."

"You're lying."

"I'm fine. Should you be driving, though?"

"I don't drink when I come to these things with Ali. She gets wasted, so I always stay sober."

"Oh…where is Ali?"

"Don't know. Don't care."

Kierra sat straighter. "Are you two okay?"

"Are *you* okay?" I countered.

She frowned.

My fucking heart shattered. "Penguin…"

"Can we just drive, please? I don't want to be here, Gabriel."

I wanted to argue, but the slight tremble in her tone made me feel sick. I turned on the ignition and drove off. "That place was filled with dicks. You shouldn't have been in a place like that," I scolded as I drove the drunken girl home.

"Why not? You were there."

"Yeah, well"—I shrugged—"I'm a dick."

"The dickest dick that ever dicked." She gently giggled as she curled her knees in to her chest. Right as the laughter faded, a somber look invaded Kierra's drunken eyes and she turned to look out the window. Her head rested against the headrest, and she sniffled slightly.

A knot formed in my gut. "Did he hurt you?"

"What?" she asked, not turning to face me.

"Brett. Did he hurt you?"

When she looked over her shoulder at me, her eyes were filled with tears. She raised her left shoulder and allowed it to drop. "It's fine."

The amount of anguish that shot through my system was alarming. I pulled the car over to the curb and put it in park. I took off my seat belt and turned to face her. "What did he do, Kierra?" I asked softly, trying to not scare her with the amount of rage I felt building up inside me.

A few tears slipped out and she quickly swiped them away with the collar of her shirt. "Nothing. It's fine. He just... He was trying to..." Her voice cracked as she shut her eyes and more tears fell down her cheeks. "It doesn't matter. You got there before he could get my clothes off."

"He forced himself on you?" I asked.

"Gabriel..."

"Kierra. Tell me now. Did he force himself on you?"

Her brown eyes reappeared and they were dripping with the truth that she seemed scared to say out loud. She broke her stare from mine and nervously fiddled with her hands. She slowly nodded. "I just went into that room to get away from the crowd, and he followed me. I didn't even know it was his room, but when I tried to leave, he blocked the door and tried to kiss..."

More tears from her.

More rage from me.

My hands gripped the steering wheel. "All right," I stated calmly.

She placed a hand on my forearm. "It's fine, Gabriel. I'm okay."

"He forced himself on you," I sniped, my anger not for her, but for Brett.

"It's fine. I'm fine," she lied.

"You're not. You're drunk and sobbing because that fucking asshole tried to take advantage of you, Kierra. That's fucked up."

"You showed up in time. You made sure nothing happened. So, it doesn't matter."

"It does!" I shouted, slamming my hands against the steering wheel. I shut my eyes and took a deep breath. "*It fucking matters, Kierra.*"

"I know," she whispered, her voice shaky. "I know."

When I opened my eyes, I saw how scared she'd been. I reached over and pulled her into a hug. She wrapped her arms around me tightly and held on as if she'd never let go.

"Thanks for saving me, Gabriel."

"Always, Kierra. Just make me a promise, all right? If you ever need me, you'll call me. I don't care if we're in some kind of fight over something big or little. No matter what, we have to be there for one another, all right? We have to look out for each other. You can call me no matter what, and I can call you no matter what."

She wiped away her falling tears and nodded slowly as she tugged on the sleeves of her shirt. "Okay. I promise."

Kierra

When I showed up to school on Monday, Brett had two black eyes. Gabriel had swollen knuckles. We never talked about what happened. We never talked about that party again. Yet, I figured that was when it began to happen for me. That was the moment I'd begun to fall in love with my best friend.

11

Gabriel

PRESENT DAY

After a day that did not go as planned, I lay on my couch around ten at night, sipping a beer as I watched a movie and Bentley lay on top of my feet, snoring. My eye still stung from that damn punch.

My phone, set beside me, dinged. I lifted it up, surprised to see a text message from an unknown number.

Unknown: Are you still alive? Do you have a concussion?

I sat up slightly.

Gabriel: Kierra?
Kierra: Yeah. Sorry. I had your business card with your number on it. I just wanted to make sure you were alive.

I saved her number instantly.

Gabriel: Alive and somewhat well.

Kierra: Good. No concussion?

Gabriel: How would I know if I had a concussion?

Kierra: Symptoms include confusion, headaches, memory loss, nausea, vomiting, sleepiness, confusion, ringing in the ears, and dizziness.

Gabriel: Did you just WebMD that and copy and paste?

Kierra: I might have copied and pasted from WebMD.

Gabriel: Well, don't worry. I think I'm okay. Just a bruised eye and a bruised ego.

Kierra: Okay. Good.

Kierra: I mean, not good that your eye and ego are bruised, but you know what I mean.

I chuckled a little.

Gabriel: I know what you mean.

Kierra: Good.

Gabriel: I'm also sorry for getting a little too personal earlier. I didn't mean to make you uncomfortable.

A few minutes passed with no reply, and I felt like an idiot for even bringing that up. That was until my phone started ringing, and her name popped up on the screen. I hesitated for a moment before answering, thinking it was an accidental call.

"Hello?"

"Hi," she murmured, her voice carrying the weight of exhaustion. "Sorry, I don't mean to bother you."

"Not a bother. I just wasn't sure if the call was accidental."

"Yeah, no. It's not. I mean, I don't know. I don't know what I'm doing."

"Are you okay?"

"Yes… I mean, no… I mean…" She seemed disoriented as her words stumbled from her tongue, but I waited patiently for her to collect her thoughts. "Ava's at her grandmother's house, Henry is out drinking with a few colleagues, and my pillowcase smells like her."

"Like who?"

"Lena."

"Who's Lena?"

"Our private chef."

Oh.

Fuck.

"I also found one of her earrings," she said. "She wears a certain type. It was under my blanket and poked me in the leg when I crawled beneath my blankets to sleep."

"Kierra—"

"Can you ask me again?" she cut in.

"Ask you what?"

"If I'm happy."

I felt nervous to ask for some reason. Maybe because I knew she'd answer, and I wasn't certain she was ready to answer. I wasn't certain she was ready to express her truth out loud.

"Are you happy, Kierra?"

"No," she quickly replied. "But maybe some people aren't meant to be happy. Maybe some people are just meant to be heartbroken."

"Maybe that's true. But I don't think those people are you."

"How can you be so sure? You hardly know me."

"I know," I agreed. "It makes no sense, but I *feel* you, Kierra. I don't know how to explain it, but I can tell the type of person you are, and you aren't a person that's meant to be unhappy."

"You feel me?" she asked, slightly perplexed.

"Yes," I told her. "I feel you sometimes even when you aren't around."

"Gabriel?"

"Yes?"

"I feel you, too," she whispered.

Fuck my heart…

It just did a million somersaults in my chest.

"Why are you staying with him?" I asked. "If you're so unhappy. If he's cheating. If he's a complete shit in all ways."

"Because of Ava."

"You could be without him and still have Ava. She's still your daughter."

"Yes, she is. But not on paper, and he's told me repeatedly that he'll take her away from me if I leave him."

"He can't really mean that."

"You must not know my husband."

"Why would he make Ava suffer, though? It doesn't make sense."

"Because it would hurt me…and that would please him."

"There must be a way out, Kierra. We can figure out—"

"We don't have to figure this out now. It's not even your

responsibility," she cut in with a weighted sigh. "I just wanted to hear someone else's voice to drown out the heaviness of my own thoughts."

"Okay." I paused for a moment, considering what else I could say to keep the conversation moving away from Henry. To lighten her spirits. To give her some kind of peace when her world seemed to be nothing but storms.

"What's your favorite thing to do when you feel overwhelmed?" I asked her. "Something that's just yours."

"Sit by the ocean and draw. I haven't done it in so long. I used to drive out to the coast and stay for hours, just listening to the water crashing against the shore. It stilled everything else for a while. It calmed down all the commotion in my head."

"I'll be by your place in twenty minutes."

She laughed. "No, Gabriel. That isn't—"

"Kierra."

"Yes?"

"Put your shoes on and bring your sketchbook. I'll see you soon."

I found her waiting on her front porch. She headed to the car and hopped in. When she looked over to me, she shyly smiled and thanked me for coming to get her.

"Always," I told her.

Oddly enough, I felt that was true.

I didn't know I could say *always* to a person I hardly knew—and mean it. Yet there I was, promising it.

She kept smiling but didn't reply. She held her sketchbook

close to her chest and tilted her head toward me. She reached out and gently touched my eye. "Are you okay?"

"I've been worse."

"Well, we'll take that answer tonight."

"Are you okay?" I asked.

Her full lips fell slightly. "I've been worse," she echoed.

I snickered. "We'll take that answer tonight."

I pulled off and we drove back over to my property that sat right on the coastline.

Kierra's eyes widened in amazement as she looked at the cabin-style ranch home with large windows and a wooden porch that wrapped around the whole house. The place wasn't huge, but it was comfortable. I owned a good handful of acres, and I could've expanded the size of the house if I wanted to, but it was just me and Bentley inside the place. I didn't see the point of having a huge home that would just feel empty most of the time.

It was lit up by the string of lights I had set up around the porch, and two rocking chairs facing the backyard had drawing tables. I spent a lot of my nights out there sketching for hours, listening to the waves crash against the shoreline. My boat was sitting at the dock, floating back and forth slightly from the waves.

As Kierra walked around the porch, her mouth hung open. "This is home?"

"This is home," I said as I slid my hands into my pockets. "It's not much, but it's—"

"So perfect," she breathed out. We'd reached the back of

the porch, and the moment she saw the water, she couldn't help but smile. Her hands fell to the porch railing and she took in a breath. "This is perfect, Gabriel."

"It's home."

"When I was younger, I wanted a place like this. I wanted something rustic and authentic, with lots of windows for natural sunlight. A place that felt like home." Before I could reply, Bentley started barking at the back door. She whipped around to face the door. "You have a dog?"

"Yeah, sorry. I should've mentioned that. Are you afraid or allergic? I can keep him inside—"

"Let him out," she urged.

I opened the door, and Bentley came jumping all over me. I bent down and snuggled him. "He's a big teddy bear and loves giving kisses," I informed her as I was attacked with dog slobber. "Okay, Bent, chill, will you?" I chuckled.

Kierra stood still, and the moment Bentley looked over to her, he headed straight for her. "Bent is his name?"

"Bentley," I corrected. "Bent for short."

Her brown eyes locked on mine. They looked as if they were seconds away from being flooded with tears. "His name is Bentley?"

"Yes?"

"And he's a...German shepherd?"

"Yup. He's my best friend."

Kierra choked out a sob and covered her mouth. "Sorry. Gosh, I'm so emotional lately." She bent down and began to pat Bentley. He rolled over to his back for belly rubs, like the little pet whore he'd always been, wagging his tail back and forth at a wild speed. Kierra's tears released from her eyes as she petted Bentley all over. "Hey, sweet boy," she whispered. "Aren't you the perfect creature."

I stood back, watching the interaction between the two. She seemed embarrassed by her emotions, but I didn't think that was anything to be shy about. I found it refreshing—how someone could feel so much, so deeply.

Kierra had a lot going on in her life. It wasn't shocking that tears found their way down her cheeks often. She was in a season of hardship. Hell, she'd just found another woman's jewelry in her bedsheets. I'd be a bit off-kilter, too. I just felt glad that she allowed her tears to fall around me. As if I were some kind of safe place for her to feel the deepest of feelings.

She stood and rubbed her arms up and down. She smiled my way and wiped her tears before crossing her arms. "He's a sweetheart."

"He's my best friend."

"I'm so happy for you, Gabriel. I'm so happy that you have this life and Bentley."

I smiled and gestured toward the two chairs with the drawing tables set up. "Do you want to sketch with me?"

"Absolutely."

"Wine?"

"Absolutely," she repeated.

I walked inside and grabbed two glasses, a bottle of red wine, and a sweatshirt because I saw Kierra slightly shivering.

She slid on the sweatshirt—so big that she swam in it—and

thanked me as I poured her wine. She opened her sketchbook, and I was stunned by her drawings.

"Fashion designs?" I asked, taking my seat.

"Yeah. I used to want to be a fashion designer."

"How does one go from wanting to be a fashion designer to becoming a therapist?"

"I ask myself that all the time." She paused and shrugged. "I guess I wanted to do something that helped people feel better."

"Great clothes can do that—a confidence boost of sorts."

"True, but after I went through something hard, I turned to therapy. It helped me so much that I wanted to help others. I still design pieces for Ava. Most of the stuff you've seen her wearing was made by me."

"No way. That's amazing, Kierra. These designs are amazing. I see where Ava gets her sketching talent."

She laughed. "She's a million times better than me."

We began drawing as we listened to the water crashing against the shore. There were periods of time when we were silent, yet that didn't feel uncomfortable or awkward. It just felt...right. There was something so welcoming about a peaceful silence. I hated forced conversation.

Every now and then, I'd catch Kierra looking my way out of the corner of my eye, and I didn't know why, but when she looked at me, my whole body heated up.

"Okay, drawing-hand break. Time for a game," she said, placing her drawing pencil down. "Two truths and a lie."

I put my pencil down, laced my fingers together, and stretched my arms in the air. "Game on. You first."

"I am deathly afraid of roller coasters. I played softball all through high school. I won a whistling competition."

I narrowed my eyes. "You can't whistle for shit."

She arched an eyebrow, seemingly stunned by my pick. Then she licked her lips multiple times, puckered her lips together, and blew. And not a damn whistle came out. Only the sound of her blowing air.

I chuckled at the worst attempt at whistling I'd ever heard in my life.

"Okay, not a professional whistler," she confessed. "Your turn."

I rubbed my palm against my chin. "I'm allergic to shellfish, I don't like peanut butter at all, and I used to smoke cigarettes."

"Easy, you never smoked."

"That's true."

"Okay, my go." She rubbed her hands together as she turned to face me more in her chair. She folded her legs into the chair and got comfortable. "*Heart and Souls* is one of my all-time favorite movies, I love puzzles, and I'm in love with my husband."

My chest tightened from her last one. "You don't love him."

She tugged on the sleeves of my sweatshirt and slowly shook her head. "I don't love him."

"Have you said that out loud before?"

"Not until now. Not until here."

"Why now?"

Her shoulders rose and fell swiftly. "I guess you just make it easier for me to be real." She bit her bottom lip and looked down at her hands in her lap. "Your go."

"All right, um...." I took a big chug of my wine before setting the glass down. "I want to draw you right now, I've had multiple dreams about you, and I love grilled-cheese sandwiches."

Her eyes widened with astonishment as she whispered, "You hate grilled-cheese sandwiches."

"I hate grilled-cheese sandwiches."

Her full lips stayed slightly parted. "Which means the other two are true?"

"The other two are very true."

"Okay." She tugged on the sleeves of my sweatshirt more, before standing and pulling her chair back away from me. She then sat and posed. "You can draw me."

I gathered my materials and began to draw her. We sat in silence again for at least twenty minutes as I sketched until she said, "You really dream of me?"

"Often," I stated, staring down at my sketchbook.

"What are the dreams about?"

I paused my pencil strokes and looked up toward her. "About me loving you."

"Oh," she murmured. "Do you wake up happy after them?"

"No," I quickly confessed. "Because when I wake, I know that the dreams aren't true."

Her lips turned down as a somber thought found her. She looked like she had a lot to say. As if her thoughts were spiraling so fast that she wasn't certain what words would make the most sense to express. She glanced at her phone. "What time is it?"

I glanced at my watch. "Two in the morning."

"Geez, I should get going. If Henry comes home and I'm not there, it will be a whole thing." She stood from her chair and smoothed her hands over my sweatshirt. "Sorry."

"No, it's fine. Not a problem."

I drove her home in silence while my mind debated repeatedly whether I'd overshared during the two truths and a lie game. I was beating myself up with my thoughts about it the whole time, but what was I supposed to say? *Sorry for telling you the truth, Kierra. Oh, also by the way, not only do I dream about you, but I think about you every waking day of the week. No big deal.*

As I pulled up to her place, she thanked me once more before she opened the passenger door.

"Gabriel?" she asked, turning back toward me.

"Yes?"

"Sorry, there's something important that I need to get off my chest. It's been bothering me for a while. I've been thinking about it for hours tonight, ever since you've brought it up, and if I don't say it, I'll explode."

Nerves built up within me at an alarming speed. "What is it?"

She bit her bottom lip and sighed. "I think it's really, *really* creepy how you don't like grilled-cheese sandwiches. It's toasted bread with melty cheese. What's not to like?"

I laughed. "Add it to my list of flaws."

A slight smile touched her lips. "It's a very short list."

"I'm sure you'll find more things to add to it over time."

"Not too sure about that. Good night."

"Good night, Penguin."

Her whole body froze. "What did you just call me?"

What *did* I just call her?

Penguin?

Where did that come from? What did that even mean?

Fuck, I didn't know why I said that. My eyes narrowed in confusion. "Sorry, I meant good night, Kierra. I don't know where that came from. I'm sorry, my brain's fried."

She gave me a small grin and nodded as she climbed out of my car. "Good night."

Her hand stayed on the car door, and she cleared her throat and said my name once more.

"Yeah?" I asked.

Her brown eyes fluttered open and closed as she murmured six words that would keep me up for the remainder of the short night. "I've had dreams about you, too."

12

Kierra

Good night, Penguin.

It was two thirty in the morning when Gabriel took me home. We'd sat under his porch lights sketching for hours. We talked a little but drew more. The only reason I'd left was because my eyes grew heavy and I knew I'd hate to deal with explaining to Henry why I was out all evening.

Yet to my surprise, when Gabriel dropped me off, Henry's car was not in the driveway. As I headed to bed, I realized I was still wearing Gabriel's sweatshirt that smelled like him. As I pulled it off, I held it close to my chest and breathed in deeply. If I had it my way, I would've stayed at Gabriel's house. If I had it my way, I would've never left him all those years before.

I stayed wide awake for a while, thinking about my time with Gabriel and how he'd called me Penguin.

He was remembering.

Maybe not fully, and maybe not clearly, but he was recalling pieces of us slowly but surely.

I couldn't help but wonder if that was a good or bad thing. Every day that passed, I found myself resenting Amma more. She needed to tell Gabriel about Elijah. He deserved to know, and the more time I spent around him, the more I felt like I was betraying him, too, by withholding that information. When I saw Amma again, I'd push for her to tell him.

Each day I fought demons in my mind, feeling heavy levels of guilt for the secrets that were being kept from the kindest man I've ever met. Gabriel deserved to know. He deserved to grieve.

I wavered back and forth about the idea of telling him everything. Even the parts that would make him hate me. Because Elijah deserved it. He deserved to be known by the brother who loved him the deepest. But then the other side of guilt filled me up, knowing that Amma ordered me to stay quiet because I was the cause of it all…

I was the one who took her son away from her. I was the reason Gabriel no longer had a brother. If it were Ava who had been lost, I didn't know how I'd react. Death changed individuals into versions of themselves that weren't even recognizable. Grief shifted a person's soul in a million different directions. Who was I to tell a mother how she was supposed to heal from the hardest heartbreak of her life? Who was I to determine her timeline?

But this was Elijah, and Gabriel loved that little boy so very much…

Gosh, he deserved to know.

I knew it wasn't my story to tell, yet if Amma didn't step up and do what was right, I would be left with little choice but to speak up on Elijah's behalf.

Because a boy like him deserved to be remembered.

Even if that meant Gabriel would never speak to me again.

———————

When I woke in the morning, Henry's side of the bed was messy, but he wasn't there. I heard a commotion in the kitchen and pulled myself out of bed. He must've come and gone quite quickly, only resting a few hours.

When I reached the kitchen, I found Henry sitting at the counter with Ava. Lena was scrambling up breakfast at the stovetop.

I raised an eyebrow, walked over to Ava, and kissed her forehead. "Morning, Sunshine. I thought you were staying at your grandmother's until this afternoon."

"It is afternoon, Mom," she said. "Lena's making us brunch."

Was it already noon? Had I slept in that long? "I could've made brunch," I urged, looking over to Lena, who had enough nerve to smile at me as if she wasn't sleeping with my husband. *Husband* being a term I was using very loosely.

"It's not a problem. I love spending extra time here," Lena said. "You're my favorite family that I'm able to cook for."

I bet we are, Lena.

I walked over to the coffeepot and filled a big mug for myself.

"Get me one, too, will you?" Henry requested. I did as he

said and slid it over to him. He looked up toward me with a big grin. "You look like shit."

"Dad," Ava said, "that's mean."

"Yeah, that's mean," I echoed. "I was up late."

"Doing what?"

"Sketching," I said.

"Are you making more fashion sketches?" Ava asked. "You haven't done that in a long time."

"Yeah. I guess watching you sketch your architectural designs inspired me to get back into it."

"But hers could lead to a profession. Yours are just doodles," Henry said, undercutting her. That was his favorite pastime—downplaying whatever I loved.

"Hey now, be nice. Kierra is an amazing designer. I'm hoping she makes me an original piece one day," Lena said, winking my way as she headed around the corner to the pantry.

I wanted to vomit from her wink. The last person I needed to back me up was the woman who was sleeping with my husband. Oddly enough, what bothered me most was that they used my bed. We had a whole guest room where their scandal could've taken place. I bet Henry got off on the idea of it though—having another woman on my side of the bed.

Henry and Ava headed out of the kitchen to give Lena space to cook. While she was in the pantry, I hurried upstairs to grab the jewelry I'd found. Then I headed back to the kitchen.

"Thanks for making brunch, Lena," I said as I walked toward her.

She turned my way with a vibrant smile. "Not a problem. I was going to make maple-glazed bacon for you. I know you love that."

"Wow, thank you. That's so sweet. Also, I think I found one of your earrings." I held it out toward her.

Her eyes widened with excitement. "Oh my goodness, I thought I lost this. Thank you, Kierra."

"Not a problem at all," I smiled sweetly. "I found it in my bedsheets."

Lena's facial expression filled with shock as the words rolled off my tongue. She parted her lips to speak, but nothing came out at first.

I kept smiling, even though a part of me was breaking. Sure, I didn't love my husband, but I really, really loved Lena. I felt blindsided by that betrayal.

"Kierra…" she whispered. Seeing her eyes flood with tears was enough of a confession for me. I didn't need to hear more, but I deserved to hear more. "I'm so sorry about that. We… I–I don't know what to say."

"Just say you're sleeping with my husband in my bed while smiling in my face and making me maple-glazed bacon."

"It's complicated."

"It's not. You slept with my husband. That's the least complex thing ever to exist."

"He said… He said you two weren't happy." The tears began to flow down her cheeks, and I hated her for crying. What did she have to be sad about? Not only was she paid well for her services, but she also was getting bonuses from my husband. If anything, she should've been thrilled. A solid paycheck and orgasms. A win-win.

"Oh, okay. That's good to know. I just wasn't aware that my unhappiness opened up the right for you to sleep with him in my bedroom."

"I didn't mean for it to happen. It was an accident." She lowered her head and wiped away her tears. "I can quit if you'd like—"

"Yes," I cut in. "I'd like that. After you finish Ava's eggs Benedict. She loves them."

She nodded. "Right. Of course. Not a problem."

I started to walk off but turned toward her. "Lena?"

"Yes?"

"We're not happy, Henry and me. But I did have the stupid idea that you and I were friends. I think that's what hurts the most."

We all ate brunch together. I pretended I was okay, and Lena pretended that she wasn't going to quit within the next few hours.

I spent the remainder of the day with Ava, reading our novels and discussing them during snack breaks. That brought me the comfort I needed the most. Whenever I felt lost and alone, that girl brought me home again with her laughter and love.

13

Kierra

I hated flowers.

My husband's apology of choice was always flowers. Roses, to be specific.

Henry grew up in an unstable home. Sometimes, I wondered if that was why he was the way he'd been toward me. So hot and cold. His father was abusive toward his mother and beat her until the day he died. During a night of drinking, Henry once told me he was happy his father was dead so his mother could finally live a happy life. He told me he'd lived his whole life being afraid of the man who raised him. It wasn't often that my husband shared his emotions with me. He hardly talked about how he grew up. His most tender moments came when he was drunk, as if he didn't even realize he was letting his shields down.

His father, Jack, never laid a hand on Henry. He never understood why, but I knew the moment I'd met Jack Hughes. That man adored other men; it was women he found fault in. Jack thought his gender was the smarter of the two and that a woman's place was in the kitchen or on her knees—Jack's words, not mine. If misogyny was a person, his name was Jack Hughes. I'm not saying Jack was attracted to men; he just didn't like women that much. He looked down on the whole sex in such a demeaning way. As a therapist myself, I could've gone into all the reasons why he was the way he'd been, but just because people had reasons for the way they were didn't mean that they had excuses.

I had the firm belief that if we excused people from their actions due to their personal traumas, we'd end up with a domino effect of passing on trauma to every single person. Even with his reasons, they didn't excuse Jack for his harmful ways.

When I first met him—the first and last time before he died—he told me I was a wasted seed unless I gave Henry another child. In his head, the only reason for a woman's existence was to bear children for the man to raise. Jack called me a weak, stupid woman when I mentioned I wasn't certain I wanted to have children. Henry cussed him out for the comment, yelling so loudly that his veins were popping out of his neck. I'd never seen a man so angry, and a part of me felt protected in that moment. He stood up for me to the man who raised him, the man he'd always feared. That felt important. It made me feel safe.

Henry apologized to me the whole ride home. He told me he never wanted me to see him lose his temper like that—where rage met the deepest forms of heartache. That was the first time I'd seen him cry. I remembered him falling apart once we got to the house, and him wrapping me in his arms, telling me that he never wanted me to see him in such an angry state. That he never wanted to raise his voice toward anyone, like his father had done Henry's whole life.

Oddly enough, Jack seemed proud of his son for standing up to him—for shouting the same way Jack seemed to shout at Henry's mother, Tamera. He smirked as if thinking, "That's my boy." That's why I figured Jack never laid a finger on Henry—because he held a part of his DNA. His poor wife, however, was a punching bag.

We didn't go to the funeral for Jack. All Henry did was light a cigar and smoke it on the back patio the night of his father's service. "I hope he burns down there," Henry muttered before putting out his cigar.

It took years for Henry to lose his temper again.

We started visiting his mother a lot more. To this day, Ava still visited with Tamera every weekend. The two were as close as close could be, and I loved that. I loved Tamera. Even with everything she'd been through, her heart never hardened. If anything, after Jack's passing, she found ways to give more love away.

Over time, I'd noticed during our visits that Henry began to nitpick things about Tamera's home. How unorganized it had been and how old-fashioned the property was. He offered time and time again to buy her a new house or to renovate her current one, but she wasn't interested. That only annoyed Henry more. Tamera didn't think much of it and waved off her son's demeaning comments. Sure, Tamera was a bit of a hoarder, but she seemed comfortable with her collections. She knew exactly where everything was, too.

I think after Jack's passing, she went out and bought everything that her husband told her she could never have. I thought it was fine and brave to live fully as herself after years of being a shadow to a man's wrath. Who was I to tell her how to live her life? I figured women who lost so much of themselves to a man deserved happiness more than most—no matter how it looked to others.

One night Henry asked me to come over and help organize Tamera's home. He said it wasn't safe for Ava to be staying over there when there was so much junk.

What he called junk, Tamera called treasures.

The two ended up in a big argument, and I saw Henry explode at his mother, leaving her in tears. I'd never seen him blow up at a person like that, not even when he shouted at his father. Even when he saw her crack, he kept yelling, bringing a newfound fear to me. He broke one of Tamera's vases in his fit of rage and told her he didn't understand how his father put up with her.

"There's no space to even move in this death trap!" he shouted. "*Fucking A, Mom. Get your fucking shit together!*"

We rode home in silence.

My mind was swirling with a million scattering thoughts.

At one point, he reached his hand over toward mine.

I held his hand.

It felt wrong.

I felt sick.

The next morning, I woke to a bouquet of flowers beside my bed and a note that said he was sorry for losing his temper toward his mother. He sent her flowers, too. Later when he came home from work, I quietly asked him if he'd ever do that to me—lose control and batter into me the way he had with his mother. If he'd keep yelling even when I broke down.

The look of pain in his eyes showed me how much my questions shattered his heart.

"Never, Kierra. Never," he swore as he broke down. "I'm not like that. You know me. I'd never hurt you or Ava. You *know* that. You have to know that."

He cried.

I cried, too.

We never talked about the situation again, but it changed me. It made me much more aware of everything we'd done or gone through. I should've been wiser. I was a therapist, after all. I was trained in knowing the signs and seeing how they formed. I should've known that that wasn't the last time I'd see Henry explode. I should've known the outbursts would become more and more frequent. I should've known that the longer I stayed, the more he'd let loose because he was learning just how much I'd allow. Just how much he could get away with.

Then he'd buy flowers.

Then he'd cry.

Then I'd cry.

I always cried longer than him, though. The cuts sliced deeper every time, and the flowers always died.

At least he never yells around Ava.

At least he apologizes.
At least he never hits me.

Those were the troubled thoughts my mind began to create as I tried to lift myself from the effect of his hurtful words. The one that meant the most to me was his relationship with Ava. In her mind, Henry was her hero. The man who would protect her from anything and everything bad that ever happened to her.

As for me, though, my husband became my monster. I was imprisoned in his realm, and I never knew what was going to set him off. I walked on eggshells, and I changed myself repeatedly based on who he wanted me to be in that moment. The problem with abuse and control from one's partner is that often you can't see all the warning signs until you look back on them. It started small. Him commenting on my outfit and telling me I should've dressed more like a mother and less like a twenty-year-old. Him offering me a gym membership to help me drop a few pounds—pounds I hadn't noticed. Him mentioning how his work colleague's wife always had dinner on the table when he arrived after work.

Then, there were the mind games. He'd tell me time and time again how I could just be…better. A better wife, a better friend, a better person. He told me he loved when I wore red lipstick, and other colors looked odd on me. So I wore red lipstick. Then, he'd tell me that he hated the red lipstick, and I'd remind him of what he stated before, to which he'd reply, "I never said that. You're remembering it wrong." If I were a client of mine, I'd tell me that I was being gaslit. But that's the issue with advice: it's easier to give it to others than to give it to yourself.

Besides, I could handle Henry's mood swings because I had my Ava. During one of our arguments, when I'd expressed that he was hurting my feelings, he told me I should just leave and let him and Ava move on without me.

He knew that was the quickest way to make me shut up—threatening to take away the one thing that meant the most to me, my daughter. He even cut as deeply as to say that she wasn't mine. But she *was* mine. Just as much as I was hers. Sure, we didn't have the same nose or the same eyes, but our hearts beat in sync. Ava Melanie Hughes saved my life when I was drowning. I'd never known a little girl's smile could heal the broken little girl within my own soul. I'd never known a love like that.

So I stayed.

I stayed when I wanted to leave him. I didn't speak up when he hurt me. I didn't fight back anymore because I couldn't lose her. I couldn't lose my heartbeat.

It wouldn't be forever. One day, Ava would be eighteen. One day, she'd be free to choose who she wanted to be with. One day, I'd be free from the chains of Henry's hurtful ways and still have my daughter.

When the following Friday rolled around, Ava was off to Tamera's house for a sleepover. I'd had a long day at work and was feeling extra tired. My clients that day were dealing with heavy issues, and even though I tried my best not to take on their emotions, I sometimes struggled. I just needed the evening to recharge and come back to myself. Still, I knew Henry would want dinner, so I put a pizza in the oven when he texted me that he was on his way home.

"I can't believe Lena quit. All you could whip up was a frozen pizza?" Henry yipped behind me as I was bent over in the oven pulling out the pizza. The sudden sound of his voice made me leap out of fright, causing my hand to hit the top of the oven, pain shooting through me at the searing burn. The pizza pan dropped from my grip, causing a mess inside the oven, which led Henry into a fit.

"Are you fucking kidding me, Kierra? Look at the damn mess you made!" he barked as I rushed to the sink to run cold water over the burn.

"You act like I tried to hurt myself," I snapped back without thought. My main focus was to make sure my hand wasn't suffering from second- or third-degree burns.

"If you weren't so lazy and actually cooked a real meal, this would've never fucking happened." He huffed, walking over to the stove and shutting off the oven. "Now that cheese is burning, and the house is going to smell awful. How do you even manage to screw up a frozen pizza?"

I stood there frozen in place from his words.

He glanced my way and the moment I locked eyes with him, I saw the emptiness that existed there. Maybe he had a bad day at work. Maybe some deal fell through. Maybe that's why he was snapping. Maybe that's why he blamed me instead of checking in on my injury.

His eyes fell to my hand, where blisters were already forming on the delicate skin. His brows lowered, and when he looked at me once more, there was a moment of sorrow in his eyes.

Say it, I silently begged.

Look me in the eyes and apologize for snapping at me.

Ask me if I'm okay. Get me some ice.

Do anything, Henry.

Anything to show that any piece of you still cares.

Instead, he grumbled under his breath, turned to walk away, and said, "I'm going out for dinner." He left the house, leaving the burning smell growing more intense around me.

———

He didn't sleep in our room that night. He took the guest room. It was probably for the best. He was the last person I wanted to wake up beside. We played the part of being a loving couple as much as we could when Ava was around; yet when she was gone, so was the make-believe love story.

When I awakened the next morning, there was a bouquet of roses on my table side and a tube of soothing cream for burns.

I lay still on my side of the bed that morning thinking about Gabriel, Bentley, and the idea of a life without Henry involved. As I looked at the bouquet, I wanted to throw up.

Roses were becoming my least favorite flower.

14

Kierra

After the burn to my hand, I did exactly what I did every time Henry had an episode. I went on as if nothing had happened. Though, truthfully, each time something happened, it felt as if a piece of me was fading. Still, life had to go on, and our house continued to be built as the foundation of our lives continued to crumble.

Over the next few weeks, we had concrete poured. A frame of the house was going up quickly. June sped past, and as summertime settled in, I was getting used to the idea of being around Gabriel. Of course, it wasn't hard to be around him. He made it shockingly easy. From meetings with Henry over the house details to treating Ava like a princess at the mentorship program, Gabriel went above and beyond to make sure everyone felt taken care of.

That even included having a cinnamon muffin and coffee with me at least twice a week. When the bakery was running low on muffins, we agreed to go halfsies with the one that was left. When we met up, conversations always came easily. He'd ask me about myself and my likes and needs. It was nice to talk to someone besides Joseph, Rosie, and Ava. My parents were wonderful, too, of course, but a few years back, they'd moved out to Austin, Texas. But talking to Gabriel felt different than with all those people. It felt like coming home after a long, cold winter. He still laughed the same. Still rubbed his thumb and pointer finger together when he was in deep thought. Still frowned with his eyes before his lips.

Still felt like home.

The guilt I harbored because a man other than my husband felt like home still ate at me, even though Henry wasn't always the best toward me. Even if my marriage was loveless, I shouldn't have felt so strongly connected to someone else.

I tried my best to battle those feelings toward Gabriel. I tried to push down the conflicting thoughts that raced through my mind. For me, the best way to do that was to focus as much as possible on my clients, rather than on myself. I liked to push my own struggles as far back as possible with a TBDWAALD sign on them: to be dealt with at a later date.

Claire Dune was having a good day. Those seemed few and far between, but I loved it when she walked into my office with a sense of confidence. She still fiddled with her hands when she talked, and at moments she'd slip into self-deprecating pity, but more than not, she'd catch herself and not let her mind spiral into a mess.

"Peter asked me out," she said nonchalantly. Her smile

stretched from ear to ear as she shook her head in disbelief. "Can you believe it? Can you believe that he actually asked me?"

"Of course I can. You're an amazing person with a heart of gold."

"I also have a lot of baggage," she commented as she sat back in her chair. "Sometimes, I think I'm too much for love. That I'm so screwed up from my past traumas that no matter what, I'd screw up any relationship I get in."

"Where do those insecurities come from? Are those your own thoughts or the thoughts of another?"

She shrugged her shoulders. "Sometimes, in my head, it's hard to know what my own thoughts are and what thoughts came from my parents."

"You know the cool thing about thoughts?"

"What's that?"

"They don't have to define you. They can come and go without attaching them to yourself and your worth. Not every thought is worthy of a response. You have the power to say, 'No, thought. You are wrong and you must leave this instant.' You are the navigator of your life, and you can shut down any person, place, or thought that makes you feel lesser. A good trick is to say out loud the opposite of any negative thought, three times in a row, to cement a better belief into your system."

Her brows knit together. "So, when the voices in my head are calling me ugly, I'd say…?"

"I am beautiful, I am beautiful, I am beautiful." I smiled her way and nodded once. "And you are beautiful, Claire. But it doesn't matter what I think, or even what Peter thinks. It matters what your core belief is about yourself. And if you learn to combat those negative thoughts, you can change your life."

"I am beautiful, I am beautiful, I am beautiful," she repeated, closing her eyes. She placed her hand over her heart and let out a small breath. "I am good enough, I am good enough, I am good enough."

"Yes, that's it."

Her eyes fell to the picture on my desk of Henry and Ava. She smiled a little and shook her head. "Your daughter's lucky to have you in her life. I bet you teach her these kinds of things, too."

"I do my best to remind her how amazing she is."

"My parents never did that. I don't think if I had a daughter before now, I would've been able to do that, either. I would've been hard on them, because hard was all I knew how to be. It's good that mothers like you exist. You are saving lives and raising kids who will be stronger than the ones before. You're really a good person, Kierra."

I smiled and leaned toward her. "Now, say that to yourself, because it's true."

Her eyes flashed with emotion as she nodded and said the words.

We worked through all her thoughts that afternoon, and surprisingly enough, helping her lifted a bit of pressure off my own chest. I felt as if she had given me a reminder to be kinder to myself, too.

Because I was good enough, I was good enough, I was good enough.

No matter what the voices in my head tried to convince me of.

———————

One afternoon, Gabriel was stopping by to drop off some paperwork for Henry. Henry was running late to work, which was something that always happened. He'd sent me a text message, instructing me to stay home to retrieve the paperwork. He didn't have to twist my arm to greet Gabriel that afternoon, that was for sure.

"Hey, come on in," I said as I opened the front door for Gabriel. "How are you?"

"Good, good. I was just going over some paperwork that Henry wanted, so I figured I'd bring it and get him to sign it before I'm back in two days to check in on the foundation and build." He raked his hand through his messy hair and grinned. "You look nice."

I glanced down at myself. I was wearing my oversized sweatshirt and sweatpants. "I look like a slob, but I appreciate the compliment."

He held the folder out toward me. "Thanks for letting me swing by to drop th—"

"*Mommmm!* I have cramps and I hate everything and being a girl is the worst thing in the world, and if I could cut out my insides I would if that meant no more..." Ava froze in place as she stomped into the living room. The moment she saw Gabriel, a flash of horror and embarrassment spread across her face.

Gabriel held up a hand toward her. "Hey, kid."

Ava's eyes darted between Gabriel and me before her jaw dropped and her eyes filled with tears. "*Oh my gosh! Mommm!* Why didn't you tell me he was here?" she said as humiliation seeped throughout every inch of her being. "This is so embarrassing!" she screamed as she stormed back to her bedroom, slamming the door behind her.

Hormonal teenagers were not something I was ready for. Then again, Ava seeing Gabriel as she talked about her period cramps was not something she was ready for, either.

"Sorry about that. That time of month makes her a little on edge," I said.

"Not a worry. I'm pretty sure if men had periods, we'd start wars to get out our rage. Her slamming a door is nothing. I hope she's not too embarrassed by it."

"Oh, she is, and I'll have to beg for her forgiveness, even though I didn't know she'd come out saying that stuff."

He smiled and rubbed his jawline. "Anyway, I just wanted to drop those off."

"Do you want a drink?" I offered. I wasn't even certain why. I shook my head. "Sorry, that's a weird thing to ask. I'm sure you have other things to do, but it felt odd to have you come all this way and not offer you anything."

He paused for a moment. "I'd take a drink."

I grabbed him a beer and myself a vodka soda, and we walked outside and sat on the ground in front of the house being built. Our legs were bent as we rested our arms on top of our kneecaps as the sun set overhead.

"I do love this land," I said as I stared forward. "There's something about nature that brings me a lot of peace. I didn't have that at our old home."

"I'm a nature guy myself. There's something about sitting in it that makes all my worries fade for a little while."

"Do you have a lot of worries?"

"Luckily, no. I live a pretty happy life. I do what I love. It just…" His words faded as if he realized he was oversharing.

"It's just what?"

"Sometimes, it's lonely. I work a lot. I keep to myself a lot. Most of the time, it's fine. But then I work on projects like this one, and I see families like yours, and I wonder what it would be like to be…more than just me."

If only reality was as great as the exterior imagery that Henry painted our family to be.

"I think some people in families are still very lonely," I told him.

"But you're not," he said. "I'll admit I'm a bit envious of the life you have, and how far from lonely it seems."

Oh, Gabriel. If you knew the shadows of my realm…

"Yes," I nodded, "Ava makes it easy to not be lonely."

"And Henry," he added.

I smiled and I lied. "Yeah, and him." I shifted a little and stared toward the build. "Do you think it will feel warm like a home and less like a mansion? It's very big, and sometimes I worry about a house this big feeling cold and lonely."

"It *is* massive," he agreed. "But it will be warm."

"How can you be sure?"

"Because you'll be there."

I smiled at him.

He smiled back at me.

I felt his smile in my chest.

I felt him in my soul.

And then, it happened.

That was the exact moment I began to fall in love again with a man who could never be mine. Then again, I didn't think I'd ever stopped loving Gabriel. That love for him always sat quietly in my heart and would stay there for the rest of time. Loving him wasn't simply a choice; it was my destiny. I was born to love him, and for a short period of time, I thought he was born to love me, too.

"Gabriel?" I whispered.

"Yes?" he whispered back.

"I really like the person that you are."

His smile stretched, and I fell for him more.

"Kierra?"

"Yes?"

"I really like the person that you are," he echoed.

And just like that, I fell some more. Tripping, tumbling, spiraling for him.

And within that moment, I felt the strongest urge to tell him everything. To tell him about us. To tell him about Elijah. Because when love was real, secrets did not exist.

I swallowed hard and released a weighted breath. "Gabriel, there's something I have to te—"

"Sorry if I'm interrupting," a voice said from behind us,

making me abandon my thoughts and slip back into reality. I looked over my shoulder to see Rosie standing there with a big, cheesy grin on her face.

I stood, and Gabriel followed.

"Rosie, hey. What are you doing here?" I asked, walking over to my friend.

"Wow," she breathed out quietly. "Well, I'll be."

"Rosie," I whispered before giving her a stern look. A look that read, "Act as normal as possible and don't make this a thing."

Unfortunately for me, Rosie would always make something a thing.

She poked her tongue in her cheek before saying, "My parents were finally clearing out their garage and found some old boxes you stored at their place during college. I just dropped those off with Ava. She told me you were back here with…?" She grinned from ear to ear, arching an eyebrow as she smiled toward Gabriel.

He stepped forward and held a hand out toward her. "Gabriel Sinclair. I'm the architect on the Hugheses' project."

Rosie shook his hand. "I've heard a lot about you, Gabriel."

He laughed. "Hopefully good things."

"Only the best." Rosie was staring at him as if she'd just seen a ghost. I didn't blame her. I, too, was in a state of shock when Gabriel made his return to my life. She placed her hands on her hips and shook her head in disbelief. "Wow, you're handsome."

"Rosie," I said, nervously laughing.

"No, really. You're damn handsome. And built." She wrapped her hand around his bicep, because the word *boundaries* was not in her vocabulary. "Do you work out?"

Gabriel kept laughing and flexed slightly. "Here and there."

"Here and there," Rosie snickered, nudging me. "Those aren't here-and-there muscles. Those are always-there muscles."

"Rosie!" I shouted, smacking her hand away from Gabriel. I felt my cheeks heating up from the whole exchange as I gave Gabriel an apologetic smile. "Sorry. My best friend has a lack of boundaries and tact."

"Not everyone can be as humble and sweet as Kierra," Rosie said. "Some of us are a bit more dickish."

"I appreciate the honesty," Gabriel stated. "Honestly, I don't think most people are as humble and sweet as Kierra."

"Damn straight. That's why I always have to cuss people out on her behalf," Rosie stated.

Gabriel smiled, seemingly unfazed by Rosie's antics. Which only reminded me of how he put up with her when we were younger. It felt odd standing there with my two best friends. It was almost as if I'd stepped into a time machine and been sent back before tragedy took root in my life.

"You look kind of familiar," Gabriel mentioned, arching an eyebrow toward Rosie.

Nerves bubbled in my gut as those words left his mouth.

Rosie didn't seem moved at all and she struck a pose. "Well, you are looking at Channel 12's weather girl in the flesh."

"Ah, yeah. You remind me to pull out an umbrella every now and again," he said.

"Keeping humans dry for the last seven years," Rosie replied.

"I appreciate it. It makes for better hair days." Gabriel glanced down at his watch and then nodded. "I should probably get going, though. Thanks again for the drink, Kierra. I'll see you soon. And Rosie, it was a pleasure meeting you."

"The pleasure is all mine," Rosie sang as I rolled my eyes. Gabriel walked away, and Rosie peered at him until he was out of sight. Then she turned to me and swatted my arm. "*Shit! Shit! Shit!* Kierra, you didn't tell me Gabriel got hot. Like supercharged hot!"

"He's pretty good-looking, yes."

"No. Don't downplay this. It's like Henry Cavill and Kofi Siriboe had a love child and Gabriel Sinclair was born. He's like a fine wine: better with age and much more intoxicating. My panties literally almost somersaulted off my body and straight to his mouth from just a hello."

"Rosie."

"I almost loosened my jaw and asked him to stuff me like a Thanksgiving turkey with his beef sausage."

"Rosie."

"I almost begged him to call me a good girl before he spat in my mouth."

"*Rosie!*"

"If I wasn't engaged and your best friend, I would've humped his leg."

I blankly stared at her. "Are you done now?"

She nodded. "Yes, I guess I'm done."

"Good. And I'm very happy you didn't hump his leg."

"I want you to know I thought about humping his leg multiple times within those few minutes."

"Well, we can stop talking about humping his leg now."

"Oh." She nodded. "Okay. But...oh my gosh. He's beautiful."

Yes, he was.

It wasn't only his looks that made him so attractive, though. It was his kindness, his heart. I wasn't sure how it was possible, but Gabriel was even kinder than he had been when we knew each other all those years ago.

Rosie's vibrant personality simmered a little as she placed a hand against my shoulder. "How are you handling all of this? Being around him?"

"Fine," I lied.

"Liar," she replied, patting me on the back. "You are officially screwed, my friend."

"He doesn't know about Elijah," I whispered, rubbing my hand up and down my arm.

She arched an eyebrow. "What do you mean, he doesn't know about Elijah?"

"Amma never told him that he had a brother after the accident...and when I saw her, she made me promise I'd never bring it up."

"Um, that's insane. What the hell? Gabriel deserves to know that. You have to tell him."

"I want to, but...I can't."

"Yes you can, Kierra. Why do you think you can't—"

"I killed him," I choked out, shaking my head as the emotions hit me. "I'm the reason Elijah's gone. I'm the reason Frank left Amma. I'm the reason Gabriel doesn't remember… She asked me to do this one thing, and it's the least I can do after ruining her life."

"It was an accident, Kierra. You didn't mean for it to happen. You're not a monster, and you can't hold that guilt."

"But that's the thing," I said, "I *am* her monster. And if I told Gabriel, even though I truly want to, I would be causing her more pain."

Rosie sighed and pulled me into a hug. "I love you, but I hate this. I hate this so much."

I nodded as I cried against her shoulder.

Because I hated it, too.

I hated it more than words.

15

Kierra

THIRTEEN YEARS OLD

Three painful, unruly years of suffering, and I was officially free from the torture and agony of wearing braces.

Brace Face was officially retired.

"They look great, don't they?" Mom mentioned as I stared in the bathroom mirror after we got back from the orthodontist's office. I had a hard time realizing that it was my reflection staring back at me. My teeth were straight, white, and beautiful.

I could smile without having a whole wire contraption move up with the curve of my lips. The kids at school would no longer have the pleasure of calling me names, even though their stupid nicknames for me weren't even creative. Getting dressed, I wouldn't stretch out my shirts anymore, either.

Life was about to be better than it ever had been, and I couldn't stop giggling to myself about it.

"I am so hot!" I exclaimed, striking a pose in the mirror.

Mom laughed but agreed. "You are beautiful," she said. She kissed my forehead. "But you were always beautiful, Kierra."

"Yeah, yeah, you're my mom so you have to say that, but look at me!" I grinned as big as possible. My cheeks rose so high that my eyes closed from how hard I was smiling.

I headed to school feeling as if I were on top of the world. The whole day, I walked around with the biggest smirk on my face ever. I wanted everyone to see that smile of mine after all they'd seen were braces.

After school, I headed to the locker room and switched into my white outfit for softball practice. I never felt more confident in my life as I headed out for practice. As our team practiced, the guys' baseball team and the track team were outside warming up, too. There were dozens of my peers around, and I made sure to smile toward as many as I could.

That was until people started whispering and pointing in my direction. At first, I thought it was due to my bright, shiny new smile, but then I realized they weren't smiling at me, they were laughing at me.

Rosie came darting over toward me with a frown on her lips. "Uh, Kierra?"

"Yeah?"

"Don't freak out…" she started.

Which was enough to make me want to freak out.

"What? What!"

"You got your period, and it's leaking through your white pants."

What?

What!

I glanced down at my pants and then looked up to see

everyone laughing at me. My stomach knotted up from panic as their laughter grew more and more. Everyone was laughing except for Gabriel. When I looked at Gabriel, he was frowning and looked sorry for me, and that only made me angrier and more embarrassed.

I dropped my catcher's glove and darted toward the locker room, completely humiliated by the whole thing. You could imagine my surprise when I heard Gabriel's voice in the locker room calling out toward me.

"Kierra? Are you in here?" he asked.

"Just leave me alone, will you!" I barked, feeling tears building in my eyes as I hid in a bathroom stall, completely mortified that I'd finally became a "woman" the day after I'd finished being called Brace Face. Only to have that reveal happen so publicly in front of all the kids who bullied me for years.

What was even worse was that Gabriel had witnessed the embarrassment. I'd have to keep my window shade pulled for months for fear that he might actually see me and mock me.

I sat in the bathroom, sobbing my eyes out, as Gabriel stood on the other side of the door. "You're not even supposed to be in the girls' locker room!" I shouted.

"You think I want to be in here?" he grumbled. I hated the sound of his voice, and I hated how it squeaked every now and then, too. Some days, Gabriel's voice sounded like a five-year-old's, and others like a fifty-year-old's. And in between those two, he sounded like my favorite thing in the world. I didn't understand that part, yet. But sometimes his voice made me feel safe.

"If you don't want to be here, then just go," I ordered.

"I am," he stated, but I noticed his feet not moving at all.

"No, you're not."

"Yeah, I am just... Here," he spat out, holding his hand beneath the bathroom stall. In his hand was a duffel bag.

"What's that for?"

"I had some clean stuff I was gonna wear after football practice. Some sweats and boxers. I figured you might want it. I stuffed some of those pad things in there, too. My mom had some extras in her car."

My chest tightened as I froze. Was he...offering me his clothes? So I wouldn't have to walk out of the locker room completely embarrassed? Was he helping me out?

"Is this some kind of trick?" I asked.

"Look, if you don't want the freaking clothes, then fine. I'll take them bac—"

Before he could rescind his offer, I leaped from the toilet seat and snatched the bag from his grip. I held it close to my chest, uncertain what to say. I combed my hair out of my face and opened my mouth to speak, but before I could, Gabriel's feet disappeared. The locker room door opened and shut quickly after, showing that he pretty much darted out of the room.

The tears kept falling from my eyes as I changed into Gabriel's clothes. I wore his briefs, slapped the pad on them, slipped into his black sweatpants, and then tossed on his football shirt with our school logo on it.

After calming myself enough to exit the locker room, I hurried out to the parking lot, where Dad was waiting to pick me up.

The moment he saw me, he arched an eyebrow. "Whose clothes are those?" he asked me.

My cheeks heated as I slid into the passenger seat and snapped my seat belt on quickly. "It doesn't matter. Drive, Dad."

He shook his head. "Those are boy's clothes. Kierra Elizabeth Hughes, why are you wearing—"

"*I got my Aunt Flo, Dad!*" I shouted at him, bursting into tears. Even with the change of clothes, I still felt humiliated and tired, and in a hurry to leave the school premises as soon as possible. The last thing I needed was my father asking me why I was wearing some boy's clothes. I was still traumatized from the past fifteen minutes, which felt as if they'd lasted for fifteen years. I couldn't believe that I'd have to return to school the following day. If anything, I should've been online finding a one-way ticket to Iceland or something.

Dad still didn't drive. He just did that dad thing that dads did when they appeared completely clueless to the reality around them. "Wait, why are you crying? What does that even mean, Kier—"

"*My period, Dad!*" I said as I tossed my hands in the air in complete defeat. "I got my period in the middle of practice, and everyone saw it on my white uniform, and now I am humiliated and need you to drive right now because I need to get as far away from this place as possible."

Dad blinked a few times as he gripped the steering wheel. "Ohhh." He nodded. "Got it. Now look, Kierra. I know this is more of a mother-and-daughter conversation that should take place. But I want you to know that getting your period is a beautiful, natural thing and—"

As he spoke, a few girls walked past the car and pointed at me, giggling.

I leaned toward him and slammed my hands on his shoulders. "Dad, please. This is not the moment for you to be all awesome and girl-dad, okay? I need you to drive."

"Right, okay, let's go." He put the car into drive and I slunk deeper into the leather seat of his car, wishing that I could melt into the fabric and never be seen again.

After we got to the house, I hurried inside with the duffel bag and shot straight past Mom in the direction of my bedroom.

"Well, hello to you, too, Kierra. Are you—" Mom started, but I didn't stop at all.

As I hurried away, I heard Dad say, "She got her Aunt Flo today."

I slammed my door shut quickly before I could hear anything else.

"What is it?" Gabriel asked, opening his bedroom window that I'd been pounding on for the past minute or so.

I shoved the duffel bag his way. "Here."

"Oh. Thanks." He scratched at the back of his neck. "You all right?"

"Why do you care?"

"*I don't,*" he said, shrugging his shoulders. "But my mom told me I should ask you if you were all right."

"I don't want you to just ask if I'm all right because your mom told you to ask me."

"Fine, pretend I didn't ask." He went to close the window.

"Wait!" I yelped, darting my hand through his window to stop him from shutting it. "I have something else for you. One second."

I hurried back to my window, climbed inside, and grabbed the plate of cookies Mom made for me from my desk. I darted out the window and headed back to Gabriel. "Here."

"What's this?"

"Period cookies."

His eyes widened with complete disgust. "You made cookies with your period?!"

"What? No, weirdo. My mom made cookies to celebrate me getting my period. It means I'm a woman now."

He narrowed his eyes. "Oh." He picked up a cookie and bit into it. "Cool."

I wasn't sure what else to say to him, so I said, "Whatever. Bye, dick."

"Bye, Penguin," he replied before snatching another cookie. He shut his window as I climbed back into mine. Then I thought about him all freaking night.

The next month, there was a knock at my window. I went to open it to find Gabriel standing there with a plate in his hands.

"What's that?" I asked.

"Cookies. For…you know…"

I scrunched up my nose. "How do you know I need cookies now?"

"Because I guess that thing happens to girls every month around the same time, so I made cookies with my mom so you wouldn't become a grumpy ogre."

"Oh…" How sweet and kind of mean? I didn't know. Gabriel confused my mind more than any other person ever did. I took the cookies and I bit into one. "Thanks."

"Are they good?"

"Yes, but I like oatmeal cookies the best."

"Nobody likes oatmeal cookies the best, except for old ladies who live with fifteen cats."

"And me," I said, taking another bite. "With raisins. But these are good, too."

"Okay."

"Okay."

"Well…" He took a deep breath. "Bye."

"Bye." I stood still as he turned around and started walking to his window. "Hey, Gabriel?"

"Yeah?"

"Do you want to be friends or something?"

He scratched his chin and shrugged. "Okay."

He made me oatmeal cookies every month after that.

With raisins.

16

Kierra

PRESENT DAY

Two days later when Gabriel came back to check on the construction process, he stood in my kitchen with a container in his hands.

"You made Ava cookies?" I asked, stunned.

"Yeah. I hope that's okay. I figured with her current state…" He shook his head. "Sorry. It's probably odd, but it just felt like the right thing to do. If I crossed a line—"

I darted toward him, unable to hold back from wrapping him in his arms. He was probably confused by my actions, since I was coming off as a complete freak as I held him in my arms.

He was still there…my sweet Gabriel who I grew up to know. He'd baked Ava cookies the same way he used to bake them for me when we were kids and I was PMSing. I couldn't help but hug him. I couldn't help but forget for a small moment that he didn't remember me from all those years ago. Yet, somewhere inside himself, he did remember. Somewhere in his subconscious, little Kierra still existed. He still knew her. He still had those memories. He was still mine.

What a stupid thought, Kierra.

Let that man go.

I pulled back from him, teary-eyed and feeling foolish for tackling him in the way I had. I had a momentary need to tell him about us. I wanted to unload all the details to him about how we were only best friends, but also in love. I wanted to tell him about all our adventures, our highs and lows, our best and worst days. I wanted to tell him about Elijah.

Oh, how I wanted to tell him about Elijah. I wanted him to know all the moments we shared with his little brother. I wanted him to know how I still wrote letters to Elijah every single year. I wanted him to know that every New Year's Eve, I could hardly watch fireworks without bursting into tears.

I wanted to tell him about Elijah's laughter. How it could fill a room and make even the grumpiest person soft. I wanted to tell him how close the two of them were. How it was a surprise when his mother and Frank told us she was expecting another kid when Gabriel was fifteen. How he freaked out at first, but then fell in love with the idea. How he used to sleep by Elijah's crib to make sure his little brother was breathing. How he'd taught Elijah how to throw a baseball, how to ride a bike, and how to tell bad knock-knock jokes.

I wanted to tell him so much about Elijah that my chest ached thinking about it.

I knew I couldn't though, because of Amma. That was the last thing she'd want me to do.

"I'm sorry," I said as I let Gabriel go, feeling completely idiotic for forcing myself on the man. "I think I'm just having a lot of feelings lately."

"I should've made you some cookies, too," he joked. He smiled and didn't for a moment seem fazed by the fact that I'd all but tackled him. He held the cookies out toward me, and I took one.

As I bit into it, I almost cried again. A part of me wondered if he knew that I wasn't always this way. I wasn't always this oddity that lived in a gilded cage. I wasn't always this broken bird fearful that it would never fly again. I wasn't always damaged.

He'd known me when I still dreamed. When I still imagined. When I still felt alive. He knew the best and worst parts of me and called them beautiful. He knew me when I didn't even know myself. And now he was there, baking cookies for my daughter, unaware that such a small act meant so much to my fragile heart.

Gabriel smiled and brushed his thumb against his chin. "Good, bad, inedible?"

"Perfect," I told him.

His smile stretched wider, and I wanted to tell him how much I missed him.

Then again, who knew how much damage that would do? Who knew how much that would make him spiral. Besides, what was the point of telling him that we had a shared past? A whole life story where we existed as each other's person. It wouldn't change our current situation. If anything, it would push him away further. If he knew what I'd done all those years ago, if he remembered the accident, he would hate me. He would blame me the same way his mother did. That terrified me.

"And thank you, Gabriel. For being so kind to Ava. I know she struggles a bit with being social. Her anxiety gets to her. Probably a trait she sadly picked up from me," I mentioned before taking another bite from my cookie.

His brow furrowed. "Are you okay, Kierra?"

I tilted my head. "What?"

"Are you okay?" he repeated.

Nothing else followed those three words. His brown eyes stayed locked with mine, packed with a tenderness that flipped my world upside down. I couldn't remember the last time anyone outside of my family asked me those questions.

I didn't answer. I didn't know why, but I couldn't bring myself to lie to him. So I remained quiet.

He frowned as he placed the plate of cookies down on the counter. Then he crossed his arms across his chest and leaned against the kitchen island. "Are you safe?"

Those words made me stumble backward slightly. "What?" I choked out with a slight shake to my head. "What's that supposed to mean?"

Before he could answer, Ava hollered from her bedroom. "Mom! I need you!"

Those words shook me away from the interaction completely as I fell back into my role as a mother. I didn't have time to answer his questions. I didn't have time to dive deeper into how I wasn't okay and how I hadn't ever felt safe.

Being a mother meant you pushed your own problems so far away to take care of others. Being a mother meant you lost yourself to save your babies. How dare Gabriel even ask me that type of question. Of course I was all right. It was the only thing us mothers were ever allowed to be—at least on the outside. On the outside we'd pretend that everything was amazing and wonderful, even though the world within us was crumbling into a million pieces.

"Sorry, I have to—" I started, but he shook his head.

He picked up the plate of cookies and held it out toward me. "Go ahead. I hope she's feeling better. I'll let myself out."

I grabbed the plate and thanked him once more, before hurrying toward Ava's bedroom.

"*Mommmm!*" she hollered again before I walked into her space.

"Is there a fire, or are you just really into yelling lately?" I remarked.

Ava sat on her bed with a box in front of her. Within said box were photo albums and old yearbooks. "What in the world are you doing with those?" I asked her, completely confused. I hadn't seen those things in so long.

"Rosie dropped them off the other day. She said she was clearing out her parents' garage and found some of your stuff that you stored there when you were in college together. I've been looking through it."

I placed the plate of cookies on her dresser and then walked toward her. "Wow, I haven't seen these in—"

"Mom," she urged, looking at me as if I had three horns on

my head. "Are you kidding me? Are you really going to act like everything's normal?"

I narrowed my eyes. "Is everything not normal?" I asked her, nervous that perhaps she'd overheard the argument between Henry and me earlier that morning. He shouted at me for showering before him, since he had a big meeting to get to. I didn't yell back. I never did, and normally Henry wasn't one to raise his voice when Ava was in the house, but his anxiety over his meeting was loud and clear that morning. I did my best to hide those moments from Ava.

"Of course, it's not normal!" she said, tossing her hands up in defeat. "It's very, *very* far from normal."

I sighed and sat on the edge of her bed. "Listen, sweetheart—"

She slammed a stack of photographs into my hands. "When were you going to tell me that you and Gabriel knew each other?"

Her words left me in a tailspin as I looked down at the stack of pictures in my hand. Pictures of me and Gabriel as kids. Pictures of us as teenagers, wrapped in each other's arms. In that moment, I was transported back to my childhood as I stared at his smile.

"Well?" she said. "Are you going to explain?"

"Ava…" I felt my stomach fill up with knots as I placed the photographs back in the box. "Don't tell your father."

"Were you two in love?" Ava asked, her words dripping in confusion. "*Are* you two in love? Oh my gosh!" she gasped as she leaped up from the bed to begin pacing the room. "Are you two having an affair?" she shouted.

"*Shhh!*" I ordered as I leaped up and shut her bedroom door. "No, we are not having an affair. I would never do that, Ava. Come on, be serious."

"I am being serious, Mom! What the heck? Why are there pictures of you with Gabriel all cuddled up with each other? And why are you both pretending that you didn't have a past together?"

"We aren't pretending. Well, he's not pretending. I'm just..." I was just what? Pretending. I was pretending. "It's complicated, Ava."

"Then uncomplicate, Mom." Her eyes were packed with so much confusion, and I couldn't blame her. "What's going on?"

I sighed, debating the best way to unpack everything for her. How much was too much to share with a fourteen-year-old girl? It was clear that Ava was very wise for her age, but she was still, in fact, an adolescent. The balance between being a mother and a friend was always up in the air for me, but in that very moment, I went with the only option that felt right—the truth.

I sat back on the edge of her bed. "We grew up next to each other. He was first my enemy, then my friend, then my very best friend, and then...we dated for a short time."

"Oh my gosh," she remarked, taking a seat beside me. "Tell me everything."

So I did. I told her every single memory of the man I once called mine. I told her the ups and downs of our story. And then I told her about the night that changed everything. I told her about Elijah. I told her about the promise I'd made to Amma, even though it made me feel awful. I told her everything and begged her to keep the secret, too, until Amma spoke about it to Gabriel.

By the end of me sharing, Ava had tears in her eyes.

Her hands sat in her lap as she shook her head. "You loved him."

"Yes, I did."

"And he loved you."

"Yes," I agreed, "he did."

"And then he just…forgot?"

I nodded. "The accident was terrible. I'm stunned that we made it out of that wreck alive, truly. But Gabriel lost all his memories. He forgot everything about our relationship. His mom had a hard time with it and blamed me for the accident. They moved away shortly after, and I never heard from him again."

"Until he showed up as Dad's architect?"

"Yup."

"And…he still has no clue who you are?"

"Nope."

"*Oh my gosh!*" Ava gasped, covering her mouth. "This is some *The Notebook* shit."

"Language, Ava."

"Mom." She groaned. "You can't tell me that the first love of your life doesn't remember you, but he randomly showed up as your architect years later and expect me not to cuss."

You know what? Fair.

"It doesn't matter, really. It was a long time ago, Ava. Ancient history. We've both moved on with our lives, and we both are happy where we are. That's all that matters."

"But, Mom—"

"No buts. We can't keep looking to the past if we want to make it to the future."

She frowned and shook her head. "But don't you kind of wonder what would've happened if you two found each other again before meeting Dad? After you saw him, did you daydream a little about the what-ifs?"

Yes.

Repeatedly.

Even five minutes ago.

"No," I lied. "I let him go the moment he moved away all those years ago. So, we should leave it at that. But it does kill me, him not knowing about his brother. It's not my place to tell him, and I promised his mother I'd let her tell him, but I don't think she ever will."

"But he should know," Ava said, "You should keep pushing his mom to tell him. I'd hate not knowing the truth."

"I know. Me too."

But I also knew that pushing Amma wouldn't bring about anything good. Yet I tried.

For the next few weeks, every single day when I showed up to Gabriel's building to drop Ava off, I'd stop by Amma's office and exchange a few words with her.

I'd told her how important it was for her to tell Gabriel.

She told me to go away.

I'd begged.

She'd ignored me.

Still, I tried.

The last time I saw her, I told her that if she didn't tell Gabriel the truth soon, I might have to do it myself.

She told me to go to hell.

Though, for some odd reason, I already felt as if I was living in the burning fires.

17

Gabriel

Kierra: Ava is going to be staying home today. She has a small cold.

Gabriel: I hope she feels better.

Kierra: A day of rest will do it.

Gabriel: Wild question for you.

Kierra: Shoot.

Gabriel: Do you want to eat a cinnamon muffin with me this morning?

Kierra: Be there in twenty.

The problem with Kierra was that there weren't any problems with Kierra. The more time I spent around her, the more time I craved. I knew it was an issue, and I knew I was making up a million reasons to be in her presence, but I couldn't help it. She felt like sunbeams in the middle of the night. Unusual and bright, showing up at the oddest of times, but still it felt right. My whole life has felt like darkness. I didn't even know it until her light came around me. It was ridiculous how I felt, and I couldn't stop it. That fact alone was extremely alarming.

One Saturday, Ramona and I had planned to help Henry and Kierra pick out fixtures for their property. Normally, Ramona handled the interior design aspects of projects, but I couldn't help but want to be involved this time around. Was it an excuse to spend a full Saturday with Kierra? Perhaps.

We'd met up at the first stop—bathroom fixtures at Arch Tubs Supreme. The four of us had stood in front of the shop, and I'd rolled up the sleeves of my button-down before shaking Henry's hand.

"Good to see you both," he said as he shook hands with me and Ramona.

"You too," I replied. "Good morning," I said, smiling toward Kierra.

She smiled back and nodded slightly. "Good morning."

I clapped my hands together. "Today is going to be a long day, but a successful day if we tackle it right. We'll start with the bathroom fixtures and move on to the fixtures for the kitchen. This area is packed with all those types of stores, so we'll be able to walk to a few of them from here. Lastly, we'll end up at the marble shop for countertops and tiles. How does that sound?"

Henry was looking down at his phone, half listening to me. "Sounds good," he said, tapping away at his phone. "Sorry, work never ends."

"Gabriel knows that better than anyone," Ramona mentioned.

Kierra raised an eyebrow. "A bit of a workaholic?"

"It keeps me on my feet," I joked.

"Yeah, not everyone works a basic nine-to-five like you, Kierra. Some of us have careers, not jobs," Henry said as he opened the door and held it open for us all to walk through.

"I'd confidently say her job is the most important out of all of ours," I said, feeling annoyed at how he tried to undercut Kierra and her position. She was the one with a PhD, after all.

That little comment was enough to make me realize it was going to be a long, long day.

And a long day it had been.

After watching Henry downplay every choice that Kierra picked out, I had watched him completely gaslight her out of choosing the options she wanted to go with—the better options if you'd asked me. Unfortunately, whenever I had tried to vouch for Kierra, Ramona would go into deep interior-design talk about why Henry's option was the better one.

The only time Kierra seemed to be enjoying herself was when she and Henry split up in the stores. As Ramona and Henry went off to discuss sink faucets, I found Kierra completely laid out in an oversized tub that seemed big enough to fit a football team. Her eyes were shut. She seemed so relaxed that I almost felt bad interrupting the moment.

"Comfortable?" I asked, making her open her eyes. The soft smile on her lips showcased that.

"Oh yes. This is my kind of heaven."

"It's in your price range." Truthfully, everything was in their price range. "And it would look amazing with the other items you chose," I said, stepping into the tub and sitting on the opposite side of her. We still had ridiculous amounts of room surrounding us both.

"Oh no. Henry would definitely not go for something like this."

"Why not?"

She laughed slightly. "Because I like it."

I didn't laugh. That seemed to be the theme of the day. Anything she thought was amazing, her husband was quick to shut down. I disliked the guy more and more with every passing second.

"Does he do that a lot?"

"Do what?"

"Undermine you and speak down to you."

Her eyes flashed with surprise for a moment. Then her lips parted and she said, "Yes."

I stared at her for a moment, not saying a word. I found myself doing that often. Getting lost in the mere existence of her.

Kierra released a timid chuckle. "What is it that you're thinking about?"

"Nothing. It's just that you remind me…"

"Remind you of what?"

"Everything."

Before she could reply, Ramona and Henry reappeared. Ramona smiled at the tub. "Holy big tub!" she remarked. "You could fit a whole football team in that thing."

"It's pretty large," I agreed, standing up from the tub. "A nice one, though. I think it's the best of the bunch," I confidently stated, feeling as if Henry would take my opinion with more weight than his wife's.

"What do you think, Kierra?" Henry asked with his brow furrowed.

Kierra looked at me before darting her eyes back to Henry. She shrugged. "I think it's too much."

Henry grumbled slightly and rubbed his chin. "I think it's perfect. Let's go with this one, Gabriel."

"You got it," I said, smirking toward Kierra, who was biting her bottom lip to hide her snicker. What a damn idiot Henry was.

"Henry and I were discussing... We still have a lot of stops to make, and he has to go into the office for work tonight, it turns out," Ramona mentioned.

"I thought you had the whole weekend off," Kierra said to Henry.

"I know, but things came up. I have a big call next week with executives in China. I need to prepare for the meeting," he explained.

"You're so hardworking," Ramona said. I almost rolled my eyes to the back of my head. "Regardless, maybe we should split up to handle the tasks. I can take Henry to the marble shop if you two want to finish up here and hit up the hardwood flooring."

We agreed.

I felt the difference in Kierra when Henry wasn't around as we finished all the tasks of the day. She seemed...happy.

Kierra came over to my house to sketch for a few hours once a week. Her talent was blowing my mind, and I couldn't help but want to see one of her pieces come to life. Bentley seemed to be her biggest fan, too, because he always chose to lie on her feet instead of mine. Some nights, we'd just sketch without talking. Others, we'd talk over sketching. She was becoming more and more a part of my life, and I loved it.

"You really need to add some life to your house," she said one night in my kitchen after we ordered a pizza. "There's no artwork or color."

"I haven't gotta around to decorating it yet."

"How long have you lived here?"

"Ten years."

Her eyes widened. "Ten years and you haven't found anything to decorate the house with?"

I shrugged. "It wasn't at the forefront of my mind."

"You just need someone to come into your life and add a bit of color," she confidently said. "It just needs a little bit of a woman's touch."

I didn't tell her that she was the woman that I wanted to touch my life. But the thought crossed my mind.

"I want to see one come to life," I told her another night, after she packed up her things to head home. "One of your dresses."

"Oh gosh, no." She shook her head. "I haven't actually sewn in a very long time."

"I'm sure it's like riding a bike."

She bit her bottom lip.

I wished she wouldn't do that.

It made me want to bite it, too.

"Maybe," she said with a weighted sigh. "Maybe I'll try."

"Please do," I said. "And then I want you to wear it for me."

———

Summer was coming to an end, which annoyed me, because that meant Ava would be going back to school, spending less time at GS Architecture. The whole team was getting used to having the kid around, and I was almost certain it would feel a little emptier with her gone. A part of me debated telling her to drop out of school and become a part of the staff, but I had a very strong feeling her parents would be against that idea.

Still, the kid would be missed.

"How was today?" Kierra asked both Ava and me as she walked into the office space. "Any new adventures?"

"I got to shadow Bobby for the whole day and he taught me how to use the computer programs. Mom! Can you buy me the programs for at home? I need them. Oh! And I'm helping plan the baby shower for Eddie and his wife, Sarah! Do you know they are having a girl? Oh, Mom, you should come to the baby shower! Gabriel, can my mom come to the baby shower? Oh! And Mom, can you—"

"*Slow*," Kierra laughed, seeing how excited Ava was growing from sharing the details of her day. "This all sounds amazing. And rumor has it that a certain boss man is gifting you the programs for you to use," she mentioned, gesturing toward me.

I'd texted Kierra earlier about the programs. They weren't cheap, but I wanted Ava to have the best of the best. Over the past few weeks, she'd shown her passion for architecture, and I couldn't help but want to give her all the keys to help on her journey. She'd be ahead of most people before she even hit sixteen years old.

"No way." Ava's jaw dropped open before she darted into my arms. "Thanks, Boss Man!" she exclaimed hugging me as tight as possible. "Oh man, I have to go tell Bobby before we leave! He's going to be stoked that I can practice at home." She then darted out of my office and hurried off to go tell Bobby the news.

Kierra's smile didn't slip after Ava's departure. "I think you just made that girl's life complete."

"I'm glad I could do it. She's extremely driven. I've never seen a fourteen-year-old as focused and talented as she is. She has a gift."

"She's much more organized than I was at her age, that's for sure."

"I'm not even that organized at my current age," I joked. I leaned back against my desk and crossed my arms. "So I was wondering—"

"Can we be friends?" she blurted out.

I arched an eyebrow. "What?"

"Sorry. That was random, but the best nights I've had in a long time are going over to your house and sketching with you. The best I've felt lately is in situations where you and Ava are present. You're a good person, and I have no doubt that you'd be a great friend, so I'd like that. I'd like to be friends with you."

I chuckled slightly and shook my head.

She bit her lip again.

Fucking stop that shit, Kierra.

"What's so funny?" she asked.

"Nothing. It's just that I thought we were already friends."

She raised an eyebrow. "You did?"

"I did."

"Oh. Well. Okay." She grinned from ear to ear, and that smile was enough to make me want so much more than a friendship with her. I wanted to spend the rest of my life somehow making those lips of hers curve up in that way. I wanted to spend the rest of my life working to get a chance to taste those lips, to feel that smile against my own. I wanted her to be mine and mine alone.

But for now, friendship would work.

18

Gabriel

SEVENTEEN YEARS OLD

"Don't push me, don't push me, don't push me," Kierra cried out as she held the swing rope over the edge of the cliff. She stood in her yellow swimsuit on the verge of tears as she peered over the cliff and looked down at the water.

"Don't overthink it," I said, laughing. "You just swing and let go."

"Oh, right, okay, Gabriel. It's just *that* easy," she sarcastically remarked, rolling her eyes. When she was scared, her sarcasm hit new heights. It was kind of cute, watching her lose her mind over rope swinging. Rope swinging was her idea, by the way. I told her she was batshit crazy for wanting to do it, and I knew she was a scaredy-cat and it would end up exactly how it was.

Yet that summer, she was determined to get out of her comfort zone, to try something new before we entered our senior year of high school. She was convinced that she'd spent her life being a loser who never took risks, so all summer we'd been doing the stupidest things together.

I didn't mind much because I never minded hanging out with Kierra every day. Even if she came up with bad ideas and pretended they were mine.

"Listen, you're the one who wanted to do this, not me. I wanted to go see the new Spielberg movie," I joked. "But since we are here, you have to swing and let go, Kierra."

"But..." She hesitated. "What if I fall?"

"That's the whole point, I think."

"*But*," she said again, "what if I fall and break my neck?"

"Well, it will happen so fast, you won't even realize you're dead, so you're all good."

She shoved my shoulder with one hand as she held on to the swing with her other. "Don't make jokes. I'm scared."

I wanted to keep teasing her, but the fear in her eyes made me feel bad. So, I moved in, placed my hands on the rope, and held her close to me. "Okay," I whispered, my voice low. "You don't have to do it."

Her eyes flashed with heavy emotions. "Really?"

"Yeah, really. You can be a little chickenshit if you want."

Her mouth dropped open. She shoved me against my chest. I didn't mind. A part of me liked whenever she touched me. A part of me teased her strictly so she'd react that way and touch me. I lived for her shoves. "I'm not a chickenshit, Gabriel Sinclair!"

I started making chicken noises.

She flipped me off.

I wanted to kiss her.

Whatever.

Ignore that impulse, Gabe.

"I'm just teasing," I told her. "You don't have to do it."

She pouted. "And I'm not a chickenshit."

"You're not a chickenshit, no." I wrapped my arms around her and inched her closer to the edge without her knowing. "You're brave. And strong. And tough and—"

Before she could respond, I tightened my hold on her and the rope and launched us over the edge of the cliff. She held on to me, screaming the whole time as we flew through the air, until we hit the water with the biggest splash ever.

Kierra came to the surface splashing like wild, screaming at the top of her lungs. "Gabriel Ayodele Sinclair, I'm going to kill you!"

I couldn't help but laugh at how livid she was.

She tossed her arms all over the place, shoving water at me. "You're such a jerk!"

"I was just trying to help you cross this off your bucket list."

She whined as she crawled out of the water and scrambled to get her towel. I was somewhat disappointed when she wrapped it around her. I liked the view without it.

I climbed out of the water and headed over to her. She gave me a stern look and pointed a finger my way. "I hate you."

"You don't."

"I don't," she agreed. "But I could've died! We could've died!"

"We didn't."

"We didn't," she agreed. "But, ugh! You're crazy."

I smirked and nodded. "I'm proud of you, Kierra."

"Yeah, yeah. Whatever." She threw a towel at me, and I wrapped it around myself. I went and sat against a rock, staring out at the water. A few other people were swimming in the lake, splashing around like wild. Kierra came and sat beside me.

She grumbled and pouted.

I nudged her arm. "Sorry if I scared you."

"It's fine." She sighed. "A part of me knew you'd get me to go over the cliff."

"It was your idea, not mine. I just wanted you to have something to cross off your summer bucket list, seeing how you chickened out of the last five tasks."

"Listen, four-wheelers seem very unsafe, okay?"

"No judgment here." I bent my knees and rested my arms on top of them.

Kierra leaned against me and rested her head on my shoulder. "I'm just sick of being a loser."

"Who the hell said you were a loser?"

"Everyone."

"*But*—"

"Everyone but you," she corrected. "I mean, we are about to start senior year, and I have nothing to show for it. I've never been kissed. My softball career is in the crapper. My fashion designs probably won't go anywhere, and I won't get into the fashion school I want because they want the greats and I'm just okay."

"Your designs are fucking phenomenal."

"Don't make me feel better just because you pushed me off a cliff, Gabriel."

"I'm not. I think—"

"Gabe."

"Yes?"

"I'm PMSing. Let me rant."

I nodded. "Continue."

She sighed. "My grades aren't even good. I'm an average student. I'm an average person. I'm just a mid-list human."

"What's a mid-list human?"

"You know. The people who are the background characters in other people's stories. The mediocre ones who never did anything exciting with their lives."

"You know what? I dream of being mediocre. I want a mediocre life."

She laughed. "No, you don't."

"Yeah, I do. I want a basic life, with basic life achievements."

"Okay." She raised her head from my shoulder and turned toward me slightly before laying out her towel. She lay on top of it. "Tell me about your basic dream life."

I put out my towel beside hers, then lay down, placing my hands behind my head. "All right. First off, I'll take on a normal job. If I could do something in architecture like my dad, I'd be happy. I'd like to be Midwest successful, not California or New York successful. You know, a decent salary, enough to have a life, but a life no one else would envy. A small house that I'd get on about an acre of land. Would I like it on water? Yeah, but that's just me being a water sign, as you would say, since you believe in all that zodiac mumbo jumbo. Nothing wild with the house, either. I'd want it to feel warm and inviting. Mansions feel empty to me. Lonely. I want my house to feel like a home. Kind of like my dad did for Mom and me. I want a wraparound porch and rocking chairs so I can come home and complain to my wife about my crappy day at work. Then, we'd plan out our yearly vacation to Florida for us and the kids."

"That's *very* basic of you."

I smirked. "Thanks."

"How many kids?"

"One or two. Nothing too wild, otherwise we'll never make it to Disney without them draining my bank account for Mickey ears. What about you? What's your dream?"

Kierra

What's my dream?

"I want a nice husband," I told Gabriel. "A really nice husband who doesn't mind if I'm moody. And a simple house, too. I want kids and a dog named Bentley, who we'd nickname Bent, so I can tell people to go 'get Bent' when I want them to go catch the dog. He'd be a German shepherd, with a heart of gold. My grandpa had a German shepherd named Swirl who I loved, so I've always wanted one."

"See? There's nothing wrong with a mediocre life. I think they are more fun. Corny Easter egg hunts. White elephant games on Christmas Eve. Fourth of July barbecues. I think sometimes people think the bigger the event, the better it is, but I don't know. Sparklers on Fourth of July and lighting small fireworks in your driveway is more fun than cramming into an overpacked park to watch a display where kids are crying and people are drunk and ridiculous."

The more he expressed the idea of a mediocre life, the more it didn't seem like a bad thing. Maybe being a background character wasn't an awful thing after all. But then again, Gabriel made anything sound better. I could listen to him talk about his mediocre dreams for the rest of my life and never get bored.

"I guess it's not that bad," I agreed. "But before I can get me a husband and a basic life, I should at least get my first kiss before I'm fifty."

"It's not a big deal that you haven't been kissed yet."

"Said the boy who has been kissed many times."

"Yeah, but not by anyone that meant a lot to me. Meaningless kisses. Your first kiss is important. It should be from someone who cares a lot about you."

"Good luck to me finding that, when guys don't even notice me unless they are super drunk at parties."

"I notice you," he murmured. "I notice you all the time. So, I'll kiss you," he said as he sat up.

Butterflies began to swirl in my stomach as I bent my arms and sat up slightly on my elbows. "What?"

"I'll kiss you," he repeated. "Then you can get your first kiss out of the way. Besides, I figure I owe you for throwing you off a cliff."

I bit my bottom lip and narrowed my eyes at him. "I can't kiss you, Gabriel."

"Why not?"

"Because you're my best friend."

"Even more reason to kiss me. Like I said, it should be from someone who cares about you. I care about you, Kierra. I think I care about you more than I care about anything."

Why did that create more butterflies in my stomach? "Oh, well…okay?" I said, but it came out as a question. I felt flustered and shy, which was new when it came to being around Gabriel. I sat up more. "What do I do? Should I chew gum first? Should I get ChapStick or lip gloss? Should I—"

Before I could reply, Gabriel cupped my face in his hands and pulled me closer to him. His lips brushed against mine and he kissed me slowly, tilting my head up toward him. His lips were soft, and he didn't press them too much to mine. I kissed him back, my hands falling against his bare chest. My eyes closed as I fell into the kiss, allowing my thoughts to stop spiraling in that moment. Gabriel Sinclair. My very best friend. My very first kiss.

He kissed me deeper, his tongue slightly parting my lips. My heart pounded against my chest. I didn't know what to do next or how to act, but luckily Gabriel took the lead in every way possible. His kisses felt like a promise. A promise that he wouldn't hurt me. A promise that he'd always be there for me. A promise that he cared.

Even though he wanted a mediocre life, his kisses were nothing like that. His kisses were…passionate. And real. I'd thought about first kisses a lot, but I never knew they could feel like that. I never knew kisses could travel and send tingling sensations throughout your whole body. I never knew kisses could make life seem less scary and love seem more real.

If I could only have one kiss ever, I'd want it to be this one. With him.

With us.

When he pulled back gently, it felt as if time had slowed down. My eyes fluttered open, and I found his brown eyes locked in on me. His lazy smile fell against those lips. Those lips that for a moment had felt like mine and mine alone.

Gabriel brushed his thumb against his bottom lip. "Cross that off your bucket list."

Trust me, Gabriel. I will.

"And I'll cross it off my list, too," he said.

I laughed, trying to shake off the nerves I still had shooting through my system. "You've kissed people before. That was already crossed off your list. Multiple times."

"That's not what was on my bucket list," he said, pushing himself up to a standing position. He held a hand out toward me. I took it. He pulled me up.

"Then what do you mean you're going to cross it off?"

"My list only had three words on them."

"And what were the words?"

"Kiss Kierra someday."

I emitted a soft, reserved laugh. "Why would that be on your list?"

His eyes softened, reflecting a depth of emotion that I'd never seen from him before. He slowly shook his head. "Come on, Kierra," he replied, his voice gentle yet firm. "Why wouldn't that be on my list?" His words hung in the air, a poignant reminder of the unspoken bond between the two of us.

Was it possible that he felt what I felt, too? That even though we'd never spoken about it, he was falling, too? Maybe that was the thing about falling in love with your best friend. You didn't have to speak about it because there were not enough words to express what that kind of love felt like. It was too big for syllables, too strong to be articulated. The love just kind of formed over time and fell into place, like perfectly placed puzzle pieces.

He was still holding my hand.

I was still holding his.

"Kierra?" he asked.

"Yeah?" I answered.

"Do you want to go get some sandwiches?"

"Yeah. I do."

We gathered our stuff, and he drove us to our favorite diner, where we ate turkey sandwiches on rye with ruffled chips and Diet Cokes. We talked for over an hour about everything but the kiss, yet the kiss stayed on my mind. I figured it would stay there for as long as I lived.

Afterward, Gabriel drove us home, and I thanked him for pushing me off a cliff. He made me brave. Even when I didn't want to be.

"Kierra?" he asked.

"Yeah?" I answered.

"If I were your husband, I'd be nice to you. I'd make you coffee in the morning and get you a dog named Bentley. And

I'd tell you to get Bent, so we could go to the dog park. And I'd kiss you good morning and kiss you good night. Every single morning, and every single night, I'd do those things."

I felt my cheeks heat up from his words. "Yeah, Gabe. I know."

"Good night."

I sighed. "Good night."

———

The next day, I saw Rosie. She came over to gossip and flip through magazines.

As she sat on my bed, I said, "I kissed Gabriel last night."

She looked up for a moment and paused. "Really?"

"Yeah."

"Oh." She went back to flipping through her magazine. "About fucking time, Kierra."

19

Kierra

PRESENT DAY

Ava had been bouncing up and down all morning with excitement about the baby shower. She'd been telling me repeatedly how cool Eddie had been and how nice he was. When we showed up to the baby shower, Ava darted off quickly and made sure that everyone was having a grand time. She put herself to work right away, helping with appetizers and the setting up of games.

It was so good to see her so light and free lately. It was as if she'd stepped out of her shy shell and was able to laugh more with others without any concerns. That was the greatest gift to a parent—seeing their child not only succeeding in life but doing so with such happiness.

That was the word of the day for the baby shower: happiness.

"They look happy," I mentioned to Gabriel as we leaned back against the same cabinet drawer. I crossed my arms as I studied Eddie and Sarah giggling like teenagers as they opened their gifts. "They're so cute."

"They're going to make remarkable parents."

"I'm slightly envious of them. I never got this part of parenthood. I was never able to do the baby shower and the silly games. Or pick out the nursery or things like that. I wish I would've had that chance with Ava. I bet she was a perfect baby."

"You would've been a perfect new mom."

I snickered a little. "No, I would've been a mess. Worrying about every single breath she took. I would've been neurotic."

"You would've been a perfect new mom," he repeated.

My lips quivered into a faint smile.

There was no reason he should've been giving me as many butterflies as he had lately. I hadn't even known my body still knew how to get butterflies.

I placed my hands on the edge of the cabinet and gripped it, trying to shake off said butterflies. "Have you ever wanted to be a father?"

"Yes," he said confidently. "It's something I still think about. Even if I don't find my person, I've thought about adoption. I just wish I had my own father around to help me through it."

"That has to be hard...you not remembering him."

"I think the hardest part is knowing he was such a good man. I wish I could remember the good things from my past. It feels unfair to hear great stories yet hold no memory of them at all."

He placed his hands against the cabinet edge, gripping it as I had. Our arms brushed, and I didn't pull away. He didn't, either. I liked it, too. I liked our proximity. I liked the warmth that flowed throughout my whole system from small touches from him.

"Do you want more kids?" he asked me.

I let out a burst of laughter, abrupt and uncontrollable. "Absolutely not with Henry."

"What about if it was with someone else?"

The question made me pause because I never thought of that. I never thought of a world where I wasn't chained to Henry Hughes. A world of make-believe, where I could have the family of my dreams.

I lowered my head, feeling a tug at my heart. "One more kid," I whispered. "I always envisioned myself having two kids and a dog."

Gabriel laughed. "That's so strange. I've envisioned the same thing."

I know, Gabriel. I know.

His words broke a part of me. I wondered what would've happened if I'd never left all those years ago. I wondered what he and I would've become. If he would've been the happily to my ever after. If we would've been sitting side by side, opening baby shower gifts and playing silly games with each other. Acting like teenagers in love, being wowed by pacifiers.

"Can I tell you a secret, Kierra?" he asked.

"Of course."

"It's difficult to be near you at times," he confessed quietly.

"Why's that?"

He paused, a look of resigned affection in his eyes. "Because once you're gone, you have a way of occupying every thought I have for the rest of the day."

Oh, Gabriel.

Why do you have to be so…you?

My hands began to sweat as panic filled me up from within. I couldn't hold it in anymore. I pushed myself away from the cabinet drawer, locked eyes with Gabriel's perplexed stare, shook my head, and marched out of the room. I needed air. I needed space. I needed him.

Oh, how I needed him more than he'd ever know, and I couldn't keep going on as if he wasn't the biggest part of my life for the longest time.

"Hey, hey, what's going on?" Gabriel asked as he followed me down the secluded hallway. I turned to face him, and the puzzlement in his eyes made me feel awful. "Did I… I'm sorry. I should've never said that, Kierra. It was inappropriate and—"

"We were best friends," I blurted out.

He froze in place and blinked a few times before arching an eyebrow. "I'm sorry…what?"

I gestured back and forth between him and me. "We were best friends. You and me. Me and you. We were best friends for the longest time."

"What are you talking about?"

"When we were kids. And teens. And…" I took in a deep breath. "We were each other's everything."

His brows knit together and he shook his head. "Bullshit."

"It's true."

"For how long?"

"What do you mean?"

"How long were we friends?"

I blinked and shook my head. "Since a little before your father passed away."

"You knew my father?"

"I loved your father."

The pain in his eyes sliced straight through my heart. I couldn't imagine what his thoughts were. Oh my gosh, what was I doing? Why did I confess to him about our past? Why did I find the need to open that can of worms and unleash it on him? I just couldn't keep pretending like I didn't feel everything he felt, like I didn't see him the same way he'd been seeing me. It was all becoming too much.

"When did we stop being friends?" he asked me.

I swallowed hard. "After the accident."

"You knew about the accident?"

I caused the accident.

"Yes," I whispered. "I did."

His brows knit and he appeared annoyed with whatever thoughts were clouding his head. I wished I could read his mind. I didn't know what it was like in his head. In the past, I could read all the thoughts of the boy I fell in love with. Nowadays with this new man, it felt almost impossible to know what he was thinking.

"You're confused and upset," I commented.

"It's fine," he huffed, seeming angry.

"Gabriel. Please. I get that you're angry with me—"

"I'm not angry with you," he spat out.

I stood taller, somewhat shocked. "You're not angry with me?"

"No." He brushed his thumb against the bridge of his nose as he looked away from me. "I just don't get it."

"Get what?"

"How my fucked-up mind could forget about you."

My heart skipped a few beats as I kept my stare on him.

When his head lifted and those dark eyes locked with mine, I almost began to weep from the idea of what we could've been.

"Can I ask you a question, Kierra?"

"Yes. Of course. Anything."

"Did I love you?" he softly asked.

A tremble hit my bottom lip as my eyes filled with tears. I nodded slowly. "Yes."

"Did you love me, too?"

"More than words."

He fiddled with his hands and nodded as he sniffled a bit. "And then we fell out of love?"

"No," I urged. "I don't think people like us ever fall out of love."

"Then what happened to our love?"

"I ran from it."

"Why?"

Because I've caused so much pain.

When I couldn't reply with words, Gabriel kept talking. "It makes sense that I loved you, because when I first saw you...I didn't know you, but I could *feel* you." He cleared his throat and sniffled some more. "And when I felt you, I didn't feel lost anymore. I don't know a lot, and my mind is still messed up, but I think that's what love is. Something that makes you feel a little less lost."

"Gabriel—"

"Did I hurt you?" he asked. The pained expression in his eyes showed the level of guilt he was feeling. "Was it my fault?"

I rushed over to him and took his hands into mine. "No. Oh my goodness, no. Not at all. I swear. It was me, Gabriel. I was the one who left. You did nothing wrong. You could've never done anything wrong."

"Then why didn't you stay?"

If only I could tell him everything. But I knew Amma would've hated all the details to come out, and it would've damaged her relationship with her son. I didn't want to cause her more pain than I'd already had. Still, I couldn't continue acting as if Gabriel and I didn't have the connection that we'd had for the longest time. He was one of the largest parts of my life—if not the biggest, after Ava.

Truthfully, a part of me resented Amma, too. Her keeping such a massive secret hidden from Gabriel seemed so deeply cruel to me. The more I thought about how much Gabriel had missed out on, how he didn't have memories of his little brother, the more it irritated me.

"I made a lot of mistakes back then. I was young and scared."

"Sounds like a bullshit excuse," he murmured as he rubbed his hand against his temple. "So, wait. Time out. If we were that close, did you know my mother?"

"Yes."

"And when you two met again, did you recognize each other?"

I knew where he was going with this. I knew that his mind was starting to piece together the deceit that had taken place over the past few weeks since we reconnected at the dinner party.

I nodded slowly. "Yes."

"So. My mother knew you but pretended she didn't?"

"Gabriel, it's more complicated—"

"Thanks for sharing this," he said, his voice growing colder than before. I saw the shift in his body as he tensed and stood taller. "I should get back to the shower."

"Gabriel, wait—"

"No, it's fine. It's not a big deal. I'm fine."

"You're not."

"How the hell would you know? You knew me before, Kierra. You don't have a damn clue who I am now," he snapped.

That hurt, but I couldn't blame him. I'd just watched him go through a tailspin of emotions within a few minutes. It was a lot for him to take in all at once, and now he was transitioning straight into anger.

But he was Gabriel, after all, so his anger wasn't loud. It simmered behind his stare. It raked repeatedly through his hair. It sat against his clenched jaw.

"You're mad," I whispered.

"I'm not," he lied.

He wouldn't look at me. I couldn't blame him. I went weeks without telling him the truth. I didn't expect him to simply roll over and take the reveal without an array of emotions.

"Gabriel…"

He held up a silencing hand and began to pace. He rubbed his hands against his face repeatedly, mumbling under his breath.

"Gabe! We are about to cut the cake and we can't find the…" Amma came around the corner to find Gabriel and me standing in the hallway. Her gaze locked with mine for a second, confusion swirling in her brown eyes, before she looked at her son. "Is everything okay here?"

"Yeah, everything's fine," Gabriel huffed, shaking his head as a short chuckle left his mouth. "Did you know that Kierra and I were in love in the past?" He kept laughing. "Who am I kidding? Of course you knew, but for some reason, you both thought it would be best to lie to me about it. So, yeah. Everything's fine. I'm just surrounded by fucking liars. Let me go help with the cake."

He stormed off, leaving me standing there speechless. Amma's eyes locked with mine. I saw nothing but rage shooting through her.

I took a step toward her. "Amma…"

"What is wrong with you?" she whisper-shouted. "You told him?"

"I had to. He kept going on about how he felt a connection with me, and it felt wrong to lie to him."

"I didn't ask you to lie. I asked you to stay away."

"I know, I know. It was impossible to do that, though."

"No," she said. "It wasn't. You're just so selfish that you couldn't stop yourself from pushing back into his life."

My stomach knotted up and I shook my head. "I didn't tell him about Elijah, Amma, but I you need to. You should tell him everything. He deserves to know. I love him, and I can't keep Elijah from him. You shouldn't want to, either. Even though it's hard. He deserves to know his brother."

"You can't do that…"

"One week," I warned. "I'll give you one week to tell him. Otherwise, I will."

"We were fine while you were gone. We were good." Her eyes shut and she shook her head in disbelief. "You were dead to us. Why couldn't you just stay dead?" she whispered, her body slightly trembling.

As she walked away, my chest filled with heavy levels of guilt as if I'd made a mistake by telling Gabriel. But I knew I hadn't. That made it hurt even more.

I stayed in the hallway for a few minutes longer. I didn't know if I could find the strength to walk back into the baby shower to see Gabriel. To face Amma again. Maybe she was right. Maybe I should've stayed out of Gabriel's life, but it felt like the universe had brought him back to me. How was I supposed to simply walk away again after I was given a second chance?

"Mom? Mom!" Ava called out, hurrying into the hallway. The moment she found me, her lips turned up in the biggest grin. "Hey! What are you doing here? It's time for cake."

I pushed out a fake smile and tried to keep myself from sobbing. I wrapped an arm around Ava as I nodded my head. "Yes, okay. Let's have some cake."

20

Kierra

When one week passed by, I didn't get the chance to make sure that Amma told Gabriel about Elijah because he didn't show up at Florence Bakery. When I texted him, he ignored my messages. If he came to my house to check in on the property, he'd do his work, say hi to Ava, and be on his way. When I picked Ava up from GS Architecture, he was always mysteriously busy and nowhere to be found.

I was officially being ghosted, and I wasn't sure how to handle it.

A part of me thought he couldn't go on forever avoiding me, but then again, why couldn't he? There was no real reason for him to be forced to interact with me. Plus, with what he'd learned, I didn't blame him for wanting nothing to do with me. Still, it hurt. Still, I missed him. It was like having a wish come true only to have the dream ripped away.

"You need to try harder," Rosie told me as we met up for our monthly spa trip. "You need to go all nineties rom-com and tell him he has to see you and talk to you." She tightened her robe as we walked into the Zen room to wait for our massages.

I grabbed a glass of lemon-and-lime-infused water and shook my head. "I'm not going to push myself into his life. He's made it clear he wanted nothing to do with me."

"Did he? Or are you just deciding that on your own? Maybe he just needed a little time, Kierra."

"It's been two weeks."

"Exactly. So now you push into his life. Men are stupid. They don't know when they've had enough time. Show up at his house, stand on his porch in the pouring rain, tell him how much he means to you," she ordered, flopping down into an oversized chair. "Otherwise, we'll be ninety in nursing homes talking about how you never took a shot at building another friendship with Gabriel…or more than a friendship."

"Rosie. Stop. I'm married."

"To a fucking dick, Kierra. I'm not saying it's right, but you should dream about the possibilities at least. One day, God willing, Henry is going to be out of your life. Wouldn't it be nice to have Gabriel be in it? I'm telling you…" She shrugged her shoulders. "You two were the reason I ever even believed in love—real love, that is."

"I just…" I didn't know what to say or what to do.

Rosie grew somber. "Just consider trying to talk to him, Kierra. And tell him how sorry you are for not telling him sooner."

"Okay. I will." If anything, Gabriel deserved an in-person apology.

She smiled. "Good. But also, Kierra…if you go to him, you have to tell him the truth. The whole truth."

I sighed. "I was afraid you'd say that."

After my massage with Rosie, I headed over to Gabriel's house, uninvited. A part of me was hoping his car wouldn't be there. It would've given me a reason to turn around and drive away. Yet his pickup truck sat in the driveway, and the lights were on in his house.

It took me a solid five minutes to build up enough courage to climb out of my car and go knock on his door.

The moment I did knock, more butterflies formed in my gut. The nerves rocking through my whole system made me want to break into hives.

When he opened the door, he seemed somewhat surprised to see me. He narrowed his stare. "Kierra. Are you okay?"

Are you okay?

What an odd first question to ask.

He seemed to ask me that more than not. I couldn't help but wonder how many I'm-not-okay vibes I was giving off daily.

"Yes, well, no. I mean, well, hi," I breathed out, tugging on the ends of my long sleeves.

Bewilderment showed in his stare. "Hi? What's up?"

What's up? You ignoring me for two weeks. That's what's up.

"I, uh, we haven't spoken?" I said, but it came out as a

question. "I mean, not since I told you about...us. And I know you're probably mad—"

"I'm not mad."

I released a nervous chuckle. "Come on, Gabriel. I know you are. I don't blame you for being mad, either, and—"

"I'm not mad," he coldly cut in again.

"Gabriel—"

"What do you want, Kierra?" he said, his voice dripping with annoyance. "Did you come here to relieve yourself of guilt? Fine. Be free of the guilt. Because I'm not mad."

"That's not why I came."

"Then why are you here?" he snapped, clearly mad, no matter what he was telling me.

"I wanted to say I'm sorry," I said, swallowing hard.

"Okay. Thanks." He went to close the door, and I placed my foot in the way.

"Gabriel, wait."

"Why? You said what you needed to say, and I said thanks. End of conversation."

"But it's not... It's clear you're still mad."

"*I'm not mad!*" he said once more. He grumbled under his breath and stepped out onto the porch. "Fine. You want to talk. Let's talk. You want to believe in your head that I'm mad when I'm not mad. I just need you to get that into your head, Kierra. I'm not mad."

"Then what are you?" I whispered. "Because it's clear you're not okay."

"*I'm fucking hurt,*" he shouted, tossing his hands up in

defeat. His voice cracked as the word *hurt* fell from his lips. He turned away from me and rested his hands on the porch railing. He shook his head a few times before he turned back my way. His brown eyes were flooded with emotion as he bit his lip and swallowed hard. "I'm fucking hurt, Kierra," he murmured.

"I get it."

"No, you don't. You don't *get* it. You don't understand." He shook his head in disbelief. "I *needed* you, Kierra," he cried out, pounding his hand against his chest. "I fucking needed you, and you left. You walked away without looking back, leaving me with this emptiness that I couldn't make sense of. You left me after I went through a traumatic event, and I fucking needed you."

The strain in his voice shattered any little piece of my heart that was still beating.

He lowered his head. "I had no one," he whispered. "I had no one to help guide me back home. I struggled for years. I thought I was losing my mind, too, because I'd dream of you and then wake up feeling more lost than ever before. You've fucking haunted my dreams for two decades, Kierra. So, forgive me if I didn't answer your messages over the past few weeks, but this is a lot to process."

"Yes, yeah. Okay. I know."

"You said we were each other's everything, and then you had the nerve to say you just had to leave. You gave me that bad excuse, and what? Did you just expect me to be okay? To shrug it off? Things were hard so you just left? I would've never done that to you. I know that I don't remember us, but I feel us," he said, putting his hand against his chest. "I feel you, Kierra, and I would've never left you at your lowest. I would've been by your side, reminding you day by day who we once were."

Tears streamed down my face as I came to realize how much I'd screwed up. "There's more to the story," I told him, shaking my head. "There's so much more to the story, Gabriel, and that's why I'm here. I want to tell you everything. I want you to know all the ins and outs of who we were and what happened that night. I need you to know that if I do that, you may never want to speak to me again, but I want you to know the whole truth. The whole story. You deserve that."

His brows narrowed as he tilted his head and crossed his arms over his chest. "You'll tell me everything?"

"Yes. Everything."

He hesitated for a moment, then invited me into his house. I sat on his living room couch and he sat across from me on the coffee table. "Okay. Tell me."

The moment I started, I wanted to stop. I wanted to erase the memories of the night of the accident. I didn't want to recall every single detail. I didn't want to go into the darkness again, but I also wanted him to understand why I left. I wanted him to understand why all those years ago, I chose to walk away. I wanted him to understand why it was nearly impossible for me to ever come back to him.

And I wanted him to know about Elijah.

Even if it hurt me to speak his name.

21

Kierra

NINETEEN YEARS OLD

"This was the best birthday ever!" Elijah exclaimed, covered in snow as Gabriel carried the three sleds on his back. I held Elijah's hand in mine as we danced through the snow. "Thanks for bringing me, Kierra!"

"And to think your big doofus brother wanted to stay home and watch the ball drop on television," I remarked with a big grin at Gabriel.

He smiled back, knowing we'd just had the best time. Elijah's joy was worth it.

Gabriel walked beside me and nudged my arm. "You did good, Penguin."

"I did, didn't I?"

He leaned in slightly and kissed my earlobe. "You did."

I was still getting used to the kisses he'd deliver to me. We'd officially been dating for a year now, and I still got butterflies whenever he came near. I loved him. I loved him so much that sometimes it made me tear up.

"It's snowing again!" Elijah said, dropping my hand and tilting his head up to the sky. He opened his mouth and stuck out his tongue. I did the same as him, catching as many snowflakes as possible.

"Okay, snowmen, let's get a move on before the snow comes down too fast," Gabriel ordered, dragging the sleds.

"She's a snowwoman, Gabby," Elijah said. He was the only one who was allowed to call Gabriel Gabby. Anyone else would've received a punch to the gut. "Not a snowman."

"You're right. My bad. Snowman and snowwoman, let's get going."

"We should make snow angels first," Elijah remarked, flopping down into the snow.

I arched an eyebrow at Gabriel with a wicked grin.

He pointed a stern finger toward me. "Don't you dare, Kierra."

I shrugged. "I can't help it. I can't say no to this little dude." I then plopped beside Elijah, and we began making snow angels together, waving our arms and legs out in sync. "Come on, Gabriel. There's room for three."

"It's almost one in the morning. We need to get home," he said.

"Snow angels! Snow angels!" Elijah chanted.

I joined him in the chanting. "Snow angels! Snow angels!"

Gabriel rolled his eyes. "This is peer pressure."

"Only the best kind of pressure," I said, patting a spot beside me. "Join the madness."

With a big huff, he surrendered, dropping the sleds next

to us. He then plopped down and began making a snow angel beside me.

I couldn't think of a better trio to make snow angels.

We stayed in the snow too long, and the snowfall increased. "Okay, we should actually get going," I said.

Gabriel stood first, helped Elijah up, and then held a hand out toward me. I grabbed his hand, and he pulled me up to his chest and kissed my nose. "My favorite snowwoman."

Butterflies.

This man would never *not* give me butterflies.

"Enough kisses, more walking," Elijah ordered, tossing the sleds toward Gabriel, one at a time.

"Don't worry, boys! I'll drive us home," I said, knowing Gabriel left his glasses at home. He couldn't see when it wasn't snowing outside, let alone in what was turning out to be a blizzard.

We hopped into the car, and I cranked the heat up as Gabriel made sure Elijah was buckled in. He checked and double-checked, even though Elijah was old enough to buckle himself in. Amma was very overprotective of her kids, and if Elijah showed up with a mere scratch on him, she'd freak out. Truthfully, after Gabriel's father passed away, Amma had become a helicopter mother. She made sure to almost always know where her boys were. If she'd known about our trip that evening, she would've shut it down quickly.

After Elijah was safe, Gabriel hopped into the front seat.

We took off down the road, and I was quick to realize how slippery everything had gotten. I was moving slower than ever, and the radio was turned down. As we approached a stop sign, I paused, looked all ways, and when it was my time to go, I went very slowly.

"Turn up the music!" Elijah requested with a yawn.

I glanced over my shoulder toward him and smiled. "You should be sleeping."

As I went to turn back to the road, I heard the blaring of a horn. I glanced to my right and saw the headlights coming straight toward us. It only took a second. I'd only looked away from the road for a split second.

One moment.

That was all.

The car slammed into Elijah and Gabriel's side of our vehicle. We began to spin around from the impact, and before I knew it, I lost complete control of the car. We went shooting down the street, and before we could stop, another car hit us on my side.

My head flew forward and hit the steering wheel as our car skid forward and slammed into an oak tree. I heard Elijah screaming and crying as I tried to lift my head up. Everything was blurry as smoke escaped from the smashed hood.

"Ouch," I whimpered as I tried to move my body. I looked over to Gabriel, whose head was smashed against the window. Blood dripped down the glass as panic filled me. "Gabriel... hey, hey, look at me," I cried as I tried to unbuckle my seat belt. It was jammed, though, and I was unable to move.

The whimpered cries in the back seat came to a stop. I turned to see Elijah who was covered in broken glass with cuts all over him. "Eli," I sobbed, trying harder and harder to get out of my seat.

They were quiet.

So quiet.

Too quiet.

Cry, Elijah.

Make a sound, Gabriel.

Move.

Please.

Moan.

Grumble.

Anything!

Say something!

"No, no, no," I sobbed, tugging on the seat belt. My head hurt. My heart felt as if it was going to leap out of my chest.

Once the seat belt finally let me go, I reached over to Gabriel and checked his pulse. His heart was still beating.

With pain stinging my whole body from the impact of the second car, I forced myself to climb into the back seat beside Elijah to check on him. The broken glass sliced my hands as I fell into the seat. "Elijah, wake up. It's me. It's Kierra, okay? You're okay. Hey, wake up," I cried, checking for his pulse.

Cry, Elijah.

Make a sound.

Move.

Please.

Grumble.

Anything. Say something!

Breathe, Eli. Just breathe.

Nothing.

There was nothing.

I choked on my next breath as I fell over Elijah's body. My world began to crumble into a million pieces as I held his little body in my hands.

"Help!" I screamed at the top of my lungs. "Help me!" I cried out to anyone who might've been around, to anyone who may have heard me. "We need help! He's just a kid! Help us! He needs help! We need help! Please," I sobbed uncontrollably as I held Elijah in my arms.

My face fell to his chest, searching for his heartbeat, searching for any sign that he would be okay. I sobbed into him as I whimpered repeatedly, *"Please help."*

22

Gabriel

PRESENT DAY

As Kierra finished telling me the story, her whole body shook and tears poured from her eyes. I stood there, shocked by the words rolling from her tongue. I couldn't fantom what she was telling me.

A brother?

I had a little brother?

That was too bizarre for me to even wrap my mind around. How was that even possible? Why would Mom never tell me about this?

It wasn't until Kierra pulled out the photographs from her purse and began to show me actual photos of me, her, and Elijah together that I fully began to believe her. I felt sick to my stomach as I flipped through the photographs. Dozens and dozens of the three of us, laughing together. Dozens of pictures showing me the truth of my brother. My little brother.

Fucking hell. I had a little brother.

How...?

Wait…?

"*What?*" I said, tossing a hand through my hair. "And my mother told you to stay away from me?"

"Don't blame her, Gabriel. Before the accident, she already struggled with worry. She was constantly afraid of something happening to you due to your father's passing. That fear only grew after Elijah was born. Then, after the accident, she fell apart. It was too much for her."

"Too much for her?" I huffed. "She erased my memories pretty much, making sure they stayed gone. If I'd never run into you, I would've spent the rest of my life never knowing about Elijah. So forgive me for not being so forgiving of her."

Kierra grew quiet, not pushing the topic. Truthfully, I was in a state of shock from the whole situation, but that didn't dismiss the fact that I could see the hurt in Kierra. The level of guilt she'd felt over the whole thing. It wasn't as if she wanted to abandon me; she'd felt she had no choice.

Still, I wonder what I would've done if the situation were flipped around. Would I have listened to her parents if they told me to stay away? Would I have left without trying everything possible to reach out? Or would the guilt and depression of the whole accident have been so traumatic that I would've buried my head in the sand and run as far as I could from any memories of what happened?

"Thank you," I whispered, clasping my hands together. "Thank you for telling me the truth. I'm sure that wasn't easy."

"It was the worst thing that ever happened, Gabriel, and if

I could, I'd turn a million clocks back to change the outcome. If I could, I would've switched spots with Elijah. I wished it were me. I still, to this day, wish it were me and not him."

"This is a lot to process."

"Yes. I get it. I don't want you to feel pressure to keep talking to me, either. I understand if you want space, and I'll respect that. I just wanted you to know the whole story."

I thanked her once more. "But I think perhaps you should go. I have a lot going through my mind right now, and I'm not sure how to process it."

"Yes, of course. Not a problem. Just…if you need anything, you have my number."

I stood as she did. "Yeah, for sure. Good night, Kierra."

She almost smiled but it fell short. "Good night."

After Kierra left, I didn't sleep.

I stayed up all night trying to make sense of the life that I'd forgotten and how much it influenced the life I now lived. How would things have been different if I knew about Elijah? What choices would I have made?

How could I look at my mother the same after this, too? It was all too much.

The next day at work, I was still lost in a whirlwind of confusion. As I walked into the hallway, I saw my mom coming my way. She was the last person I wanted to see. The moment I saw her, I felt sick to my stomach.

She raised an eyebrow. "Gabriel, what's going on? You look—"

"Did I have a brother?"

The color drained from her face as she froze in place. Her mouth parted but no words came out. I knew the answer before she told me, but I needed to see how she'd respond once I brought it to her face-to-face.

I nodded once. "Yeah, all right."

"Gabriel..." She reached toward me, but I pulled my arm away.

"Don't touch me. Don't talk to me. Just..." I released a weighted sigh. "*Don't.*"

23

Kierra

Gabriel: Hey. Can we meet up to talk?

The moment Gabriel's name appeared on my phone screen, I sat up straighter in my chair at the dining room table. I hadn't heard from him in two weeks, since I'd told him everything about the accident. I didn't think he'd reach out again, if I being honest.

I couldn't blame him if he kept his distance.

Kierra: Of course. When and where?
Gabriel: Eight tonight at my place.
Kierra: See you soon.

———————————

I was nervous the whole time I drove over to his house, and when I showed up, he asked me if I wanted to sketch with him on the back patio. I agreed, and we walked around to where he had his sketchbooks set up.

We didn't talk for a while. I wanted to give him the opportunity to speak when he was ready. Yet I'd be lying if I said I wasn't holding my breath the whole time as I waited.

"What would've happened if you hadn't left?" Gabriel asked after a while.

"What do you mean?"

"After it happened with Elijah…after the accident. After my mom pushed you away and I struggled to find myself. What do you think would've happened if you had stayed?"

My chest ached from the thought. I'd played that what-if game repeatedly for many, many years. I'd crafted images in my mind of what life could've looked like for us both. I visualized different scenarios. Ones where we baked fresh bread on Sunday mornings, and he attended my fashion shows on Friday nights. Ones where we laughed at stupid jokes over coffee and lay on the couch watching bad films. Ones where our kisses never stopped. Ones where forgiveness was possible. Ones where guilt no longer lived.

"We would've been happy," I whispered. "Maybe not at first, but we would've found a way to be happy again."

"I would've loved you through the dark days."

I released a nervous chuckle because I knew that was true. Maybe that was why I left. I didn't think I deserved the kind of love Gabriel would've given me. "I know," I nodded. "You would've."

"And you would've loved me through harsh nights."

"Fully."

He looked down at his hands sitting in his lap. He fiddled with his nails and shrugged. "I'm glad that didn't happen."

His words threw me off slightly and stung my heart. "You are?"

"I mean, sure. We would've had more years to love each other, we would've had more memories, but I'm glad you didn't come back. I think we needed to be apart to really appreciate this now. Besides…you wouldn't have Ava if we'd stayed together back then. What a crime that would've been."

"She saved me," I confessed. "I don't think I would've made it through life without you if it wasn't for her."

"She was your foundation."

I raised an eyebrow, wanting him to expand on that thought.

His smile slipped out. "The solid ground that you needed to begin again. Before her, things probably felt rocky and unstable. Ava's your solid ground. She's not your house; she's your home."

"*Home*," I softly sang. "Yes. She's home to me." I shook my head, still feeling guilty. "I just feel as if it's so unfair to you, though. You've missed out on so much. On your memories, on Elijah. And I still feel so awful, Gabriel, for not telling you."

"Kierra," he whispered, "stop."

"I can't. I am so sorry for everything I've done, Gabriel. I am so sorry for—"

"It wasn't your fault," he said. "And I forgive you."

I looked up at him, shaking my head. "How can you forgive me for that, though?"

"Because I'm almost certain you've spent the last decade or two beating yourself up over the accident. You don't have to carry that anymore, Kierra. I forgive you. Now it's up to you to forgive yourself."

I knew that would take time, and it would be hard for me to do so. Self-forgiveness was one of the hardest things to do. I'd watched my clients deal with the heaviness of guilt, and I worked endlessly to help them break through their past mistakes. Yet, as with most things in life, that was easier said than done.

"I'll work at it," I swore. "At forgiving myself."

"Good." He crossed his arms. "Can you do something for me, though?"

"What's that?"

"Tell me about Elijah. Any and every little detail about him."

I tilted my head toward him and smiled shyly. "Well, he loved superheroes. He hated cats. He thought Legos were the greatest invention ever. He always wanted a dog. He loved swimming and was a better swimmer than both of us combined. He refused to eat anything green but liked to eat onions like candy."

"Weirdo," Gabriel laughed.

"Total weirdo," I agreed with a smile. "Our favorite weirdo. I have notebooks of letters I'd write to him every week since he passed."

"Do you still write the letters?"

"Yes. No matter what."

"Why do you do that?"

"Because I miss him," I confessed with a slight nod. "Writing him letters felt like a way to still be connected to him. It's silly, I know."

"It's not silly. It's beautiful."

I tugged on the edge of my long-sleeved shirt and shrugged. "In the early stages, I wrote down every single detail about who he'd been. I wanted to remember everything about him. I wanted a time capsule of sorts to hold on to the memory of him forever. If you'd like, you can read them."

"You'd let me?"

"I'd let you do anything that made life easier for you."

"I'll take you up on that soon." He turned toward me and raised an eyebrow. "Did I used to call you Penguin?"

I smiled. "Yes. Since we were kids. We got into a fight and you said I waddled like a penguin. It sort of stuck."

"That's why it keeps popping up in my head."

"Yeah. Definitely."

"Well…" He took a deep inhale. "Thanks, Penguin."

My heart wanted to cry at hearing the nickname. I wanted to fall apart in his arms and hold him for all the days I hadn't gotten to hold him before.

Instead I simply said, "You're welcome."

"Friends again?" he asked.

I sighed.

I nodded.

"Friends again," I agreed.

Even though, truthfully, all I wanted was *more*.

24

Gabriel

"Hey, Boss Man?" Ava asked, tossing some M&M's into her mouth as we took a work break to play video games.

"Yeah, kid?"

"Do you think you can help me with something?"

"What's up?"

She placed the game on pause and turned to face me. "I know there have been a lot of parties happening, but I think there's one more big party that should happen before school comes back around, and I need your help planning it."

"And what's this party for?"

"My mom's fortieth birthday. I feel like that's an important birthday for old people, and well, Dad isn't the best at throwing surprises for her. If anything, she's always planned her birthday stuff, but I don't know. Dad always gets his dinner parties and stuff to show off. Mom gets nothing. I just want to make sure it's a great birthday for her."

"Did you ask your dad to help? I don't want to step on any toes."

"Whatever. I don't want his help," she said snappily. That was odd. Normally, it seemed like Ava and Henry had a great relationship. They weren't as close as Ava and Kierra, of course, but it seemed as if Ava had a strong love for her father.

"Is everything good with your dad?"

"Dad's just Dad. It doesn't matter. Do you want to help or not?"

"Sure, of course. We can start planning as soon as possible."

Ava's smile spread across her face. Any irritation she had about Henry disappeared as I agreed to help her set up a party. "Really?"

"Of course. I'd do anything for Kierra." The words rolled off my tongue without thought, and then I realized how damn insane they sounded. I shook my head. "I mean, I'd do anything for you if that means helping your mom. My client."

Ava nodded. "I think you meant the first comment, too. Which is fine, Boss Man. I'd do anything for her, too. There is one small issue, though."

"And what's that?"

"I only have one hundred dollars for the budget."

I laughed. "I think I can manage to cover the rest."

"Sweet! Thanks, Boss Man."

"Welcome, kid."

She tossed more M&M's into her mouth and unpaused the game. "Let's get back to me beating you."

The day of Kierra's party, Ava and I spent hours setting up. Of course, Henry knew about the party, but he did little to be involved. Though, when everyone showed up, he acted as if he'd been involved in every little detail, taking credit for the creativity that Ava had spent weeks on. It was damn annoying to say the least. As I helped Ava with the last tasks, I noticed Henry out of the corner of my eye, greeting everyone with his over-the-top personality.

"I hate that he's doing that," Ava grumbled as we finished checking on the champagne table for the birthday toast later in the night.

"Who's *he* and what is he doing?"

"My dad. He's acting like this was all his idea."

Oh.

So she'd noticed, too.

"You know what's crazy?" Ava asked as she lifted a glass of champagne as if she were going to drink it.

I took the glass from her hand. "What's that?"

"Mom laughs with you. Like, her real laughs. The kind where she tosses her head back in a giggling fit. I can't remember the last time I saw her do that with Dad."

My gut tightened. "I'm sure your parents laugh all the time together."

"They don't," she replied. "If anything, all Mom does is cry because of him. She tries to hide it, but sometimes I hear her." She turned toward me after staring at her parents across the room. She crossed her arms and shook her head. "You don't like him, do you?"

I swallowed hard. "Your father is a brilliant man. He is decades ahead with his tech—"

"That's not what I asked, Gabriel. I said you don't like him. Him being smart doesn't make him a good person."

I grimaced, uncertain of what I was supposed to say. I wasn't there to shit on her father. I wasn't there to make her feel bad about the fact that her dad was some awful human being that most people thought was a saint. I wasn't going to tell her about his cheating with their former chef, or him treating Kierra like she was nothing. He was a disgusting pig. But how could I convey that to his daughter?

"We're just different people," I told her.

"Yeah," she agreed, "you are. You're better than him."

I arched an eyebrow and shook my head. "No, I'm not."

"Yeah, you are. Based on that response alone. If I told my father he was better than you, he'd agree. Which would in turn prove that he wasn't."

"Ava…"

"I caught him screaming at Mom a few weeks ago," she mentioned, her eyes flashing with tears. "He thought I was gone to my friend's house for the weekend, but I came back to pick up my book." Her voice began to crack as she spoke. "They didn't know I came into the house, but he…" She dropped her head and shook it in disbelief. "He was screaming at her for something, as if Mom had ruined his entire life. I hid in the foyer because I didn't know what was happening. I waited to see what she'd done that made him so angry. But then I found out why he was yelling so loud. Why his rage was at a boiling point. Do you know what Mom did wrong?"

"What's that?"

"She burned herself getting a pizza out of the oven. Her hand hit the top of the oven, and she dropped the pizza, making a mess in the oven. She had a solid burn on her right hand, and he screamed at her for it. For a mistake. And the way he did it…It was so clear it wasn't the only time he'd yelled at her like that when I wasn't around. For the first time ever, I saw my dad as something new."

"What did you see him as that day?"

"A monster."

I didn't know what to say. I wasn't going to lie to the girl. Her father was a major dick, and knowing that he'd screamed at Kierra after she injured herself made me want to rage. It was taking everything inside of me to not march across the room and slam his head through a window.

Henry Hughes wasn't a man. A grown man would never shout at his wife in that fashion. They'd never hurt someone they loved so deeply and humiliate them in public or private. I could only imagine how Kierra felt terrified and embarrassed and hurt by the outburst that he'd unleashed when he thought he was alone to torture her. How often did those kinds of things happen between the two of them?

How often did he hurt her? With and without his words?

"I'm not always the best with my words, Ava, and truthfully

I don't even know what to say right now because what I want to say isn't child-appropriate."

"It's just funny to me." She sighed and picked up a glass filled with punch, finally surrendering to the fact that I wasn't going to allow her to down champagne. "He was my hero for the longest time. How could my hero be my other hero's worst nightmare?"

I wanted to comfort her, but mostly I wanted to find Henry and make him feel how he made my two girls feel—small and scared.

My two girls.

Realistically I knew they weren't mine, but my heart disagreed. I felt protective of Kierra and Ava.

My eyes began to dart around the house in search of Henry, who seemed to be quickly on the move as he interacted with guests. I figured it was about time I gave him one or two birthday greetings.

"I'll be back, kid," I told Ava as I picked up my own glass of champagne, downing it and placing it back down on the table.

As I walked around the house, I saw a ton of people laughing with one another. Some were dancing. Others spoke highly of Henry as if he was the greatest thing since sliced bread. The more positive comments I heard about him, the more my rage built.

When I looked across the way, I saw Kierra standing next to Henry's mother, Tamera. The two smiled as they interacted. When Kierra looked up at me, her eyes flashed with a stillness. Her smile faltered for a second before her lips turned back on.

She held up her hand, waving slightly. I waved back. I still felt uncomfortable after our last exchange. All I wanted to do was be near her, and I knew it was inappropriate to say the things I said to her, but I couldn't help myself.

I just needed to let her know that I felt more whole whenever she was near me. There was something about Kierra and her eyes. I'd never known locking eyes with someone could feel so much like home.

She excused herself from Tamera and began to walk over toward me. "Hey, stranger."

"Happy birthday, Kierra."

"Thanks. This is amazing. Ava is a sneaky devil. I can't believe she pulled this off all on her own." She then narrowed her eyes. "Which is exactly why I don't think she pulled it off by herself."

"She may have asked for a little help. I may have made a few calls."

"Gabriel...you didn't have to do this."

"I know. I wanted to. You look amazing, by the way."

She was wearing a fitted deep-red gown that highlighted every curve of her body. My eyes had moved up and down her frame many times since I'd spotted her that evening. "Oh, this old thing? It's a Kierra original."

I arched an eyebrow. "Bullshit. You made this?"

"Finished it last week. I finally dusted off my machines."

"It looks beyond fantastic. You look beyond fantastic. I'm so fucking proud of you, Kierra."

Her eyes teared up. "Thanks, Gabriel." A small breath released from between her lips. "Can I tell you a secret?"

"Always."

"For the first time in years, you make me feel seen. You make me feel…good enough. I haven't felt like that in such a long time."

I bit my bottom lip, debating if I moved in too close to her seeing as how there were so many others around us. What would our proximity appear like to them? What would people say if they saw me so close to Kierra? What would they think?

"Kierra—"

Before she could reply, the room filled with people singing "Happy Birthday." We looked over our shoulders to see Henry and Ava coming out with a giant cake being guided on some robotic table. The three-tiered cake was covered in white, gold, and pink fondant with sparklers sticking out of it, making the whole cake seem remarkably luxurious.

Kierra's eyes widened with surprise as she clasped her hands together and placed them against her mouth in awe.

As she moved closer to Henry and Ava, placing her hand against her heart, everyone in the room sang "Happy Birthday" to her, leaving her near tears. After the singing came to an end, Kierra blew out her candles. I couldn't help but wonder what she wished for.

If I had a wish, it would be for her.

Damn, that dress looked phenomenal.

After the candles were blown out, everyone began cheering and shouting, "Speech, speech, speech!"

Kierra waved her hands bashfully. "No, no!" They kept chanting until she gave in. "Okay, okay, fine. Though most of you should know I'm not the best at public speaking. When I was sixteen, I had to give a speech during a softball awards ceremony, and I threw up all over myself." Snickers were heard throughout the room. Kierra's smile seemed so gentle. Her shyness only made me fall harder. I watched her lips slightly part as she continued to speak. "I am just really, truly grateful for you all. This surprise, you all showing up, means the world to me. My life is happier because you are all in it. Now, go eat, drink, and be merry."

Everyone clapped and cheered once more.

Someone walked over to me and tapped me on the shoulder. I turned to find an older gentleman dressed in the most impeccable suit I'd ever seen in my life. And the most impeccable gray beard I'd ever seen in my life, too. This dude looked like a *GQ* model.

He smiled. "You're Gabriel, right? The architect."

"That's me."

He nodded and held his hand out to me. "I'm Joseph. I work at the clinic with Kierra."

I shook his hand. "Oh yeah. I've heard about you from Kierra."

"Hopefully good things," he said as he lifted two beers from the robot that kept circling the room. He held one toward me and I accepted.

"Only the best. She really looks up to you and your work ethic."

"She's one of the most talented and compassionate individuals I've ever had the pleasure of not only working with, but knowing."

"That's not hard to believe," I said, staring over to Kierra who was giggling with Ava as they cut the cake. "She's quite extraordinary."

"'Extraordinary,'" he repeated as he removed his glasses and rubbed the bridge of his nose before placing them back on. "Yes. That's the perfect word to describe her."

Before I could reply, Henry played a few keys on the piano, grabbing the attention of the room. He then stood on top of the piano bench with a glass of wine in his hand. "Sorry to interrupt, but I think we can all agree that my wife's speech was a little lackluster," he said with that smug smile that seemed to be always plastered on his face. "And if you have ever been to one of our dinner parties, then you understand I love a good toast. So, I figured I'd take a moment to make a toast to the most splendid woman I've ever had the grace of knowing." He held his glass up in the air. "You know, when I met Kierra, I was a single father trying to figure out life. She came in like a rocket and made my life brighter. Made our lives brighter," he said as he gestured toward Ava. "So, tonight we toast to my beautiful, gifted, caring wife, Kierra. The woman who puts everyone else before herself. Cheers!"

Everyone cheered and drank their wine. Joseph stood beside me, shaking his head in disapproval. "'The woman who puts everyone else before herself,'" Joseph said, echoing Henry's words. "It's funny. That's supposed to be seen as a compliment, but really, it's a curse."

"How do you mean?"

"It's self-harm—loving others more than you love yourself.

Kierra is nicer to others than she is herself. I've never met such an *extraordinary* woman who was so unkind to herself."

"Why do you think that is?"

"I have a million professional reasons that I could come up with. Thousands of different ways to study her. Yet, from a friend's viewpoint, it's easy. Something in her past made her feel as if she didn't deserve a certain level of love, so she overpours into others as a way to make up for her past."

"She's carrying guilt of some kind?"

"Yes, maybe." He slightly shook her head. "Or maybe it's just a heartbreak that never healed completely. Either way, her way of living will be to her own detriment. Maybe not today, but it adds up—giving so much without receiving a thing. Henry knows this and abuses that role in her life. He knows she'll do anything for Ava, which means he can get away with anything if Kierra fears losing her daughter."

"He controls her through her love for Ava."

"Precisely. Which makes him the scariest kind of person. I mean, what kind of man would use his own daughter as leverage to get his way?"

A monster. A monster would do that.

Joseph nodded once. "But who knows? Maybe I've had one too many beers." He held a hand out toward me. "It was nice to meet you, Gabriel."

I shook his hand. "You too, Joseph."

"In a perfect dream world, I'd have you build me a new home, too."

"Just call me whenever you're ready."

"I doubt I could afford you," he joked.

"I'll give you the friends and family discount."

Joseph laughed. "I'll hold you to that. Cheers, brother," he said, tapping his beer bottle against mine. Before he left, he said one more thing that stayed with me. "You know the difference? Between you and Henry?"

"What's that?"

"He only speaks kind things of Kierra when they are in crowds. He's loud about it around other people. You speak so kindly of her quietly, sincerely. And if I'm good at reading people, which I believe I am, I bet you speak that kindly of her within your thoughts, too."

As the party continued, people grew more and more intoxicated. I still hadn't had a chance to speak to Henry, but as more time moved by, I figured Kierra's birthday party wasn't the best opportunity to have it out.

Every time I looked over at Kierra, her smile was stretched wide, and she seemed surrounded by the people she loved most. It was a very different crowd than Henry's dinner party. Everyone seemed genuinely more friendly and welcoming. There was a warmth about the whole situation, and I was glad she was able to have that level of joy. I was happy to see that the attention was only on her.

She found her way back over to me at one point. She was a little tipsy and had a goofy smile of delight on her face.

"Guess what," she said, swaying to the jazz music filling the room.

"What's up?"

"I'm happily drunk."

"I love that for you."

"I love you, too," she replied. Even drunk, she realized her words and shook her head. "I mean, I love that for me, too. I mean… Well, you know what I mean. I didn't mean… Well, you know."

I chuckled. "I know what you meant." Even if I wished she meant what she'd said, I knew what she meant.

"Now, one question for you. A very serious question," she said.

"Okay. Shoot."

She leaned in closer. "Do you think I'm allowed to go change out of this dress now? Because I think my measurements were a little off and it's a little too tight and I just want to change into sweatpants so I can eat more pizza."

"It's your birthday. You can change out of anything you want."

She placed her hands against her hips and sighed heavily. "Okay, good because one more inhale, and the seams would bust and my butt would be on full display."

As if that's a bad thing, Kierra.

"I'll be back," she said, hurrying up the stairs. I watched her backside the whole time she exited, too. It didn't take long for her to return, though. Yet when she emerged from around the corner, she was still wearing that amazing red dress. The only issue was she looked as if she'd seen a ghost. Her eyes were wide with panic, and I couldn't help but walk closer to the staircase to see what was wrong.

Before I could begin to walk up the steps, I saw a panicked Ramona hurrying over to Kierra's side, pulling up the strap of her dress. My head tilted as confusion filled me. That was until Henry emerged behind her, buttoning up his shirt. Unlike Ramona, he didn't seem panicked at all. He seemed smug.

It was right then that I knew exactly what had taken place.

"Kierra, I'm so sorry. I didn't mean for you to see that. I mean, I didn't mean for..." Ramona began rambling.

Kierra didn't look at her for one second. Instead, her head rose and I caught her stare. She blinked once, and the pure shock on her face made my heart shatter into a million pieces. I couldn't imagine how her own heart felt. How much betrayal could a heart endure before it simply gave up on beating?

Henry scolded her, instead of apologizing. "Don't make a damn scene, will you, Kierra? You're always making a damn scene. Tonight has been perfect. Don't mess that up with your dramatics."

With her dramatics?

Oh, fuck this guy.

She turned to him, almost robotically, and said, "Fuck you, Henry."

He was as shocked as I was hearing those words fall from her mouth. Maybe it was the liquid courage pumping through her veins, or maybe she'd just reached her fed-up limit. Either way, she stood up for herself.

Henry quickly gripped her wrist and yanked her toward him with a force that sent a rage through every inch of me. "Don't fucking embarrass me, Kierra," he whispered as she cringed from his tight grip on her arm.

Without a thought, I headed up the stairs, straight toward Henry, and slammed my fist into his face. He stumbled backward, his body crashing to the floor. The whole party froze at that moment. The only sound heard was the music speakers, filling the space with jazz music.

The horrific situation made Kierra dart down the staircase and head outside. I followed after her. As I passed Ava, she looked just as perplexed as everyone else around us. "Gabriel, what's going—?"

"One second, kid. Let me check on your mom," I said as I sped past her.

I hurried to the backyard, where Kierra had rushed out to. She bent over and placed her hands on her sides, taking in deep breaths. Her whole body shook as I moved over to her. I placed a hand on her shoulder, and she almost leaped out of her skin as she shot around.

"Hey, hey, hey. It's okay. It's me. It's me."

The moment she realized it wasn't her husband touching her, she tried her best to shake off her nerves and catch her breath. "Sorry, sorry. I–I–I can't—" She shook her head and began to pace. "I fucking hate him," she cried. "I fucking *hate* him."

"Yeah," I agreed. "I do, too."

"He likes it. He likes when I catch him because he gets off

on hurting me. He's sick, and he couldn't stand that today was about me. He couldn't handle that something was for me and not him. He couldn't…" She took a deep breath and waved her hands wildly. "Fuck it. I don't care. I'm so tired of caring. There's nothing more that I care about."

"Kierra."

"Yes?"

"How can I help?"

Those words made her movements slow down. She looked up at me and her eyes flooded with tears. "Can you make me strong? Not this weak, embarrassing person who now has to deal with a household of people seeing me have a breakdown? I don't want to be like this anymore. I don't want to be weak."

"You're not weak."

"Yes," she said. "I am."

"No, you're not. You're strong, Kierra. And fuck him for making you feel anything but that. Fuck him for getting in your head and making you doubt the brilliant mind and person that you are. You deserve more."

She stood in front of me with tears flooding her eyes. Her lips parted, but no words fell from them. I saw the heartache in her eyes, and I hated that it lived there. If I could, I'd swallow up all her pain and take it on as my own. Eyes like hers didn't deserve to have such a broken look. Eyes like hers deserved to smile as much as her lips could. They deserved to sparkle with joy and an unattainable type of peace. She deserved *more*.

"Kierra, you feel like the whole fucking galaxy wrapped up in one human being. I'm not saying that to convince you to want me over Henry. Fuck me in this situation. Fuck everyone else in this current moment. I'm telling you this because I need you to feel how I feel for you. I need you to look into the mirror and know that you are the whole fucking universe wrapped in one. And you deserve better than anything that man can give you. So again, right now, how can I help you?"

She lowered her head lowered and tears rolled down her cheeks. "Get everyone to leave? I don't want to deal with anyone right now. I don't have the energy."

"You got it." I moved closer to her. And closer. *And closer.* So close that I could lean in to whisper against her ear. "Whatever you need from me, I'll do. Whenever you need me, call me. No matter what. I'll always answer."

I ushered everyone out of the house, making sure no one lingered too long other than Ava and Tamera.

"Is she okay?" Tamera asked about her daughter-in-law. "Did Henry do something?"

I smiled even though I wanted to tell her how shitty her son had been. But Ava was in earshot. Then again, it probably didn't look good that I slammed my fist against her father's jawline. "She'll be okay. If you can keep an eye on her, that would be great."

"Of course," Tamera said. "Always. I'll go check on her now."

Oddly enough, I believed her. She didn't seem much like her son at all.

I looked over at Ava, who looked so distraught. That broke my heart, too. I didn't know my heart could break so many times for two women in my life. "I'm sorry, kid."

"Are you okay?" she asked me, wide-eyed with concern.

"Yeah. I'm fine. I'm sorry about what I did. That was uncalled for."

"Did you do it to protect her?" she asked.

I nodded. "I did."

She darted toward me and pulled me into a hug. I held on to her tightly, wishing I could take away any hurt that was residing in her, too. "Thank you, Boss Man."

She then headed outside toward the backyard to check on her mom.

I went out the front door and started in the direction of my car.

"Gabriel! Gabriel! Wait up!" Ramona said, darting over to my car as I opened my driver's door. I took a deep breath and released it through my gritted teeth as I slammed my door closed.

I turned to face her as she stood there combing her hair behind her ears.

I didn't say a word.

That was until she began to speak again.

"Gabriel, I'm—"

"You're fired."

Her eyes bugged out. "What?"

"You heard me. You're fired."

"What? I... You can't fire me. This isn't a work event."

I gestured toward her in frustration. *"You were fucking our client at our other client's birthday party, Ramona!*" I whisper-shouted, bewildered by her comment.

"But I was off the clock," she mentioned, shaking her head, seemingly stunned. She seemed shocked that I was pissed off. Shocked that I was raging from the fact. "You can't fire me because of what I do in my private life."

"Private life," I huffed. "Are you fucking kidding me?"

She narrowed her eyes and shook her head. "I'm confused as to why you're so angry. Are you…jealous?"

"What the hell are you talking about?"

She bit her bottom lip and shrugged. "Are you mad that another man wanted me? That you lost your chance?" The wild appearance of my eyes must've given her a big reality check, because she followed it up with, "Okay, it's not that."

I took two steps toward her. "Ramona, you fucked a married man at his wife's birthday party. What the actual fuck were you thinking?"

"He…" She shook her head, looking as confused as ever. "He said they were more like roommates."

"Who the hell cares what he said? Take him out of the equation. What makes you think that's okay? How would you like it if someone fucked your husband at your birthday party?" She wasn't an idiot. Ramona was way too intelligent to be acting the way she had been, and it was pissing me off that she'd do something so cruel and heartless. "Damn, Ramona. You're supposed to be better than this."

"I messed up, okay! I didn't… We weren't thinking—"

"Was this the first time?"

She went quiet.

She shook her head.

Fucking A.

"How long, Ramona?" I asked, not even sure I wanted the answer.

"Not long. Like five weeks."

"*Five weeks!*" I hollered, stunned.

"Gosh, Gabriel. Don't make it a thing."

"You made it a thing. Again, you're fired."

"Oh, fuck you, Gabriel!" she barked, shoving me in the arm. "Stop acting like you're so high and mighty."

"What are you talking about?"

"You think I don't see it? How you look at her? Sometimes, I walk past Florence Bakery, and I see the two of you in there, laughing it up with one another. And now you're going around punching her husband. You look at her with stars in your eyes."

"I don't look at her in any other way than I look at everyone," I lied.

"Bullshit. Stop lying. And you know why I can tell that you look at her like you do? Why it's so clear to me?"

"Why's that, Ramona?"

"Because," she choked out. Her eyes teared up and she shook her head. "I've been waiting years for you to look at me the way you look at her. So, judge me if you want. Fire me if you need to. I don't care. But don't pretend that I'm the only person who caught feelings for a client."

She began to walk back over to her car and I called out to her. "Ramona."

"Yes?"

"He's not the genius you think he is. He's an asshole, and if he'd do this to his own wife, what do you think he'll do to you?"

"Well..." She shrugged. "I guess that's for me to find out on my own."

As she drove away, I couldn't help but feel as if she was walking straight into a firepit. It wouldn't take long for her to get burned.

25

Kierra

"I'm worried about you," Tamera said as I walked to the front door with her.

"Don't worry. I'll be fine. I just need to clean up a bit and then I'll head to bed."

"You should hire someone to clean this mess up," she said as she tossed on her coat. "It's your birthday, Kierra. There's no reason to be cleaning up yourself."

"It's okay. I have this handled. Just have a great sleepover with Ava. And thanks for all the help tonight. Everything was beautiful."

She smiled but it seemed to be a grin filled with questions. "Are you okay, though? Has Henry been good? To you, I mean. The last time he stopped by, we got into an argument, but I've heard a few rumors that things haven't been going well at his company."

"Oh? He hasn't mentioned anything." Not that he would. I knew as much about Henry's work as the next person. Then again, I didn't care to know. If I could, I'd erase him completely from my thoughts.

"He didn't tell me either, but I heard a few others mention it tonight as I was strolling around. I guess a big deal just fell through."

"Oh. Well, he seems to be doing okay." More than okay.

"But he's been good, right? To you, I mean? I know there was a situation tonight, but even before that…he's been okay?"

I narrowed my eyes and slightly shook my head. "Tamela, what do you…?"

Humming was heard in the living room, which was a telling sign that Henry was in a good mood. When he was outrageously joyful, he hummed. It kind of pissed me off that he was humming. It was almost as if he was mocking me.

We both looked toward the living room. A weighted sigh fell from Tamela's lips before she placed a hand on my shoulder.

"Don't mind me, love. I'm just an overthinker. Happy birthday, Kierra," she said, pulling me into a hug. Tamela was a master at giving the best hugs. They made me feel enveloped in warmth and care each time she delivered them. "I love you so much."

"I love you, too, Tamela."

Ava rushed over and hugged me from the side, holding her duffel bag on her arm. "Love you, Mom. Happy birthday."

I kissed her forehead and snuggled her. "Thanks for the best party ever."

She frowned. "Are you sure you had a good time and Dad didn't ruin it?"

"No, baby. Everything was perfect. I promise."

"Only the best for the best. Don't eat all the cake, though. We can eat it together tomorrow for our book club."

"You got it."

The two headed out, and I was left with a messy house that showed the signs of a successful party. I hated that I couldn't feel good about the situation. Because I knew what Henry had done that evening. I knew his humming wasn't due to his love for me, but for the fact that he'd had another woman in our bedroom. Another woman who'd had her hands all over him and then had enough nerve to smile in my face.

I wanted out.

I wanted to not spend my next years in the same space with such a monster. Such a vile person who could make great toasts, then be so callous.

I hated him.

I didn't know I had the kind of heart that could feel hate so deeply, but Henry brought that out in me.

"This place is a disaster," Henry said as I walked past the living room to get to the kitchen so I could grab water. He was humming vibrantly as he danced around with a bottle of champagne in his grip. He walked over to me and grabbed my wrist with his free hand. "Dance with me," he said.

Was he truly acting as if everything was okay after what had happened? How much had he actually drunk that evening?

"Henry, not now. I'm tired."

He didn't listen and pulled me in to him, humming against my ear. "Dance with me, my love."

My love.

That felt like a slap in the face.

His mouth was coated in the scent of alcohol as he forced me against his body.

"Henry, stop," I said, slightly shoving my hands against his chest. As he stumbled back, the bottle in his hand dropped to the floor. It didn't break, but the champagne began to spill all over the rug.

"Fuck, Kierra. Look what you did."

"Yeah, well, spills happen."

"Clean it up," he ordered.

I sighed. "Not tonight. I will in the morning."

"Fine," he agreed. "Leave the mess and dance with me now," he offered again, reaching out toward me.

I swatted his hand away. "What's the matter with you?"

"I'm trying to change the damn energy of this house. The energy that *you* caused. We were having a great night, and you just had to go and ruin it with your attitude."

"You were screwing another woman in our bedroom."

"Yeah, and you made sure everyone had to suffer from you finding that out. Sending everyone off. Fuck, I even got punched in the damn face because of you."

"Because of *me*?" I said, stunned by his words. A part of me wanted to argue with him. A part of me wanted to try to get through that thick skull of his. But a bigger part of me, the biggest part of me, just wanted freedom. I wanted out of the jigsaw puzzle of my life with Henry Hughes where it became more and more clear that none of our pieces were from the same puzzle. "I want a divorce," I spat out.

He paused his movements. His head tilted. He snickered. "Go to bed, Kierra."

I stood tall. "No. I want a divorce."

"We've talked about this before. If you want out, then go."

"I want Ava, too. She'll stay with me, and we can work out some coparenting thing. If you take anger management courses."

"Anger management? Oh, fuck off, Kierra."

"I'm serious."

"Me too. Fuck off. I don't have anger issues. And you aren't taking my daughter. If you want to leave, then leave. Go. But Ava stays with me."

"She's not only yours. She's mine. Just like I'm hers." If anything, I spent more time with our daughter than Henry ever had. His world was his work, and Ava received the crumbs of time that he had left after he poured all of himself into his tech company. Still, over the past few months, it seemed his anger was growing more and more intense. He seemed to snap more often, too. My greatest fear was that if I wasn't around to be his emotional punching bag, if it was only Ava and him when he came home with his issues, that he'd take them out on her.

"Nothing about her is yours," Henry argued. "Not her laugh, not her smile, not her DNA. And we agreed that if we ever went our separate ways, that Ava would be with me. Or do you not remember the documents we signed before we married?"

I remembered them. But when we signed them, I never

imagined him becoming the creature that he had become. I thought always and forever meant exactly that when we spoke our vows—always and forever. I didn't know it meant "always until Henry decided to become a whole different person."

Or perhaps this was who he'd always been. Perhaps, he was just skilled in hiding his demons for a long time until they became too loud and poured out all over the place.

"Henry—"

"Go," he ordered, gesturing toward the foyer. "Get some suitcases and get out, Kierra. Trust me, Ava doesn't need such a weak woman around her anyway. I mean, hell. What kind of woman are you? I've been cheating on you for years, yelling at you, belittling you, and you just take it because you're weak."

"I'm not weak," I whispered, trying to shake off his words and not let them implant in me.

I'm strong, I'm strong, I'm strong.

"No, you are. You're fucking pathetic, too. You're weak and pathetic, and without Ava, you're nothing. And guess what? You just lost her forever. You're nothing, Kierra. Nothing."

"Stop it, Henry."

"Nothing," he echoed, getting right in my face. His words spat out as he said it again. "*Nothing.*"

"You don't see it, do you?"

"See what?" he asked.

"How you're acting just like your father."

Without a second's pause, his hand rose and landed straight against my cheek—*hard*.

He slapped me.

I stood there frozen in place as the realization of his actions settled into both of us. My body broke into shivers as he stood in front of me, wide-eyed with panic. My cheek stung from the intensity of his smack, and my heart shattered into pieces as I realized one of the truths I'd held about Henry was no longer a reality.

~~At least he never hit me.~~

He took a step away from me and placed his hands on top of his head, stunned by his own actions.

"*Fuck*," he muttered, his eyes filling with tears. "Fuck, Kierra."

He paced slightly as I remained frozen. He then moved back over to me and forced me into a hug. He pulled me in to him, holding on as if he was trying to hold on forever. "Why did you do that?" he whispered against my ear as he pressed my body to his. "Why would you make me do that?" he cried, his tears falling against my cheek. "We were doing so fucking good tonight."

I felt sick.

I needed him off me, but I feared the consequences of my actions. What if they sent that into a deeper spiral? What if I said the wrong thing? What if my words made the situation worse? I should've kept it all to myself. I should've never spoken up about Ramona. I should've shut up and sat down and played my role in our make-believe marriage.

I should've stayed in line, but I couldn't. Maybe because I was tired. Maybe because I was betrayed. Or maybe because Gabriel was right.

I deserved more.

I didn't even know more was an option until those words fell from Gabriel's mouth. I didn't know I could crave more than imprisonment. I thought the only moments of happiness in my life could come from my time with Ava. I didn't know I was allowed to feel good except with my daughter.

"It's fine," I lied, hugging him back. Afraid that if I let go, he'd grow angry again with me for not forgiving him quickly enough. "It was my fault. It's fine. I'm okay."

He pulled back and placed his hand against my stinging cheek. He cupped my face and moved in to kiss it. His touch made my skin crawl in a way I wasn't certain I could handle. He made me sick. His lips began to move to my lips, and I felt vomit rising in my throat.

"Henry," I whispered, slightly turning my head.

"Kiss me," he ordered, his mouth brushing over mine.

"Wait," I murmured.

"Kiss me," he repeated. "I love you, Kierra. I love you."

That broke my heart.

I couldn't remember the last time those words rolled off his tongue. I didn't know he knew how to say he loved me anymore. What broke my heart the most was how those words were soaked in lies. If that's what love was, I didn't want anything to do with the sentiment. Love wasn't meant to feel this way.

"I just need to use the bathroom," I told him. "I just need a moment."

He held me tight for a second before dropping his hold.

His eyes looked empty. When did he lose it? His soul? All I saw was darkness as he stared so deeply into my eyes.

I pushed out a smile. "I'll be back in a second. Maybe I can meet you in the bedroom?"

Any doubt in his stare faded as he gave a slight nod. "Okay." I began walking to the bathroom near the foyer. "Kierra?"

"Yes?"

"I'm going to fuck you like I'm sorry tonight."

He said that as if it were a compliment before he turned to walk to our bedroom.

The moment he rounded the corner and was out of my view, I hurriedly but quietly slid on my shoes, grabbed my keys and purse, and headed out of the house.

I drove off as fast as I could.

I drove for what felt like hours, looping around in circles, uncertain of what to do or where to go. And then I remembered Gabriel's last words to me. *Call me if you need me. No matter what.*

I dialed his number.

He answered on the second ring.

I drove to his house.

He opened his screen door and stepped onto the porch the moment my car pulled up. The porch light cast a soft glow against his skin as he gave me a look packed with concern. "Hey. You okay?"

I shook my head.

He stepped closer. "Did something happen with Henry...?"

I flinched at the name as my heart pounded painfully against my chest. I swallowed hard as I pushed away the tears wanting to fall. "I was just wondering if you could... Can you... can you hold me?" I whispered, my voice breaking.

Without a second of hesitation, Gabriel wrapped his arms around me. I buried my face in his chest, feeling his warmth engulf me, feeling it comfort the chaos and instability of my mind.

He didn't say a word, and I didn't cry. Just resting against him felt like enough to keep me from completely falling apart over what had happened with Henry. I didn't want to go home. I didn't want to go back and face him at all. I wanted to stay with Gabriel in a world where I felt safe from any harm. In a world where I felt seen. In a world where a person looked at me as if I mattered more than anything else.

He took me inside and held me on his couch for hours. We didn't talk. I didn't even cry. I just stayed in his arms, breathing him in as he refused to let me go. He became my weighted blanket that helped slow down the speed of my thoughts.

I pulled away slightly from him and looked up into his eyes. "Gabriel?"

"Yes?"

"Can you kiss me?"

His eyes searched mine with a mix of emotions—shock, concern, and a deep unspoken understanding. He cupped my face gently and tilted my head up. "Kierra, all I have wanted to do for a very long time is kiss you. But I…"

"No buts," I cut in. "Just a kiss. I just need to know."

"Need to know what?"

"If what my heart is telling me is real."

His voice dropped a few octaves. "Kierra, if I kiss you…I won't want to stop."

"Yeah, I know," I murmured, moving in closer to him. "So don't stop."

For a moment he hesitated, uncertain if he was crossing a line that I'd regret. But he wasn't. If anything, he was giving me more than I knew I could want. I wanted him. I always wanted him.

Then, slowly, he leaned in, his lips meeting mine in a soft kiss that was oh so tender. He kissed me slowly, placing his arms around my body as mine wrapped around his neck. I closed my eyes, allowing myself to get lost in the moment, a moment I'd craved longer than I could admit.

The gentle pressure of his lips against mine sent warmth through my whole body. He kissed me with care, and comfort, and unspoken promises that felt like always. Then one of his hands rose to the base of my neck, and he tilted my head up more, deepening the kiss, sending my mind into a flurry of passion. He parted my mouth with his tongue as he kissed me deeper, his fingers moving to my lower back, which arched toward him. He laid me down on the couch, his body hovering over mine. Our eyes locked, his dilated and hungry as he rested his forehead against mine.

"Tell me to stop and I will," he swore, his words melting against my lips. My hips arched in his direction, feeling his hardness swipe my inner thigh. I slid my hand between us and brushed the stiffness slightly with my hand. He growled as his eyes fluttered shut. "But if you don't say stop, Kierra, I'm going to want this. I'm going to want you forever."

I pulled his mouth back to mine, kissing him hard, our tongues tangling as if they'd never wanted to part. "Give me forever," I whispered against his lips, wanting nothing more than for him to have me. All of me. The good, the bad, and the broken parts.

Without another word, he lifted me from the sofa and carried me to his bedroom. He laid me down on the mattress before he tossed off his shirt. I sat up slightly, and he reached behind me, unzipping my dress. My heart pounded at a rapid pace as my fingers grazed against his rock-hard chest. I took in his old tattoos, which were intertwined with new ones I'd never seen. My fingers landed over his heart, where penguin footprints were, and tears flooded my eyes as I was transported back in time to when he received that tattoo on his chest.

"My heart can't beat without you there, Penguin," he'd told me.

He tilted my head up as he realized I'd paused my movement. The gentleness and care in his stare made me feel safer than ever before. "You're crying," he whispered, leaning in and kissing the tears streaming down my cheeks one by one. "I hate it when you cry. We don't have to—"

"No," I cut in quickly, shaking my head. "I want this, Gabriel. You have no clue how much I really want this."

"Then why the tears?"

"It's overwhelming. It's just..." I took a deep breath as I placed both hands against his chest, against his heart. "I've been waiting a very long time to feel this way. To be here with you."

His lazy smile came and he gently swiped his mouth against mine. "Kierra...I've been looking for you my whole life."

More tears fell.

More kisses took them away.

"Can I stay the night?" I whispered, gently arching my core so I could feel more of his hardness against me.

"Kierra..." he groaned as his mouth fell to the nape of my neck. He trailed across it with kisses. "You can stay forever."

He pulled my dress down and I shimmied it off my body. He stared at me, at every inch of me, as I undid his jeans. Everything moved faster than before. His hands roamed all over me, and his mouth did, too. He tasted every inch of me as my hand slid into his boxers and wrapped around his thickness. I began stroking him up and down as he growled against me.

"Just like that, Kierra. Nice and slow," he murmured against my neck before he sucked my earlobe and slid his hand into my panties. His fingers began to rub against my clit as I moaned in bliss from the feeling. "I like that," he whispered, pressing his mouth against mine. "I like how I make you so fucking wet." He then slid a finger inside me as I rocked my hips back and forth against him. He slid in another finger. And another. My mind began swirling from the feeling of him inside me. I called out his name and he answered with his mouth against my nipple, sucking it hard as he brought me to the edge of an orgasm.

"You like that, huh?" he asked me, placing a hand at the base of my neck. "You like when my hands take control of you?"

"*Yes*," I breathed out. "I like that."

He slid another finger in, his hand still at my neck. I almost screamed out from the amount of pleasure rocking throughout my system. He locked his eyes with mine and moved to my mouth. I didn't know when it happened, but at some point I couldn't tell which breaths were his and which were mine. Yet it seemed like his mere existence became my oxygen. Without him and his touches, I couldn't breathe.

He smiled against my lips, and I licked his bottom lip before biting it. "Taste me," I murmured against his mouth. "Now."

The wicked grin grew larger as he obeyed my orders. He moved down my body, sliding my panties down my thick thighs, and tossed them to the side of the room. He placed his hands on my inner thighs and spread them apart. He buried his head between my legs and began licking, sucking, and fucking my core, rubbing his finger against my clit as I arched up toward him, wanting his tongue to go deeper and deeper inside me.

My hands tangled in his hair as I guided him up and down, loving the way he ate me as if I were his favorite sweet.

After he finished, he pushed himself up and moved over me, kissing my lips as he balanced himself. His cock brushed against my leg as I pulled down his boxers. I tossed them to the side of the room, and within seconds his cock rubbed against my clit, making me want him more and more. His eyes stayed locked with mine. I became lost in his eyes and I wrapped my arms around his body, digging my nails into his back as he slowly slid his hardness inside me. I gasped at how each inch of him consumed me. I murmured his name as my eyes fluttered shut from the intensity of his thickness and the depth at which he slid inside me.

He picked up his speed as our two bodies became one. He wasn't fucking me yet, no. He was making love to me. Taking his time, taking care, building up to the greatest climax of my life.

I wanted more of him, his touches, his thrusts, his kisses, his heart.

I wanted to wrap myself fully within him and never let go.

"Damn, Kierra, you feel so fucking good," he whispered against my ear before nibbling it. "I love how your pussy feels wrapped around my cock like that."

"It's all for you," I whispered back, arching my hips up as he thrust deeper and deeper. "I'm yours."

"That's right," he growled, moving his mouth to mine. "You're all mine. So now I'm going to fuck you and claim you forever."

The speed picked up and he hammered into me as I cried out in bliss. He made love to me as if he was making up for all the lost time. He pumped himself into me so hard and deep that I couldn't stop my legs from trembling. He fucked me so hard from the front, and then he flipped me over to my back before wrapping his hands around my curly hair and using it as an anchor point as I rocked my hips against his, dripping in sweat and wetness as I took all of him in.

Once he came, he lay down beside me, completely out of breath. I crawled on top of him and licked his lip before kissing him gently. "That was…" I sighed.

He shut his eyes and kissed my forehead. "Exactly that." He pulled me closer. "I love you, Penguin."

I smiled as I closed my eyes. "I love you, too."

"Give me ten minutes," he whispered as he nibbled my ear. "Then I'm gonna make love to you again in every room of this house."

———

After a few more rounds, we lay in the bed naked, under the sheets, me resting against his chest, completely exhausted yet at peace from the madness that was my life outside Gabriel's four walls. Every now and again, he'd pull me closer to him and kiss my forehead, reminding me that I wasn't alone. I hadn't known how much I needed that reminder every now and again.

"I wasn't able to give you your birthday gift yet," he whispered, trailing a finger slowly up and down my neck, which sent chills down my spine.

"You mean that thing with your tongue between my legs wasn't the gift?" I half-joked. If I could have Gabriel's face between my legs as my alarm clock each morning, I'd wake up a lot happier.

He chuckled. "No, it wasn't. Want to see your gift?"

"Sure."

He sat up, raising me with his body. He then stood, slipped on his boxers, and held a hand toward me. With the sheet wrapped around me, I took his hand into mine, and he led me out of the room. We walked down the hallway, and he took me into a spare bedroom that had been transformed into a sewing room.

A sewing room with vibrant, wild wallpaper of greens and oranges. There were three machines set up: a sewing machine, an embroidery machine, and a serger.

To the left was a closet stocked with fabrics. There were bins of needles, threads, and cutting shreds.

He made me a sewing room.

He made me a sewing room!

"This is for me?"

He leaned against the doorframe and nodded. "You brought some color to my life. Figured you could use a space for your creative projects."

"Gabriel?"

"Yeah?"

I walked over to him, stood on my tiptoes, and pressed my lips to his as I whispered, "Make love to me in here, too?"

So he did.

———————

The next morning, when daylight broke through the window shades, I rolled over in the bed and found an empty spot beside me. I pushed myself up to a sitting position, searching for Gabriel, but he was nowhere to be found. Though my nose was able to smell my way through the situation.

I pulled myself up from the bed, slipped on my panties and one of Gabriel's T-shirts sitting on his dresser, and then headed toward the kitchen.

A smile spread my lips when I saw him standing over the stove, scrambling eggs in a pan.

"Morning," I said loudly.

He startled and jumped slightly, dropping his wooden spoon to the floor, which flung a good serving of scrambled eggs all over the place.

"Shoot, I'm so sorry," I hurriedly said, rushing over to start picking up the mess. I reached for the paper towel and shook my head, embarrassed by the mistake. "I'm sorry, I'm sorry."

"It's fine," he said, chuckling.

I still felt awful, hurrying to start cleaning up the mess. "Gosh, I'm so clumsy. I'm sorr—"

"Really, Kierra. Don't worry about that."

"Ugh. It's all over the place. It's my fault for—"

"Hey," Gabriel said, placing a hand on my shoulder and bringing me to a halt. He leaned in, locked his eyes with mine, and gave me his lazy smile. "Hi there."

I bit my bottom lip and slowed my erratic breathing. "Hi there."

He moved a piece of my fallen hair behind my ear. "I made you breakfast."

The gentleness of his touch calmed the panic in me. If

the same situation had happened with Henry, I would've been shamed and shouted at for making him make a mess. I would've been called names and belittled for the scrambled eggs hitting the cabinets. I would've been told to clean it up as soon as possible.

Gabriel instead smiled and then kissed me gently on my lips. I didn't think he knew how much it meant to me—his gentleness.

"Good morning," he whispered.

"Good morning," I murmured back.

He raised me to standing before he pulled me into a hug and kissed my forehead.

I glanced at the countertop, which had a spread of bacon, hash browns, orange juice, and of course cinnamon muffins. Along with not one, not two, but four different types of eggs.

"Are you feeding two people or an army?" I joked as Bentley came into the room, wagging his tail as he ate up all the scrambled eggs on the floor. Turned out you didn't need a robot to clean up messes; you just needed a dog.

"Well, I was cooking and realized that I didn't know how you liked your eggs. So I made hard-boiled, over easy, sunny-side up, and an omelet. I tried poached, but it didn't work out. And well, you saw how the scrambled—"

"I love you," I breathed out, unable to hold the words in any longer. I had almost stopped believing in those three words when it came to the opposite sex. I had almost given up on the idea that I'd be able to whisper those words to another. Yet Gabriel made it easy. So easy that I cut off his words just so I could say it.

Maybe that was what love, real love, was. Something that somersaulted off one's tongue. Maybe love was messy kitchens and oversized T-shirts. Maybe love was quiet good mornings and forehead kisses. Maybe love was peace. Maybe love was him.

He smiled and pulled me closer to him. I loved how I felt whenever he wrapped his large frame around mine. I felt safe. No one in the world knew how important it was to feel safe after years of feeling the opposite. "I love you, too. You know what's crazy about that?"

"What's that?"

"I knew I loved you before I even knew your name." He slowly brushed his thumb against my bottom lip and said, "So how do you like your eggs?"

I smirked a little and shrugged. "Scrambled."

"Fuck," he laughed, raking a hand through his hair. He started for the refrigerator. "Figures. I'll crack a few more and—"

"Gabriel." I reached and grabbed his arm, pulling him back toward me. "Let's eat what's here. And next time we can make scrambled."

He snickered and shook his head.

"What is it?" I asked.

"Nothing," he replied, "I just love the fact that you said 'next time.' Because I really want a lot more next times with you."

I sat in his lap as we talked and ate the whole morning. He made me laugh, too. That wasn't shocking, though. Everything about the man made my cheeks hurt from smiling so much.

The best fact about it all?

He loved me, too.

After a while, I realized I had to leave my haven and head back home to reality. After I finished getting dressed, I headed down the hallway and noticed Gabriel standing on the back porch. I pushed the screen door open, and as I walked out onto the wooden porch, he began to speak.

"You should've found me again," he said as he leaned against the porch railing, staring out at the coastline. He slid his hands into the pockets of his gray sweatpants. "After all these years…I wish you would've found me again."

I walked over and leaned against the railing across from him. "I know."

"Why didn't you?"

"I thought about finding you many times…but I always talked myself out of it. I was young and stupid. I blamed myself for everything that happened. It was too hard knowing how much you lost…" I took a deep breath, trying to shake the image of Elijah from my mind. "After a while, so much time passed that I was all but certain you'd moved on and I'd missed my chance of ever loving you again. I had to put it to bed. I made up this story that you had a wife, a family, and you wouldn't want me again. I figured that after I walked away without looking back, you'd never forgive me. Besides, you forgot who I was, Gabriel. I was nothing but a stranger."

"That doesn't matter."

"It does."

"If I lost my memory every single day for the rest of my life, I would still find my way back to loving you. I'd love every version of you. I'd love the young version of you. I'd love the current version, and I'd love the gray-hair version, because loving you doesn't take time. Loving you just is. It's a constant in an unstable world. I'd fall in love with you over and over again, without hesitation. It wouldn't even take years to fall in love with you, Kierra. It merely takes seconds. I think that's why I ended up doing the architect project for Henry. Somehow my soul knew it would bring me to you."

"When two souls are tangled in forever…" I whispered.

"Then forever is what they'll be," he whispered back.

I lowered my head. "I want to leave him so bad," I confessed. "But I'm so afraid of losing Ava. That's why I've stayed so long."

"We have to figure out how to hit him. You can maybe use the fact that he's been cheating in your case. Plus, from what I've learned about him so far, he cares a lot about his social image."

I chuckled. "To say the least."

"What if you threatened that? What if you threatened to smear his name in the media if he didn't allow you to coparent? Do you think that's an option? You don't even have to do it; you can just threaten it."

I lowered my eyebrows as I stood there in thought. That never crossed my mind, but Gabriel was right. If there was anything Henry cared about, it was his public image. It was something to keep in mind if things shifted in a direction that worried me.

"I'll think about that," I told him.

"Yeah. And I'll keep thinking of other ways to help."

My sweet, sweet hero.

"Gabriel?"

"Yes?"

"Can we stay here for a few minutes?" I asked. "Just the two of us on this back porch together? We don't have to talk or anything… I'd just love a little more time to be here with you."

He titled his head in my direction for a moment's time. The sincerity of his stare made a wave of peace hit me as he nodded. "Yeah," he said before staring back out toward the morning. "I'd love to be quiet with you."

Who knew silence could be so loud and meaningful? Who knew comfort could come from the quiet moments of love?

After an hour or so of being still with each other, we headed to the front of the house and I kissed him goodbye at his screen door. As I began to walk away, he called after me.

"Hey, Penguin?" Gabriel asked, leaning against his doorframe, shirtless and perfect as he'd always been.

"Yes?"

"Will you come back tomorrow?"

A small smile spread across my lips. "Yes."

"Okay." He slid his hands into his sweatpants and rested his head against the doorframe. "Hey, Penguin?"

"Yes?"

"Will you come back the day after that?"

Butterflies. "Yes."

"And the day after that?"

I nodded as I gnawed my bottom lip. "Uh-huh."

"Hey, Penguin?"

"Yes?"

He raked his hand through his messy hair and walked over to me. He placed a finger beneath my chin and tilted my head up to meet his gaze. His mouth brushed against mine. "Promise…?"

"Promise."

He kissed me slowly and I melted back into his arms as he whispered against my lips, "Good."

26

Gabriel

EIGHTEEN YEARS OLD

I loved her.

A lot transpired before that fact and a lot happened afterward, but in that very moment I was in love with Kierra. And she didn't even known it.

"Remember this very moment, will you?" she whispered, her lips turning up into a big smile that matched her mom's. Kierra's straight black hair was pulled into a high ponytail as she swung around in a circle in the tree house, showing off the gown she'd made herself. The gown had been so loved by a neighbor that they requested her to make them their own Kierra original. Also known as her first-ever official sale as an up-and-coming fashion designer.

Watching her dreams come true was something I was lucky to witness. Her goofy grin and squirrelly body movements made me want to hop up from the floor and pull her against my chest and kiss her. I hadn't stopped thinking about giving her her first kiss all those months back.

I wanted to give her her second kiss, too. And third, and fourth…

I knew that was a terrible idea because kissing your best friend was always a bad idea, but I couldn't help it because I loved her.

Stupid love.

It showed up even when I told it to piss off.

"I'll never forget it," I told her, smiling at her joy.

"She's going to pay me, Gabriel. Can you believe that? With real money. Unlike the Monopoly money you used to pay me with when we were kids."

"That was my good, hard-earned money, Kierra."

"You stole it from my board game," she argued.

"Borrowed," I countered.

"You can't borrow fake money and give it back to buy something from me."

"I can and I did." I hopped up from my seat and brushed my thumb against my nose. "And I still use that blanket you made me every night, thank you very much."

She frowned and her bushy brows knit. "It was supposed to be a sweater, but I didn't know how to crochet anything but a straight line back then."

"In a few years, I could sell it for a million bucks. A Kierra original."

"Only a million? I'm offended. You should at least go for three mil—"

"I love you," I cut in.

Her eyes fluttered with confusion as her movements came

to a halt. She tilted her head and she smiled shyly. "I love you, too, Gabriel."

"No," I said, shaking my head. "I love you."

"I heard you."

"No," I disagreed. I walked over to her and placed my hands on her shoulders. I swallowed hard, feeling as if my heart was going to tear straight out of my chest as my mouth opened. "I am in love with you, Kierra. Not the kind of friendship love. Not the we've-known-each-other-forever kind of love. But the kind of love where I want to kiss you more than anything else in the world. The kind of love where I dream about you and then wake up in my bed mad that you're not there. The kind of love where I want to spend every day to come with you in my arms for the rest of forever."

"Oh," she whispered, her voice timid and low. "That kind of love."

"Yeah. That kind of love."

"Well." She sighed. "What took you so long, dork?"

I arched a brow. "Wait, wha—"

Before I could reply, she kissed me. Her arms wrapped around my neck and she pulled me in, kissing me as if she'd been waiting for that day to come. It took a few moments for me to realize what was going on, but the moment I did, I kissed her with the same intensity, if not more. My hands fell against her lower back, and I pulled her closer to me, holding her as long as I could.

When our mouths parted slightly, she brushed her lips against mine and whispered, "Gabriel?"

"Yeah?"

"I love you, too. The rest-of-forever kind of love."

"Oh. Well. *Good*."

27

Kierra

PRESENT DAY

I returned home to find a dining room table filled with flowers. The house felt eerie as I walked inside. Sitting at the head of the table was Henry, who had a glass of dark liquor in his hands. He was wearing the same outfit as the night before, but his white button-down was undone, and his sleeves were rolled up to his elbows.

He leaned back in the chair and raised his head to meet my stare. He huffed a little. "About damn time you came home."

"I needed space to clear my head."

"Let me guess, you still want a divorce."

"Yes. But you're drunk, and you look like you haven't slept. We can talk about this—"

"My deal fell through," he mentioned. "With the team in China."

I nodded slowly, uncertain of what Henry I was going to get that morning. "Tamera mentioned that."

"It was a nine-figure deal. I found out yesterday. That's why I was acting out."

"I'm sorry to hear that, Henry. But that doesn't excuse—"

"Have some compassion, Kierra. I had a bad day. The worst day. And you expect me to just be okay after that? Listen, I didn't mean to do what I did last night—"

"Which thing are you speaking about? The sleeping with Ramona on my birthday thing or the hitting me on my birthday thing? Which one didn't you mean?"

He grimaced. "Both? But more so, the second thing. I didn't mean to do what I did."

"You mean hitting me?" I cut in. "You didn't mean to hit me?"

He cringed at me stating what he'd done. Saying, "I didn't mean to do what I did," was a way for him to not use words that might make him feel guilty.

Hit me.

He *hit* me.

He closed his eyes and took a deep inhale. "I thought you would be more understanding. With your job and all." When he opened his eyes, he looked so sad. Broken. Like a lost little boy searching to find his way home again. For a moment, I felt guilty. I felt as if I saw the same broken boy who'd told me about the trauma his father had caused him. I saw the hurting soul who needed comfort. I saw the pain that he used anger to cover. I saw his pain in his eyes.

But he *hit* me.

How was it my responsibility to comfort the one who

caused me pain? Why was it my job to fix the broken man who time and time again took a sledgehammer to my soul?

"I can't do this, Henry. I can't do this," I said, gesturing toward the dozens and dozens of flowers. "I can't keep pretending that this life is normal. That we are normal. I'm not your wife, and you're not my husband. Truthfully, I think you've known that for a long time."

He lowered his head again before chugging the brown liquor in his glass. He poured himself another from the bottle sitting on the table.

"Where were you last night?" he whispered.

Was he even hearing the words leaving my mouth?

"I just needed space to clear my mind," I told him, scared of what the next few moments would unlock within him. He was acting strange. Sure, I'd seen him be strange before, but he seemed freakishly quiet and calm as his hands wrapped around his glass.

"Where did you clear your head?"

"I stayed the night at Rosie's."

"You're lying," he said.

"I'm not."

"You are."

"No," I countered. "I'm not."

His eyebrows knit together as he poured himself another glass of bourbon. "I tracked your phone," Henry whispered. The calmness of his voice sent chills down my spine. "It's just odd to find out that Rosie lives at the same location as Gabriel Sinclair."

My heart dropped to my stomach. "You track my location?"

He laughed. "That's enough of a confession to me."

"Henr—"

"Fuck you, Kierra!" he shouted, throwing his full glass of alcohol across the room, hitting a wall and making the glass shatter into a million pieces. My system went into high alert. My eyes darted around the space. I needed to figure out which direction was the quickest way out. Escape routes. I needed an escape route.

"What is it?" Henry barked, his rage echoing off the bourbon-stained wall. "I fuck Ramona, so you screw the boss? Is that how you deal with your issues? You try to get back at me?"

"I want a divorce," I echoed again, trying my best to not show my fear. "It doesn't matter what I do, or you do, because we aren't together, Henry. We haven't been for a very long time. I just want this to end."

"No," he said matter-of-factly.

"What?"

"I said no. You can't leave me. If you do, you'll lose Ava, and I know that's the last thing you want."

"I don't want this to be messy, Henry. We both love Ava. So, let's do what's best for her."

"What's best for her is our family staying together."

"No, what's best is happy parents."

"You aren't even her real parent. I am. It was me and her before you, and it will be me and her after you."

I didn't want to play dirty, but he was making it hard. He was cutting me deeply with his words, and all I had in my mind was that I needed to protect Ava. I needed my daughter. "I don't want to get messy, Henry, but our prenup talks about infidelity. And I know how important your social image is to you. I don't want to, but I will reveal the fact that you cheated on me, now that I have proof of it, to the court system. And those would be public records. I don't want to do that, so just let me go. We can make an arrangement so that we both have time with Ava. It doesn't have to be all or nothing."

"Are you threatening me? You're saying you'll smear my name?"

"I don't want to..." I argued. "But I will do whatever it takes to have Ava in my life."

He laughed and shook his head. "You don't even have proof of my infidelity. You have nothing to go on...but I do. I doubt anything you say will be as powerful as the footage I have of you actually hooking up with Gabriel."

I narrowed my eyes. "What?"

"You think I only had a tracking device on your phone with no recording abilities? I'm fucking Henry Hughes, Kierra. I'm master at technology. I see everything you do. Every step you take. Every breath you breathe. I see it all. You think last night was the first time I noticed you running off with him? No. It's just the first time I mentioned it to you."

I felt as if my heart sank to the pit of my stomach as I realized the one form of leverage that I thought I had against my husband was now in his hands. He'd been watching me? For how long? That sent a wave of fear soaring through me. I felt exposed in a way that I would've never expected.

I shook my head in disbelief. "I don't get it. You're not even happy with me. Why are you doing this? Why can't you just let me go?"

"Because you're mine," he said. "I've built plenty of machines, but you're my favorite little robot." The way he claimed me made my skin crawl. It dripped of control. I wanted to blame the whiskey, but truthfully Henry had acted that way for a long time—as if I was his. Not his wife, but his property. I was one of his little robots that did exactly what he wanted, whenever he wanted, and if I stepped out of line, he tried to tweak me just enough to return to his favorite version of me—the one who didn't talk back or speak up. The one who stood in his shadow at his dinner parties. The one who didn't have an ounce of confidence in herself because he'd drained it all. Only now he couldn't control me, because I was waking up from my deep slumber. I was waking from the nightmare of my past years. Henry was losing control over me, and that terrified him. But I didn't care.

I was breaking free.

Which meant he was losing grip on his reality as I began to step within my own.

"You can't leave me," he stated.

"Yes, I can and I am." I said the words, yet they were filled with uncertainty. I didn't know what he'd do next or how he'd react. I didn't know the thoughts swirling through his head. I didn't know the panicking of his heartbeats. All I knew was I couldn't live another year the way I'd lived the past decade. I knew I couldn't make it another four years until Ava was eighteen—let alone another week, truthfully.

He lowered his head and placed his face in his hands. "Don't you see?" he whispered, his voice cracking. "Everything's falling apart."

"Or maybe for the first time ever, everything's coming together," I said calmly, still feeling unsure of what his next outburst might be. That was until he began sobbing uncontrollably into his hands. His heavy cries broke a part of my heart that I didn't know still beat for him. Even though I studied emotions and feelings on deep levels, I still didn't always understand how they worked. How was it possible for me to feel the amount of guilt I did in that moment for the man who'd hurt me for so long? Why did I feel a need to comfort my demon? Why did it feel as if I were the one who betrayed him, and not the other way around?

"Henry," I whispered.

His body shook as he choked on his inhalations. I'd seen him cry before during drinking bouts. That wasn't uncommon. But this was a new level of panic shooting throughout his whole system.

"I don't want to be like him," he sobbed between his violent trembling. "I don't want to fucking be like him," he repeated over and over again.

For a second, I felt my own chest tighten. For a second, I saw the little boy with daddy issues sitting before me. I saw the broken child whose father messed up his brain so much that he made it damn near impossible for Henry to grow up without suitcases of trauma. For a second, my motherly instinct kicked in and I wanted to comfort him. I wanted to be there for him.

I wanted to wrap him in my arms and tell him that he could get help. That he could heal from this. And that we could learn to coparent in a healthy, safe environment.

I moved over toward him to comfort him. Not to be his wife, but to be a fellow human who saw another hurting. I knelt beside him and placed a hand against his shoulder. "Henry. We can get you help. We can—"

Before the words could finish falling from my tongue, he placed his two tear-soaked hands against my shoulders and shoved me hard, sending me flying against the wall where his broken glass had shattered. I fell to the floor, a piece of glass slicing through my hand. I yipped and picked up my hand, trying to shake off the dizziness from the impact of the crash. I pulled the piece of glass from my hand and looked up to find Henry staring my way. He still had tears rolling down his cheeks, but he looked wild. As if he was no longer there, and all I could see was his father staring back at me. A switch had been flipped, and Henry was gone.

He stood from his chair and moved over to me. He knelt and placed his hands above me on the wall, boxing me in, and lowered his face to mine. "You're not leaving me, just like she didn't leave him. Do you understand, Kierra?" he said as he crouched over me. He gripped my chin in his hand and pulled my face toward him. "You said the words. 'Til death do us part.' So, either you *die* or you *stay*. You're mine." He then forced his lips against mine, kissing me with his whiskey-drenched tongue, infecting me with his threats that felt like terrifying promises. I sat still as his mouth engulfed mine. Once he finished kissing me, he shoved my face away, making my head hit the wall behind me. "Stay away from Gabriel Sinclair, or I swear to God, you'll regret it and I'll make his life as miserable as yours."

He walked over to the roses on the table, pulled out a handful of them, and threw them at me. "And to think I bought you all these roses."

28

Gabriel

Gabriel: Hey, Kierra. Missed you this morning at the coffee shop. I hope you're doing okay.

Kierra: Hi, sorry. Crazy morning. Henry's in a mood. All is well. I'll reach out later on.

Gabriel: Are you okay? Do you need me?

Kierra: I'm okay. Can we talk later?

Gabriel: Always. How are you?

She didn't answer.

I knew I shouldn't have read into her messages too deeply, but frankly I was worried. She seemed nervous. At least to me she did. That shit worried me more than anything, based on the man she was married to and the way I knew he fucked with her mind. I could hardly imagine the mind games Henry was playing with Kierra. Her text was seemingly simple, but I could almost feel her anxiety coming through every letter she'd typed.

It wasn't until her husband showed up to my office in a huff later that day that I grew extremely worried for her safety and well-being.

"Stay away from my family," Henry said as he marched into my office. He was dressed in a designer suit and messing with his cuffs. "Do you understand me?"

"You have a lot of nerve showing up here," I said, rising from my chair. "It might be best if you leave."

"Trust me, I'm not planning on staying long. I just wanted to make one thing clear, and it's that I want nothing to do with you. I want you nowhere near my property. Your staff can handle all the details from now on, but you will not set foot on my property."

"Is that it?" I asked, crossing my arms over my chest.

"No, that's not it." He marched toward me, puffing out his chest as if trying to be the alpha. "If I find out you touch my wife again, I will destroy your life."

"From what I can tell, you don't have a wife. And Kierra damn sure doesn't have a husband."

"That's not for you to decide. I mean it. Stay away from her and my daughter. Or else."

I arched an eyebrow. "Is that a threat?"

"It's a promise," he said, sliding his hands into his slacks pockets. "You think Kierra is unhappy with me now? Trust me...I'll make her life a living hell if she keeps seeing you. I will not only destroy you; I'll ruin everything good she has going for her."

"You're a fucking bitch," I growled, feeling my protective

nature grow as he spoke about harming Kierra. "If you hurt her—"

"That's my right," he cut in. "She's mine to have, and mine to handle. So stay the fuck away and stop texting her. You sound pathetic."

"You've been reading her messages?"

"She's my wife. Mine. I'm allowed to read anything she sends out. And the last I heard, she made it clear that she wanted nothing to do with you. So, do us all a favor and stay far away from us all. You're lucky I don't press charges against you for hitting me. A punk-ass hit, too. If I'd had my footing, it would've never stuck."

Sure, Henry. Whatever you fucking say.

"Are we done here?" I said through gritted teeth, knowing he was trying to get a rise out of me. A part of me wanted to step toward the challenge, yet another part worried what he'd do to Kierra and Ava if I did step up to him. If I did knock him out. Because I would. I would knock him out faster than he could say a word.

"I think we are. Pretty sure you got the message."

"Loud and clear," I muttered.

He smirked his annoying smirk, smoothed his hands over his blazer, and headed out of the room.

My first thought was to message Kierra, but now I knew he was monitoring her phone. I didn't want to make things messier for her, but I did need to see her. So, I grabbed my keys and headed over to her therapy clinic, hoping I might be able to catch her at the end of her day.

When I showed up, I found Joseph in the front lobby, finishing up some paperwork with the receptionist. When he saw me, he smiled widely.

"Gabriel, hey there. How goes it?" he asked, walking over and extending his hand my way.

I shook it. "It's going. I was just wondering if Kierra was free for a few minutes to chat."

He glanced at his watch. "I believe she has a meeting with a client in about fifteen minutes, but I can see if she's free."

"That would be great. Thanks."

He headed back to Kierra's office, then emerged with a soft smile on his face. "Come on back, Gabriel. She's in her office waiting for you."

I thanked him once again and headed into Kierra's office. She was standing in front of her desk, pulling on the sleeves of her shirt, which I was picking up was a nervous habit of hers.

After I walked inside, I closed her door behind me and moved toward her. She stepped backward slightly, making it clear that my closeness wasn't welcome, so I paused.

"Hi," I breathed out, feeling sick to my stomach. She was so close to me, but so far away at the same time. She looked tired. As if she hadn't slept for days. Her distance made my mind want to start spiraling into a pit of despair, but I wasn't ready to go that far yet. Not until I knew she was okay. "How are you?" I asked.

Her eyes blinked, and she looked as if she was on the brink

of tears, but she didn't cry. "I'm fine. Sorry. I meant to get back to you earlier today, but I've been—"

"How are you?" I asked again, taking a step nearer to her, repeating the question I asked her earlier that day.

She took a step back. She shut her eyes and took a deep breath. When she reopened them, she looked sadder than before. That broke my heart. She was suffering in silence, yet the pain was clear in her eyes. A deep sadness floating in those brown eyes of hers. "Gabriel, don't."

I stepped closer. "How are you, Penguin?"

She stepped back and hit her desk. Her hands fell to the edge and she gripped it. "I'm fine."

"You're lying."

"I'm not."

I moved closer.

She looked down at the floor.

I placed a finger beneath her chin and raised her head so she'd meet my stare. "Is he hurting you, Penguin?"

"Only emotionally," she softly replied.

"Has he ever laid his hands on you?"

She shut her eyes and tears began rolling down her cheeks. She didn't answer me, but the slight shake to her body and the release of the tears told me everything I needed to know.

"I'll kill him," I promised.

"You won't. It's fine. I'm fine. Everything's—"

"He hurt you, Kierra. He's abusing you both mentally and physically. Nothing is fine. Not until he's dealt with."

"That's what I'm doing," she said, shaking my hand away from her face. She stepped to the side, away from me, and began pacing as she wiped her tears. "I'm dealing with it."

"Let me help you."

"You can't."

"Why not?"

"Because." She sighed. "He said if you're around me, he'll make things harder for you."

"I know. He stopped by my office to threaten me."

Her eyes widened. "He stopped by your office?"

"Yeah. That's why I'm here. I wanted to make sure you're okay, which you're not, and—"

"Did he follow you here?" she asked as she moved to her window and peered out toward the parking lot.

"What? No. Kierra—"

"You can't be here, Gabriel." A clear panic grew in her, telling me that this man had her spooked the hell out. That made me uneasy in a way that I couldn't express with words. "We can't see each other for a while. I'm sorry. There's just so much going on, and I can't risk your safety, or the safety of Ava and me. I'm working with lawyers to get things in order, but until then, you and I can't be around each other."

"Slow down. We'll figure this out together."

"*We can't!*" she cried, tossing her hands up in defeat. "Don't you see? There can't be a 'we' right now. I'm not in a good place, and I know you'd do anything to help me get to a good place, but the best way for you to help now is to *leave*."

That felt like a dagger to my chest, but I tried not to show

how much it hurt. This wasn't about me. It was about her and her safety.

"I can't leave you knowing he's hurting you," I told her quietly.

"I can handle Henry. I can handle all of this. I just can't have you in the mix with how my prenup is set up. He's threatening me big-time, Gabriel, and I just can't move so freely. So please. Just…" She took a deep breath and shook her head. "I need you to stay away from me."

"But…" My voice dropped and the hurt that sliced through my soul leaked out from between my lips. "I just got you back."

I saw it in her eyes, too. The heartbreak. The realization that we had to walk away from each other before we even had a chance to really find one another again. She was hurting just like me. She was hurting more than me. That was when it officially clicked in my mind. I found Kierra amid her storm. She was going through wars of torment when I reentered her life, and me being there was making it harder than before.

So even though it hurt, I understood her. I understood her pushing me away, because she couldn't see a path where we could be together.

"I need to let you go again," I whispered, the truth stinging my heart as it slipped between my lips.

Her tears fell at a rapid pace. "I'm so sorry, Gabriel. I should've never brought you into all of this. I should've never…" Her words fumbled off as she broke eye contact.

I moved over to her and took her hands into mine. I pulled

them to my mouth and kissed her palms gently. "I'm glad you found me, Kierra. I needed to remember."

"But this is a mess…and we just… I–I love you," she cried out, allowing herself to move in closer to me. Allowing our closeness to come back to us. She was fighting it so much, but it was no secret that whenever we were near each other there was a magnetic pull, bringing us closer.

She was home to me.

I wanted to be home to her, too. Her firm foundation that would be there when she made it out of the storm—and she would. She'd make it out.

"I'll wait for you," I swore.

"I can't ask you to do that, Gabriel. Who knows how long this whole process with the divorce might take? It could go on for a long time with Henry being petty and cruel."

"I'll wait for you," I repeated.

"I can't ask you to do that."

"I'll wait for you," I promised once more.

She tilted her head up toward me and shook her head. "I want you to live your life to the fullest. I want you to not sit waiting for me to come back to you. I'm not even a good thing right now, Gabriel. I'm broken," she cried, shaking her head in disappointment. "I don't even know why you'd want me as I am right now. I'm too much. I'm too weak right now."

"You're not weak."

"Yes, I am. I've been weak a long time. I know you think I am, for staying with a man like Henry for so long."

"No," I disagreed. "It takes strength to endure the treatment you did for so long, Kierra. But I just want you to know that you deserve better. You deserve to walk away, and I'm proud of you for doing that. And I understand, okay? The last thing I want you to feel is guilt for pushing me away. You handle yourself and Ava, and I'll be around. Even if you tell me not to wait, I'll be here waiting for you."

"Why?" she whispered. "Why would you do that?"

"Because I finally know what love is. It's patience during the storms. It's sometimes waiting. I'll wait for you."

She kissed me with a fervor born from a deeply painful realization. Her lips met with mine in a poignant seal of our shared past and uncertain future. She kissed me for all our missed yesterdays and all our unsure tomorrows. I despised the bittersweetness of the kiss. It was a perplexing mixture with the kisses whispering goodbye, yet in the same breath feeling like a promise of eternity.

It wasn't until that very moment that I understood how kisses could both heal and break one's heart at the same time.

"I love you," I whispered against her lips. "I love you, I love you, I love you," I repeated. "I love you, I love you, *I fucking love you.*"

I said it so many times because I needed her to know that when she was going through the darkest times. I told her I loved her because it was the only truth I knew. I told her repeatedly, because my soul craved for hers to imprint those words on her heart and remember them when she felt like she wasn't strong enough to continue.

"If it ever gets bad, you'll call me?" I asked.

"It will be okay," she swore.

"If it ever gets bad, you'll call me," I repeated, more as a statement.

She nodded. "Yes."

"Good. And when you leave him," I said, placing a gentle kiss against her forehead, "come home to me."

"Gabriel—"

"I'm patient, Kierra. I've waited over two decades for you. I'd wait another if I had to. Take all the time you need. Do all that you need to do to get free from his chains. Then, you and Ava come home to me."

29

Kierra

Claire Dune was having an average day. No big highs and no big lows. Just a coasting sort of day.

Me on the other hand? I was seconds away from breaking down in another wave of tears.

After Gabriel left my office, I'd only had a few seconds to pull myself together and make myself professional. I only had moments to act as if I hadn't just gone through one of the hardest breakups of my life seconds before Claire entered my office. I had to pretend that my heart wasn't shattered into a million pieces.

Unfortunately for me, my acting skills were not up to par, and Claire recognized my distress instantly. As she sat down in her chair, she raised an eyebrow. "You were crying."

I shook my head and pushed out a smile. "No, no. I'm fine. How are you?" I asked, taking my seat. I pushed up my sleeves slightly, not realizing that the marks Henry left on my wrists were still visible. We'd gotten into an argument the night prior, in which he fought with me over his business plans not going through. He grabbed my wrists so hard that he left bruises. I was happy Gabriel hadn't noticed because I could only assume that would've made him spiral even more.

Claire's eyes widened when she saw the bruises and she sat up, alarmed. "Oh no."

"What is it?" I asked.

She pointed to my wrists. "Those marks."

A wave of embarrassment swept through my system as I quickly pulled the sleeves down. It made me feel awful that Claire had noticed the bruises, especially knowing her history of abuse. "Oh, it's nothing. I was just—"

"Did he do that to you?" she asked, cutting into my words.

"Did who do what to me?"

"Henry. Did he hurt you?"

I shook my head. "No, no, it's not like that. He didn't…" My words faded as realization clicked in my head. "How did you know my husband's name?"

A flash of panic filled Claire's eyes as she shook her head before she began to ramble. "I'm so sorry, Kierra. I didn't think… I had no idea that he'd hurt you, too. I thought it was just me, and that I was some oddity, because you two seemed happy for so long. I just thought it was me who was the issue because I was so messed up, but you're not messed up, and he hurt you, too, and I didn't think he'd do that. I didn't think he'd hurt you, too. And—"

My stomach knotted up as I stared at her in bewilderment, completely baffled by the words falling off her tongue. I pushed my chair back from my desk and tried to grasp what she was saying. "Claire. What are you talking about?"

"Henry. He was the person from my youth that messed me up. He was my abuser."

No.

There was no way.

That was impossible.

How?

"What are you talking about?" I asked.

"Henry Hughes... We met when I was only seventeen and he was in his late twenties. We fell in love. Well, I thought it was love, but I realized, through you, that it was love bombing. He presented himself as something he wasn't, and I told him everything. I told him about my family trauma, and he seemed to use that to get me closer to him. When I turned eighteen...I got pregnant..."

A knot sat heavily in my gut as I kept shaking my head. "No, what? I..." I felt uncomfortable and unsafe as the words were falling off her tongue. What was she saying? Was she saying Ava was hers? There was no way.

Her eyes moved to the photograph of Ava on my desk, then back to me. Claire's eyes were flooded with tears as she nodded. "He gaslit me. He told me I was nothing and I'd be an awful mother like my own. I was depressed when I had her. I was so lost and he made me feel like scum. I signed away my parental rights, and he had a restraining order placed against me. I haven't been able to see Ava through all these years. All I could do was creep around his property to just get a glimpse of her, but—"

"No," I stated sternly. "Stop, Claire."

But she didn't.

She continued. "Then you began to raise her. I was jealous of you. I wanted to be you. I hated you for a while because you were living my life. I hated that you were beautiful and smart and everything I wasn't. When I found out you were a therapist, I thought therapy would be a good way to get in to know you. To see what you were about and to see how you were treating my daughter. I didn't expect you to save my life, too, Kierra."

"Claire, I need you to leave," I stated sternly, standing. I felt terrified and nauseous from what she'd shared.

But I saw it, too.

I saw Ava's eyes in hers.

I saw my daughter's nose against Claire's face.

I saw parts of Ava that I wished I could unsee.

She stood, too. "I hated him. I hated him for finding you and seemingly loving you right. I hated him for stealing from me and making me seem like I was the broken one, when he was really the messed-up one. I hated him for making me think I deserved to be hit because I was crazy. I hated him for hurting me and loving you. But now I see that it wasn't me. It was him all this time. Because how could he hurt you? You're good, Kierra. You're such a good person," she said with tears rolling down her cheeks.

She stepped toward me, and I stepped backward, on high alert. "Claire. I need you to go."

Her eyes widened and she shook her head. "No. Don't you

see? You're just like me! We're the same. We're victims. You need to understand. You understand, right, Kierra? I was going to tell you at some point, I swear. I wanted to figure out a way that maybe I could see Ava and—"

"*Claire*," I snapped. "Leave now."

A flash of hurt filled her eyes. "But...but you're supposed to understand."

"Joseph!" I shouted as Claire kept approaching me. I didn't know what she was going to do, so all I could think to do was call for Joseph to come and have her removed. I shouted his name repeatedly until he entered my office.

He looked alarmed as he raised an eyebrow. "What's going on?"

"Can you please remove Ms. Dune from my office?" I asked as calmly as possible.

Claire shook her head. "But I'm just like you! He messed us both up, Kierra! Don't you see?" she sobbed. "I just wanted to see my daughter. I just wanted to see her through you. And then you guys moved, and I couldn't stop by your place to get a glimpse of her, to see her..."

Oh my goodness.

She was the person on the property at our old place. The fanatic creeping on our property, going through our trash bins.

I felt sick.

"Okay, okay, it's all good," Joseph said, placing a hand against Claire's shoulder. "I think that's enough for today. Let me get you safely out of here."

"No, you don't understand," Claire cried. "He's the monster, not me! I'm not crazy."

"I never said you were crazy," Joseph swore.

Claire shook her head. "But you're looking at me like I'm crazy. I'm not crazy. Tell him, Kierra. Tell him I'm not crazy and tell him how Henry is the one who is! Tell him how Henry is hurting you the same way he hurt me. Tell him!"

I stayed quiet.

She looked betrayed as Joseph walked her away.

I stayed frozen in place while Joseph dealt with the system out front. The cops were called. They came to speak with me. I told them everything I knew without thought. My mind was a jumbled mess. I had a stalker. My client was a stalker. My client was my daughter's mother.

This was all too much.

Life was becoming all too much.

When the cops left, Joseph reentered my office. The look of heartbreak in his eyes was heavy. He walked over to me and slid his hands into his slacks pockets. "Are you okay, Kierra?"

I shook my head.

He nodded in understanding.

"Is she really Ava's mother?" he questioned.

"Yes. I think so."

"Fuck," he murmured, pinching the bridge of his nose. "Listen, I hate to ask this, because I know it's a lot, but I'm now very concerned. Claire told me to look at your wrists. She said Henry is hurting you the way he hurt her. So...I need to ask because I love you, Kierra. Is your husband hurting you?"

My eyes filled with tears, and I burst into uncontrollable sobs as I nodded my head. Within seconds, Joseph's arms were wrapped around me, and as I crumbled in his embrace, he held me tighter.

Everything in my world was falling apart.

I wasn't certain how much more my heart could take before it gave out, too.

I wished Henry had a work trip to fly off to. It would've given me a breather to gather my thoughts for a few weeks, but it appeared that he was home more than ever before. The tension of the home was indescribable. It felt as if I were walking on eggshells, not knowing what might set Henry off. Not knowing what to say or do or even think.

Ava wasn't herself, either. I couldn't blame her. Henry took away the one thing that made her happy, and she didn't even get a reason why, other than "because I said so." It was one thing when my own happiness was being stolen; watching it happen to my daughter brought about a whole other realm of sorrow.

"Why can't I keep going to Gabriel's?" Ava asked at dinner. "I don't get it."

"Well, it's not for you to get. Besides, with you back in school, you should be focusing on your studies. Not some silly mentorship."

"It's not silly. And I could go after school. I can bike over there."

"You'll do no such thing. Stay away from that place," Henry scolded.

"But—"

"Ava," I cut in. "Let it go."

"No," she said, looking at me as if I were insane. "I'm not letting it go. Why would you side with him? You know what that mentorship means to me, Mom!"

Watching her eyes fill with tears broke my heart. I hated that I had any involvement in it. I hated that I was a big cause of her heartache. "Listen, sweetheart," I started, but Henry cut me off.

"Stop babying her. I already said no, so that's the end of the conversation," he ordered.

"You're being a jerk. You can't stop me from going," Ava said.

"*Shut the hell up,*" Henry shouted, slamming his hand against the table. "I don't want to hear another word about that man in my house, do you fucking understand?"

I saw it happen—the moment my daughter began to shrink from her father's tone. It was as if a bright light was being forced to dim.

~~At least he never yells in front of Ava.~~

Her tears fell down her cheeks, but she sat tall. "You're just mad because everyone likes Gabriel more than you."

Oh no. This wasn't going to be good.

He cleared his throat. "Ava—"

"You are! You're mad that I like him more than you, and Mom likes him more than you! And did you know they were in love?" My heart dropped to the pit of my stomach. *Oh no, Ava. Please stop...* "They were in love when they were kids, and he treated her better than you ever treated her! Because he's not a monster. She's actually happy with him because he's not mean to her and doesn't hurt her feelings and doesn't—"

"*Enough!*" he hollered, slamming his hands against the table again. "Shut your mouth before I shut it for you, Ava Melanie." The whole table shook, glasses falling over. My stomach caught in my throat. The rage shooting through him sent a panic through me that I wasn't ready to face. That I wasn't ready for Ava to witness. His breathing was erratic.

Ava had tears rolling down her cheeks as the room filled with silence. She pushed herself away from the table, looked Henry straight in the eyes, and said, "I hate you."

She stormed off to her bedroom, and I was right behind her.

"Ava—"

"Why wouldn't you stand up for me?" Ava cried as I entered her room. "Why do you let him talk to you like that? Why do you let him hurt you so much?"

"It's complicated."

"It's not," she argued. "The only thing I don't understand is why you don't stand up to him. I hate him, Mom. I hate him so much and I know you do, too, but I don't understand why you'd let him do these things."

"Ava, you have to understand. I'm working to figure this out. I'm working harder than you'd ever know to make sure we are good."

"We'd be good without him," she told me. "I'm going to Grandma's. I already texted her, and she's on her way."

"Ava—"

"I love you, Mom," she cut in as she rushed to me and hugged me. She hugged me tighter than she'd ever hugged me before. I choked on my next breath, pushing down the sob that was trying its hardest to escape from between my lips. "I just wished you loved you, too."

I shut my eyes, kissed her forehead, and let her go.

I stayed in her bedroom after she headed off with Tamera. A part of me wished I'd gone with her. I wished I'd packed a bag and headed over to Tamera's, too, to escape the prison I resided in.

After she left, I headed back to the dining room to clean up the table. As I was doing so, Henry reappeared in the room, a look of disdain on his face.

"You knew Gabriel Sinclair before he began working on the project?" he asked.

Chills raced through my system, knowing that this conversation wouldn't lead to anything good. "We don't have to talk about that."

"The hell we don't. What the hell did Ava mean about that? Were you in love with him?"

"I knew him when we were young. It was a long time ago, Henry, and Gabriel didn't even remember me."

"But you remembered him," he urged. "Were you playing me this whole time?"

"What?" I chuckled slightly, stunned by the question. "Of

course not. I wasn't the one who hired Gabriel, remember? That was you."

"But you were mocking me this whole time." He moved over to me as I gathered a stack of plates. "Did you get off on embarrassing me? And did you enjoy having Ava mad at me?"

"I didn't embarrass you, Henry. Also, Ava being mad at you has nothing to do with me."

"It has everything to do with you. If it wasn't for you and your lies, this Gabriel thing would've never happened."

I turned to walk toward the kitchen, not wanting to go back and forth with him. I was burned out both mentally and spiritually. My heart was exhausted, and I was running on empty. All I wanted to do was disappear for a while. I wanted to crawl into a dark cave and stay hidden away from the world, from Henry.

I wished I were invisible.

I placed the dishes into the sink, and Henry appeared right behind me. He gripped my wrists from behind and slammed my hands against the edge of the counter, pinning them down. His body pressed against mine as I closed my eyes, scared of what he'd do next. Everything slowed whenever he pinned me down. I hated that I didn't go with Ava. I should've gone with her.

His hot breath melted against my skin, reminding me of his control over me. He tilted my head slightly and rubbed his nose against my earlobe. "Did you fuck him in our house, too?" he whispered.

What was I supposed to do when the devil was the man who I said "I do" to?

Henry wasn't strong, but he was stronger than me.

Henry wasn't big, but he was bigger than me.

And he was beginning to unravel faster and faster with every passing moment.

"Please let me go, Henry," I whispered, praying he didn't sense the fear in my tone. He fed off that—my fear. He loved to know that he made me uneasy. That he had control over my comfort level, over my feeling of safety.

He tightened his grip on my wrists.

Did he do the same to Claire?

She was only seventeen when they'd met.

A little girl.

Only three years older than Ava was now.

My mind couldn't wrap around the idea of a grown man preying on a child. Let alone someone who had been through as much as Claire had.

"I'll let you go when I'm ready," he hissed against my ear.

"Is that what you told Claire Dune?" I replied.

The words slipped through my lips and must've felt like a slam against his chest, because he dropped his hold on me.

He stepped backward and arched an eyebrow toward me. "What did you just say to me?"

"So you know her?" I asked.

"How do you know Claire?"

"Is she Ava's mother?"

He shook his head. "No. Of course not. I told you, Ava's mother was a junkie psycho."

"Yes, that's what you told me. But is that actually true?"

"How do you know Claire Dune?" he asked again, avoiding my question.

"She's a client of mine."

The confusion in his eyes was as clear as day. I was nervous about what was going to happen next, because I never knew how he was going to react. Especially as of late, because he seemed easily triggered.

He took a step back, turned away from me and muttered something before saying, "I need space. Maybe you should stay somewhere else tonight like Ava. I can't leave because I have to pack. Tomorrow I'm heading to China for work. We can talk when I'm back in town."

I didn't know what else to say except for one word. "Okay."

This release of me sent a chill down my spine as he walked away. I was thankful that he let me go, and I realized how quickly his reaction could've gone badly. Relief raked through my system as I realized the next steps I'd need to do while he was gone to China.

I had no plans to talk to him once he made it back into town. I had no plans to work things out.

The only thing on my mind now was for me—and Ava—to escape.

All I wanted was to be free.

30

Kierra

I showed up to Tamera's house with a duffel bag and a defeated smile. "Hi."

She smiled at me as she opened her screen door. Her eyes fell to the bag, and she nodded in a knowing way. "Okay, sweetheart. Come on in and tell me everything. I'll make us a pot of coffee."

"Did you know Ava's biological mother?" I asked Tamera as we sat on her back porch talking.

"Claire?"

"Yeah."

"I did. She was young. Very young. But a sweet girl. Henry painted her as a crazy woman, but truthfully that was when I realized he had some darkness in him. She was so young and naive. She had a lot of emotional stuff going on at her home, too. I figured that was why she signed over the rights for Ava."

"Do you think she wanted to do that?"

Tamera shrugged. "I think she was so damaged before and after Henry that she just wanted some form of peace. Pair that with postpartum depression and that woman didn't have much of a chance."

I rubbed my hands up and down my arms. "She showed up as a client of mine."

She sat straighter. "Who? Claire?"

I nodded. "She's been a client of mine since we've moved."

"My goodness. How did you find out she was Ava's mother?" she asked.

"She told me today. She knew the whole time that I was Ava's stepmother and wanted to find a way to get close to Ava. I guess Henry has a restraining order against her. She said she just wanted to make sure Ava was okay."

"Oh goodness. That's a lot."

I sighed and brushed my hand through my hair. "Life feels like a lot."

"I think this is the first time I'm truly realizing that my son is just like his father. I've tried to convince myself that Henry was different. That no parts of his father lived within that boy's soul, but I knew that was a lie early on. I knew there were parts of me that lived within Henry, but most of them belonged to Jack," Tamera confessed. "Do you know how much that hurts? To see the baby I once carried in my own womb turn out to be such a monster."

"Tamera…" I sighed, feeling awful for dragging her into this situation. "I'm so sorry."

"Does he hurt you?" she asked. "Does he belittle you? Has he ever put his hands on you?"

I paused for a moment. A part of me wanted to protect the image of her son for her. Yet my head nodded. Her eyes flooded with tears as she stared out into the night sky. She sniffled a little with a slight shake of her head. I felt instant guilt from telling her that.

"He scares you?" she questioned.

"More often than not."

"I thought it would be a onetime situation with his father." She fiddled with her hands. "It's never only once. It was only the first time. And you never really forget the first time. The first time Jack hit me, I almost thought I'd imagined it. We'd been married for years before it happened, and we were so deeply in love at first. I couldn't wrap my mind around the idea that someone I loved could do something so…cruel. I couldn't comprehend that. I loved him. He loved me, too. The second time he hit me, I blamed myself for making a mess around the house. The third time, I had a panic attack at the stoplight we were at. I was pregnant with Henry, and he punched me in my stomach."

"Oh my goodness," I gasped as tears began rolling down my cheeks.

"Once Henry was born, Jack was gentle again. He was kind and attentive. He promised me he'd never hurt me again. For a few years, he held on to that promise, too. For a while, I felt as if I had my husband back again. That was until he lost his job, and I realized that whenever something bad happened, he'd need a punching bag. That punching bag was me."

"He was a monster."

"He was, yet I stayed... I stayed until his very end. Do you know how often I used to daydream about what my life would be like if I had left? Do you know the dreams I'd used to dream?" She shook her head in awe as the stars sparkled over our heads. "If I'd left, I would've gone back to school. I would've finished my nursing degree. If I'd left, I would've raised Henry in a small apartment that wasn't luxurious, but it would be mine and mine alone. I would've dated. Oh, my gosh, I would've dated so many different types of men until I found one that felt right to me. I would've fallen in love, too. A real love that didn't hurt. A kind of love that healed the broken pieces. We both wouldn't have been perfect, but we would've been perfect for each other. If I'd left, I wouldn't have years of trauma to unpack. My load of scars would've been lighter. My bruises would've not been as deep. If I'd left, I would've been happier sooner."

She turned her body toward mine and took my hands in hers as she continued to speak. "Now, Kierra, I can't tell you what would happen if you left. That's your story to write, your tale to create. Your pages are blank if you leave, and you get to create that narrative. But I can tell you what will happen if you stay." Her voice lowered as she brushed away the tears rolling down my cheeks. The sincerity of each word from her made my broken heart keep beating. "If you stay, he won't change for the better. If you stay, he'll still hurt you. If you stay, he'll still hit you. If you stay, you'll lose more and more of your brilliant light."

I nodded and whispered lightly. "I know."

"But that's not all," she swore. "If you stay, Ava will notice. If you stay, she'll witness his actions. Maybe not at first, but she will eventually. If you stay, he won't even try to hide it from her. If you stay, she might try to stop him. If you stay, she might get pushed if she tries to intervene. If you stay, he might shove her. Hit her. Kick her. Punch her, too. If you stay, her spirit will start to break. If you stay, she'll either see herself in you and allow men to treat her that way, or she'll become ashamed of you and push you away or blame you for not being strong enough to go. If you stay, you might not only lose yourself, but Ava may lose her light, too."

"You don't get it, though," I whispered, brushing away my tears. "If I go, he said he'll keep her from me. She's my daughter, but not on paper. On paper she's his, and I'd lose her. That's why I've stayed so long. That's why I put up with everything I have, because the only thing I want in this world is my daughter. I can't lose her. She's my world."

"You won't lose her, sweetheart."

"Yes, I will. I know I will."

"No," Tamera said sternly, "you won't. Because when you leave, she's going with you. I will fight tooth and nail to make sure that she does. You aren't leaving him on your own, Kierra. This isn't all on you. You're walking away with a team of people who love you. Who will fight when you feel weak. Who will speak up for you when your own voice shakes. I promise you. And Ava is old enough to stand up in court and speak for herself, and I know she'll choose you."

"How can you be certain of that?"

"Because she told me so. She'd choose you over and over again, in every lifetime. Just like I would."

I stared down at my hands and shook my head. "But he's your son…"

"Yes," she agreed. "But you are my family." She placed a finger beneath my chin and tilted my head up to look her in the eyes. "And it's about time for you to learn how to breathe again. All I need is for you to say the word. Say you want to get away, and I'll put the wheels in motion. Say you want out, and we'll make a way."

"Okay." I nodded slowly as trembles found my voice. "I want out."

Tears rolled down Tamera's cheeks. She cupped my face in her hands and smiled as she kissed my forehead. "Brave girl. Brave, brave girl."

Tamera made dinner for Ava and me. Afterward, Ava and I lay out in the hammock for a few hours, staring up at the stars. We swayed slightly as she rested her head on my shoulder.

"I'm glad you came over, Mom," she whispered as she fiddled with the sleeves of her shirt. "I love Grandma, but I really needed you, too, tonight."

"I know, sweetheart. I'm sorry it took me so long to get here." I hesitated as I bit my bottom lip. "Can we have a grown-up conversation?"

She glanced my way and narrowed her eyes. "I've been wanting you to do that for years. I'm not a silly kid anymore, Mom."

"I know, but sometimes when I look at you, I still see my little five-year-old girl who I want to protect from all harm, no matter what."

"Yeah, but then who's protecting you?"

I smiled a sad smile and kissed her forehead. A small sigh rippled between my lips. "I'm leaving your father."

She sat up slightly, making the hammock rock more. "What? Really?"

I nodded. "Yeah. But it's complicated. When your father and I married, we signed a prenuptial agreement and it states that if there were a divorce, he would get full custody of you."

"What? No way. I don't want to go with him. I hate him," she barked out, sitting up completely, almost tossing the hammock all the way over. She stood. "He can't do that. You're my mom."

"I know, sweetheart. It's just a paragraph in a document that he has hung over my head for a long time. But...I spoke with a lawyer. He told me that a clause in a prenuptial agreement attempting to stipulate the rights of a stepparent in a future child custody case would likely not be enforced. There's a lot of complexities when it comes to parental rights and custody cases."

The fear in Ava's eyes settled. "Oh. Okay, good."

"But if your father gets his way, he might drag this out and keep his threats coming. You might have to testify in court that you want to be with me. I know that's a lot to ask—"

"I'll do it," she cut in. "I'll do anything for you."

The tears burned at the back of my eyes as the words left her mouth. "I don't want you to feel responsible for making sure I'm okay, Ava. All I care about is you and your safety."

"You are my safety, Mom. Besides, you said forever, right?"

I stood and walked over to her. I held a pinkie out in her direction. "Forever."

She wrapped hers around mine. "Forever," she echoed.

I pulled her into a hug and held her for the longest time. "I love you, Ava Melanie."

"I love you, too, Mom. And I'm really proud of you."

I'm really proud of you.

That was the line that made the tears fall.

31

Gabriel

I was miserable without them. There was no getting around the fact that not seeing Kierra and Ava was affecting me more than I thought possible. I'd tried to focus on anything other than the fact that my world felt dark without them, but everything felt empty. I couldn't eat, I couldn't work, I couldn't even think.

It had been three weeks since Kierra told me to stay away. Three weeks of me worrying about her well-being. Three weeks of me thinking that Henry might've done something to hurt her and Ava. Three miserable weeks of me staying up all night, terrified that I may get a call that something awful had happened.

Rosie was kind enough to give me daily updates, letting me know that she'd been checking in on Kierra. She assured me that everything was okay, but I didn't feel that way. It was almost impossible to explain, but I felt as if something terrible was happening.

I may not have had my memories with Kierra from our youth, but I felt her within me. I knew it didn't make sense, but I swore over the past years my heart only beat because somewhcrc in my consciousness I knew hers was out there beating, too. And I currently felt her heart breaking. As she fell apart, my own chest ached. As she cried, my own eyes leaked.

It made no sense.

I made no sense.

But I knew she wasn't okay.

No matter what she'd told Rosie.

"Have you heard from her?" Mom asked as she walked into my office. She looked at me the same way she'd been staring my way over the past few weeks—as if I were a sad, abandoned puppy dog who had no clue how to find my way home. We hadn't spoken since I'd learned about Elijah, and I wasn't ready to speak to her on the topic. But I was certain Bobby had informed her of what was going on with Kierra.

I shook my head, knowing she was speaking of Kierra. "No. I haven't."

She took a step toward me. "Son—"

"Don't," I urged. I couldn't look at her. The mere idea of her still made my stomach turn. "I'm not ready for this conversation, Mom."

"I know. I…" she started, but her voice cracked and faded away. I still didn't look her way, because if I had, I would've felt bad. I would've saw the hurt in her eyes and felt the need to comfort her. I wasn't ready for that. I wasn't ready to forgive. I wasn't ready to heal. I wasn't ready to hold a conversation with her that would either move us forward or forever tear us apart.

"Son, please," she begged as she rushed over to my side. "I just want to make this right. Tell me what I can do to make this right."

I rose my head to meet her stare. Tears fell down her face, and my stubborn heart still broke when I witnessed her sadness. My mother was my world...even though she robbed of my everything.

"Apologize," I sternly said.

She nodded rapidly. "Yes, yes. I do apologize, Gabriel. I am so sorry for—"

"*No*," I cut in. "Don't apologize to me. Apologize to Kierra for how you've treated her. For how much heaviness you placed against her. When you do that, when you speak with her, I'll be ready to speak with you."

She took a few steps backward and closed her eyes. The tears kept falling, and she nodded slowly. Her brown eyes that matched mine opened and she wiped those tears away, only for fresh ones to keep flowing. She lowered her head and walked toward the door. Before she left, she turned toward me one more time and said, "I love you, Son. I just truly want you to know that. Everything choice I've ever made was because of that love."

I hated that she said those words, because I knew they were true.

Love wasn't always perfect. It often came with bends and

cracks. The greatest heartbreaks always came from love more than they came from hatred.

That was why love was so hard to make sense of. It was dizzying, complex, and at times so damn difficult to grasp.

My mother left my office still struggling with a wave of emotional tears.

A part of me shouted at my stubborn heart for not saying, "I love you, too."

32

Kierra

"Amma, what are you doing here?" I asked, staring at Gabriel's mom yet again in my office lobby. The moment I saw her, I felt defeated. I was too tired to defend myself to her. I was too tired to listen to her tell me what an awful person I'd been.

I was running on an empty tank of emotions and had little of myself to give. And any juice that was left in my tank had to be given to my clients. They didn't deserve to suffer simply because my life was in flames. I'd been spending time with lawyers, making an exit strategy, making sure I had all my ducks in a row before filing for divorce. Tamera had mentioned how I should gather video footage of Henry attacking me over the past few weeks. With our home being a smart house, there would definitely be footage of Henry being violent toward me. So while Henry was gone, I'd go into his office and try to find any files that I could. I also had my own cameras set up for when he came back into town, just in case he became enraged again.

But I couldn't focus on that with Amma in my office. I needed her to know I didn't have time for whatever it was she was going to say to me.

"Listen, actually, don't tell me why you're here. I don't have the time for a talk. Or for you to tell me how awful I am," I blurted out. "Frankly, I can't really take much more of hearing how terrible a human I am, and I don't need you to—"

"I'm sorry," she cut in, making me pause and shake my head in confusion.

"What?"

She stepped toward me. "I'm sorry. For everything. I'm sorry for being so cruel to you all those years ago. I'm sorry for blaming you for the accident, because it wasn't your fault, Kierra. It was tragic, and painful, and traumatic, but it was never your fault."

"I..." My words caught in my throat. I shook my head. "It was my fault. I should've been more careful on the road. I should've—"

"It was an icy street. You couldn't foresee it, and you weren't even the car that slid out of control. You loved my Elijah so much. I know you did, and you would've never wanted a hair on his head to be out of place."

It was true.

Elijah felt like a gift not only to Amma and Gabriel, but also to me. He was the little brother I never had and always dreamed of. Everything about him was magical. From his unique imagination to his ability to make people laugh. From his kind, gentle heart, to his welcoming smile. Elijah was the definition of a perfect pure soul, and the world was a darker place without him.

"I loved him so much," I whispered.

She nodded. "He loved you, too. And I'm sorry I put that on you. I'm sorry I let my own heartbreak crash into your life. I'm sorry I allowed you to carry that burden of blaming yourself for his death. It was an accident. You didn't kill my son. It wasn't your fault."

It was an accident.

You didn't kill my son.

It wasn't your fault.

Three sentences that I'd dreamed of hearing from Amma were now rolling off her tongue. And just like that, small pieces of my own heart began to heal.

I rubbed my hand up and down my forearm. "I'm not sure what to say."

"You don't have to say anything. I just...I realized how much harm I've done. Seeing how heartbroken Gabriel is...I should've never sent you away."

"You did what you thought was best."

"That doesn't mean it didn't have dire consequences." She moved in closer to me and placed a hand on my arm. "Kierra... my son's in love with you. He's been in love with you for a very long time. And I'm sorry that I interrupted your love story. But if you give him a chance...I know he'd love you, and love you right, for the rest of your life."

I believed her. Not because of her words, but because I

knew who Gabriel had been. I didn't need him to tell me he loved me because I felt it in his actions. I saw it in his eyes. The only good thing over the past few weeks, other than Ava, was the fact that my dreams took me back to him. Some nights, I'd close my eyes and dream of his lips, of his arms wrapped tightly around me. In my dreams, we were everything we deserved to be. We were in love, we were happy, we were forever intertwined with always.

I hated when I woke each day, because that was the problem with dreams—they didn't lead to reality. They just remained within the darkness.

"I love him," I told her.

"Then go after him. He's waiting."

"I can't," I whispered, shaking my head. "I want to, Amma. Trust me, I do. But first, I have to make sure my daughter and I are safe."

Her eyes that matched her son's blinked a few times. "He'll wait for you."

"I can't ask him to do that."

"Oh, Kierra… Don't you see?" She shook her head. "He's been waiting for you for over twenty years. I have no doubt that he can wait a little bit longer. I can tell him—"

"Please don't," I urged. "Don't say a word, Amma. I don't want it to be that way. I want him to live as I try to figure out my life. I don't want him waiting for me until I know I'm able to give him all of me. And if I'm too late, well…that's something I'll have to live with."

That was the thing about love, real love, that is. One had to be willing to let it go in order to not hold the other back from finding their joy.

After work, I headed home to begin my search for documents and files in Henry's office. I wanted to find a password to the videos of him abusing me in the home. Knowing how much of a smart house we had, I knew something had to have captured Henry's abuse toward me. Those videos would go far in court.

My stomach was in knots after I got into the office and began to thumb through his things. The only issue was that everything was password protected and next to impossible to get into. It shouldn't have surprised me that a tech mogul had a high-level password system set up. Still, I was hoping that I was able to break through something. *Anything.*

"What the hell are you doing?"

I startled, looking up to find Henry standing in the doorway of his office. The look of shock on his face was heavy as he held a stack of paperwork in his hands. The divorce papers I'd had drawn up and left in the living room. I was going to read through them that night and mark down any changes I needed for my lawyer.

"Henry. What are you doing here?" I nervously asked as I stood from his office chair.

"What are you doing?" he repeated. "And what are these?"

I slowly walked toward him, uncertain of how he'd react. "I didn't know you were coming home so soon. I was hoping to have everything put together for us to go over after you came back and—"

"We already talked about this. We aren't getting a divorce."

"Yes, we are."

He narrowed his eyes and glanced around his office. "What were you doing in here? Trying to find ways to fuck me over in court?"

"It's not that… I just…" I sighed as my stomach knotted up. "I can't lose Ava, Henry. She's my world."

"She's not yours. She's mine."

I shook my head. "She's not your property. She's a human, and she wants to be with me."

The anger that flashed through his eyes made my skin crawl. His nostrils flared with his deep breaths. "You're trying to ruin me. I bet you want my money, too."

"No," I said. "I want nothing from you. You can keep everything. I just want my daughter."

"My daughter," he corrected. "Not yours."

He was blocking the door, my way out. I tried to stay calm because I knew if he saw a moment of fear in me, he'd lean into that even more.

I grimaced as I tried to casually walk past him. "We can talk later. I'm sure you had a long flight and—"

He gripped my wrist and shoved me against the doorframe. I yipped from the pain of my back hitting the door so hard.

"Ouch, Henry!" I murmured, trying to untwist his grip from my wrist. "Let me go."

"You're trying to ruin me," he said, his brown eyes packed

with hatred and fear. He smelled like whiskey, and it was becoming clear that his trip to China hadn't gone the way he'd hoped. Now I was the one who was trying to ruin him. Now I was his enemy because he couldn't attack those who truly let him down. He could only try to hurt me in the shadows.

"Henry. You're tired. Please, let me go," I whispered.

He pulled me closer to him and pressed his forehead to mine. I closed my eyes, feeling the level of danger building in my chest from his tight embrace. He rubbed his cheek against mine and brushed his mouth over my lips. "I fucking hate you," he whispered. He said the words as if they were soaked in love, in such a passionate way. "Do you hear me, Kierra? I fucking hate you."

I hate you, too.

I couldn't say that, though.

Because I was certain that would make him spiral more.

He forced a kiss on me, gripping my neck, and I didn't move. I was too nervous to do so. His kisses tasted like hatred. He kissed me like I was his greatest enemy and he was marking me with his disgusting taste.

Then he grabbed my cheeks with one hand and shoved me backward to the floor. I fell with a hard thump. He smirked down at me and shook his head. "Get up, Kierra. Stop being so weak," he said as he chuckled.

As I went to stand up, he whipped his leg out in front of my feet, making me fall back to the floor. My heart pounded rapidly as the panic began to grow in my chest. I began to crawl toward the front of the house. His laughter as he watched me crawl made me nauseous. I wanted to just make it to the front door. To get out before he could hurt me. Before he could do something to me that couldn't be undone.

As I made it near the kitchen, I gripped the doorframe and began to stand up. As I stood, Henry shoved me from behind, making me trip forward. My head slammed against the kitchen island, and I felt the blood begin to trickle down from my forehead. I felt dizzy, sick, embarrassed. Weak.

He kept snickering behind me.

"Get your footing, Kierra. You're so damn embarrassing," he hissed as he walked over to me. He grabbed my arm and began to yank me in his direction. "Let's go up to our room to talk," he said. "We should sit and have a heart-to-heart."

"Please, Henry. Stop this," I begged as tears began falling down my cheeks, mixing with the blood from my forehead.

He slapped me. Hard. Then he punched me in the face, splitting my lip open with his wedding ring. The ring I'd given to him all those years prior. Then he laughed again. "Be strong, Kierra. Stop sounding like a weak bitch." He then dragged me by my arms toward the stairs, forcing me up each one to our bedroom.

He kept dragging me until he shoved me against our wall.

I curled up into a ball, uncertain of when his next hit might come. I covered my head as my heart began beating faster and faster, reality beginning to settle in. 'Til death do us part. He was going to kill me. He was going to kill me, and Ava would have no one. He was going to kill me, and Ava would get the message that her mother was gone. He was going to kill me, and I'd never see my daughter again.

"Please stop." I sobbed into my hands as my body shook violently from fear of his unhinged actions. "Just leave me alone," I begged.

I didn't look up at him. I couldn't. Because if I did, the joy in his eyes would terrify me even more than I already was.

He began ripping up the divorce paperwork, and he threw the pieces at me. He then picked up the vase with the dead roses I hadn't gotten around to throwing away and dumped it over my head, soaking me and the paperwork. He bent down and cupped my face in his hand once more. "Before you even made it to court, I would drain you of every cent you had. Then I would ruin you in the courtroom, you crazy bitch. Don't test me," he ordered. He took a few steps back with the vase in his hand and threw it just over my head, where it hit the wall. Pieces of glass shattered all over me as my body trembled nonstop from the terrifying fact that I was stuck in a house alone with a complete madman.

He's going to kill me.

He's going to kill me.

He's going to kill me…

I kept my head down as he walked around me. He kept laughing as I stayed in a ball. "You're so pathetic, Kierra. This is embarrassing. Pull yourself together."

I didn't say anything, and he kept laughing.

"I'm going to get a drink and to meet with a few clients. Clean this mess up. We'll talk later."

He left the room, but I didn't believe that he truly left. My husband was a liar. A psychotic, monstrous liar who would probably be waiting around the corner for me to feel safe enough to get up, only so he could shove me down the stair-case. He'd tell people I tripped, too. That I was so clumsy. That I was so unstable. That I was the issue.

I was always the issue.

I heard the front door slam closed, and a car pulled away.

A short breath fell from between my lips.

When I found enough courage, I reached into my back pocket and pulled out my cell phone. I sent a quick text message. Then I waited. And waited. And waited.

How did I get here?

What had I become?

Blood trickled down my cheek as I stayed balled up beside my nightstand. The water seeped into the carpet while glass pieces sat scattered around me.

That would be another argument. Or, more so, him yelling at me, reminding me how disappointing I'd been.

"Why did you upset me so much that I had to throw that at you, Kierra? Why do you push me so much when all I do is love you? Now, look at that mess."

Mess.

Such a mess.

I shuddered as I heard the front door open, thinking Henry was back for more. I hadn't moved in the past twenty minutes. My phone was gripped in my hands as my nervous system stayed in overdrive, making it impossible for me to physically stand.

"Kierra!" was shouted, the voice alert and stern.

Within seconds, my troubled soul soothed from the sound of the voice packed with bass. Henry's voice didn't do that— soothe me.

"Here," I choked out. I felt a certain amount of shame as I glanced down at myself. My T-shirt was stretched out and ripped from when Henry's hands had twisted around it to toss me around like a rag doll.

Concern for my safety should've been the first thing to cross my mind at that moment, but truthfully embarrassment showed up first. I felt ashamed that another would see me in my current state. Especially him.

I didn't want him to see me like this. Broken. Battered. Bruised.

Damaged.

I frantically wiped at my tears, but still, I couldn't stand. Why wouldn't my feet move? Why was my body frozen? Why did I not fight back?

Weak.

"You're such a weak bitch."

So many of my thoughts weren't even my own anymore. They all belonged to him. He'd spent the past few years repro-gramming my thoughts to match his voice. Thoughts that fed me insults at rapid speeds, drenching my soul in self-doubt.

They started out so small, harmless even.

"You're not going to eat another piece of bread, are you?"

"That's an interesting hair color choice."

"Have you considered starting at a gym to up your energy more? We can go together and make it a couple's thing."

I never struggled with my energy. Still, I signed up for a membership.

Stop, I begged my own brain. There was such a small part of me that remained after what he'd done to me. Yet it still fought back, even though it was tired, even though it was hurt, even though it wanted to quit time and time again. It was that same part of me that managed to make the call that would take me away from here.

The footsteps were fast paced and then they reached the bedroom and found me.

Me.

In the corner.

Balled up like a coward.

I looked up and met his eyes. The kind eyes I'd hadn't seen in days, weeks.

Gabriel.

He came.

Reality set in that he came back for me.

Even after how everything went down.

He hurried over, his hand rested against my cheek, and I shut my eyes. Comfort. I missed that most of all.

"Kierra…" he choked out with palpable heartache.

I opened my eyes and saw the hurt in his stare. I shook my head. "Just a few bruises, that's all," I half-joked.

He didn't laugh. I didn't blame him. Nothing was funny.

"Where's Ava?" he asked, alert, his eyes darting around the space. "Is she…?"

"She's okay. She's at her grandmother's."

Gabriel pulled me closer to him. "I'm going to murder him," he growled, his nostrils flaring with a rage I'd never seen before. "I'm going to fucking murder him."

"No. It's fine."

"This isn't fucking fine," he growled, his voice dripping with desire for vengeance.

"I know. But we have to leave before he's—"

The front door opened again, and I tensed up. Gabriel glanced toward the doorway of the bedroom, then back to me. "Stay here," he ordered. Not an order from control, yet one from protection. Those orders were very different. Henry controlled; Gabriel protected.

Gabriel stood and marched out of the bedroom. I covered my ears and rocked back and forth as the commotion in the other room intensified. It sounded like a war zone with things being knocked over, things being shattered. I trembled from fear, uncertain what was going on in the other room. Seconds felt like minutes, and minutes felt like hours as I waited.

When the commotion came to a halt, the silence terrified me more than the noise prior. Footsteps grew closer. My anxiety shot higher. Then he appeared.

Gabriel.

He walked over to me, with a busted lip.

I placed my hand against his face. "Are you okay?" I asked.

A tiny curve raised his lips. "Just a few bruises, that's all."

Gabriel.

My Gabriel.

My very best friend.

"And Henry?" I questioned, a crack in my voice.

"Don't worry. You're safe."

He lifted me into his arms. I burrowed into his chest. "Keep your eyes closed until you're in the car, okay, Kierra? Don't look around."

I agreed. He carried me to the vehicle and unlocked the door. As he placed me in the passenger seat, I kept my eyes shut. He hurried over to the driver's seat and closed his door. The second he drove off, I opened my eyes and I allowed myself to breathe.

33

Kierra

I felt dirty as I sat in the police station.

They had me undress.

They took pictures of me.

They asked me questions about my husband.

Gabriel stood by my side the whole time.

He held my hand.

He answered questions when I couldn't speak up myself.

He comforted me when I felt weaker than ever before.

When I grew embarrassed, he held me closer.

When I cried, he cried, too.

Through it all, he stayed.

34

Gabriel

Henry was arrested shortly after the incident. Not only did Kierra have physical proof of his abuse all over her body, but the video cameras she had set up showed the officers exactly what they needed to get Henry locked away for a long time. Unfortunately, when a man as powerful as Henry had money and resources, there was a chance that he'd be released sooner than later. Or worse, he'd get a slap on the wrist. Justice wasn't always serviced, especially for the women who suffered silently for so long. We all had to live with that fear, but we'd face it head-on. Henry wasn't allowed to hurt my girls anymore. I'd fight to protect them for the remainder of my life. And no matter what, he lost. Henry lost the two most amazing women I'd ever encountered. That would be his imprisonment for the remainder of his days—he'd no longer have access to Kierra and Ava's light. His world would always be filled with darkness, behind bars or outside of them. He wouldn't receive any kind of happily ever after. He'd be stuck in the darkness while we danced in the light and built our future toward our happy ending.

I took her to my house to stay, and she remained quiet the whole time. I didn't blame her. I couldn't imagine what she was going through, what her mind was going through. After a while, I placed her in a shower and cleaned her up. The dried blood washed down the drain as I washed her body, which was clearly still in a lot of pain. I wished I could take the mental and emotional pain away, too. I wished I could bottle up all her hurting and toss it into the fucking ocean.

"I'm okay," she whispered as I began to massage my fingers through her hair. "I'm okay, I'm okay, I'm okay," she kept saying, as if she was trying to convince herself most of all.

I tilted her head up so her eyes locked with mine. "Kierra, you don't have to be—"

She shut her eyes and shook her head as the water fell over us. "No. Please. I'm just…" Tears began to fall down her cheeks again as she kept shaking her head. "I have to be okay. I have to be okay. Even though I'm not, I need to keep saying it, okay, Gabriel? Otherwise, he wins, and I can't let him win," she sobbed, her body shaking in my arms. "I can't have him win. I–I can't. I ca-can't let him…"

I pressed my chin to the top of her head as I pulled her in to my chest. I held her tightly as she sobbed in my arms, and I whispered, "You're okay. You're okay. You're okay."

We both knew she wasn't in that very moment, but I gave her what she needed to hear.

She took deep breaths and echoed my words. "I'm okay, I'm okay, I'm okay…"

I couldn't wait until those words were true.

After the shower, I wrapped her in a towel and led her to my bedroom. I dressed her slowly in my T-shirt and sweatpants as she sat on the edge of my bed. She didn't say a word as I did so. The defeat on her face was enough to break my heart.

I knelt in front of her and took her hands into mine. I knew she was repeating the words *I'm okay* in her mind. So, I gave her a few more words that she could repeat.

"You're safe, you're safe, you're safe," I whispered, gently kissing the palms of her hands.

Her eyes closed and she turned her head slightly away from me as tears fell down her cheeks. She nodded her head slowly.

"I'm safe, I'm safe, I'm safe," she murmured, her voice faint.

I laid her in the bed and climbed in beside her. I didn't wrap myself around her at first, because I didn't know what she needed me to do. I didn't know if she needed to be held or if she needed space to breathe.

Yet she moved toward me, curled into a ball, and fit herself directly against me, resting her head against my chest. My arms wrapped around her with no plans of ever letting her go again.

As we sat in the darkness, I tried to shield Kierra from seeing my own tears fall. But how could he do that to her? How could he be such a monster that he'd hurt the gentlest being in the world?

That was when I knew that my heart was entangled with hers.

It was at that moment I promised myself I'd never leave her side again. She'd never be that afraid again as long as I lived.

"What will I tell Ava?" she whispered against me. "How do I explain…" She sighed, shaking her head. "How do I tell her what happened?"

"With me," I told her. "You'll tell her with me. Then you don't have to do it alone."

"I can't ask you to do that, Gabriel. You've already done so much and—"

"Kierra. I'm here forever now. You don't have to do things alone anymore."

A weighted sigh of relief rippled through her system. "Thank you."

"Rest," I whispered, kissing her forehead.

She did the best she could.

During the night, she woke from nightmares, but I was there to comfort her back to sleep. And when daylight came, we told Ava together.

Ava cried and held on to her mother tightly. She apologized as if it was her fault that Henry had done what he'd done to her mother. Kierra cried, too, and seemed thankful that he would never be able to hurt Ava. He'd never be able to hurt them again as far as I was concerned.

Kierra went to court against Henry. It was the messiest situation when the media got ahold of the information that Henry

Hughes, the mogul, was an abusive monster. News articles, think pieces, and social media exploded with their own opinions on the whole situation. Kierra made Ava promise that she wouldn't go online with all the madness going on. Her main concern was to protect her daughter throughout the whole situation. My only concern was to protect them both.

I wished I could say the case sped by quickly, but it took months for Kierra to receive full custody of Ava, and Henry was sentenced to three years in prison for his actions.

There were more tears after that whole situation, but they were tears of freedom.

My girls would be safe.

"We can't just move into your life," Kierra protested as Ava ran around the backyard with Bentley chasing her. "You've already done too much for us, Gabriel. I'm grateful for you letting us stay with you, but I don't expect you to change your whole life for us."

We sat on the top step of the back porch, and I shrugged. "Why not? I want to change my whole life for you. I want you and Ava to add more color to this place."

She leaned against my shoulder. "Are you sure?"

"I've never been surer of anything, Penguin."

"I just worry that..." She lowered her head. "That I'm too broken still for you. I feel as if I should heal and become a better version of myself before we—"

"Every version of you is the best version," I told her, and meant it. "And no offense, Kierra, but I've waited long enough to have you back with me, and I don't want to wait any longer. I just want you. In every way, in every fashion, in every season. And we can work on being our best selves together. We can grow together as we move forward."

She took my hand into hers and kissed my palm. "Grow as we go?"

"Yes. Grow as we go."

"Okay...good. Besides, I doubt Ava would've let me run away from this. Especially since she now has the dog she always wanted."

I smiled at Ava, who fell over and was getting a million doggy kisses from Bentley. "It's almost like it was meant to be."

"Something like that."

"So, now that you've had more time to think about it and process, what are you thinking about Claire?"

Kierra sighed and nodded. "I talked to Ava about it. I wanted to see if it was a wise thing to do, to introduce the two. She's open to it. I just have to make sure Claire is stable enough to handle it. It's a very sensitive thing, and I don't want to put Ava in harm's way. But I also know Henry, and I can only imagine what he put Claire through. The mind games he probably played with her. And who knows what I would've done if I were in her shoes. I would've done everything possible to make my way back to my daughter, too."

"I'm learning that life's not so black and white."

"Yes," she agreed, nudging me in the arm. "Which is exactly why you should talk to your mother."

"We talk at work."

"About work things." She bit her bottom lip. "I mean you should talk about your relationship and Elijah. I think you both should really talk about Elijah together."

I sighed and pinched the bridge of my nose. "It's going to be hard."

"Yes," she agreed, "but we can do hard things."

"Penguin?"

"Yes?"

"You're my best friend."

She smiled and snuggled closer to me. "I know, Gabriel. I know." She stood up and placed her hands on her waist. "Hey, Ava? Get Bent. Let's all go to the dog park."

35

Gabriel

"I realized something," I said as I walked into Mom's office one Friday night. "About life."

She looked confused as I approached her. She put the paperwork in her hands down on her desk. "And what's that?"

I sat in the chair across from her. "It's fucking hard."

A small, uncertain smile lifted her lips. "It is."

"And nobody knows what they're doing. Not really."

"That's also true."

"I think we're all just trying our best while battling the storms. You were drowning after Dad and Elijah, and you did whatever you thought you had to do in order to somehow get back to shore. I can't say I would've done what you did, but then again, I'm not you. I've never had to walk in your shoes. I've never had to bury my partner and a son. I don't know what that would do to my psyche if I had to. I'm still processing all of this and it will take time, but with everything that has happened, I need you to know one thing."

"And that is?"

"I love you."

"Oh, Gabriel…" she whispered as her body shook slightly.

"Even when I'm mad. Even when I'm distant and processing all of this, I still love you."

Tears began streaming down her face as she shook her head. "I don't deserve that love."

"Yes, you do. We all deserve love."

"Even those who mess up so deeply and will regret their choices for the rest of their lives?"

"Maybe they deserve a little bit more love than others." I stood from my chair and walked over to her side. I bent down and kissed her forehead. "Just be honest from here on out, all right?"

"Of course."

"Okay, good. Now come on." I held a hand out toward her. "Let's go get dinner."

She raised an eyebrow. "You have a lot of work to do. You never make time for dinner."

"I'm realizing work isn't everything. I figured I should make time for those who matter the most."

She placed her hand in mine and I helped her up. "Thank you, Gabriel."

"Always." I pulled her into a hug. "Kierra has letters that she's written to Elijah every week since he passed away. I figured you and I could read through them together to help us remember him. I want to know as much about him as I can."

Her eyes widened with surprise. "She wrote him letters?"

"Yes. Every week. She loved him."

Her eyes grew teary and she nodded. "She did." She fiddled with her hands before saying, "I should probably take you to the storage unit, too."

"The storage unit?"

"It's where I had all his things stored over the years. I have to advise you, though, whenever I go there, I end up crying."

"That's okay, Mom. This time will be better."

"I don't know. I'll probably still cry."

"Yes," I agreed, "but this time when you cry, you won't have to cry alone."

36

Kierra

One Saturday afternoon, Claire walked into Florence Bakery, pulling at the sleeves of her dress. She glanced around in search of me, and I waved her over. When she saw me, her eyes were gentle and she looked relieved.

She slid into the chair across from me and gave me a small smile. "Hi, Kierra."

"Hey, Claire. Thanks for coming."

"Thanks for meeting with me. I didn't expect it, but I was happy when your email showed up. I just…" She shook her head in disbelief. "I never expected to unleash everything the way I did. I've been beating myself up about it for months, Kierra. I'm sure you think I'm some psycho who spiraled badly but—"

"You're a mother," I cut in. "You're a mother who was cut off from your daughter all those years ago."

Her eyes flooded with tears. "Yes."

"And he was a monster who cut you off."

"Yes."

I sat back in my chair and studied Claire. I knew her well enough to know she wasn't a danger. She'd sat across from me for over two years, telling me her story. I knew her triggers and I knew her joy. I knew her ups and I knew her downs. Yet, at the end of the day, my sole responsibility was to make sure Ava was safe and cared for.

"She wants to meet you," I said, speaking of Ava.

Claire's eyes released the tears as she shook her head back and forth. "Oh, gosh, no. No, Kierra. I can't do that. I didn't expect that, either. I just…" She sighed. "I only checked in to make sure he wasn't doing to her what he did to me. I only wanted to make sure she was okay. I know it's not my place to be in her life. I wouldn't expect that to be a thing. And now knowing that Henry is gone, I don't have to worry anymore. I know she's safe with you."

I smiled and nodded. "Yes, she is. But…I know she'd be safe with you, too, Claire."

She let out a nervous laugh as she wiped the tears from her face. "But you're her mother. I'm just a stranger."

"A stranger who gave me the greatest gift. Now, there's no pressure. If you don't want to meet her—"

She hesitated for a moment's time. "I mean…if it's okay. It can only be once. I just…" Her hands flew to her chest and she shook her head. "I just want to hug her one more time."

I understood completely.

When I thought Henry was going to kill me, when I thought my life was over, all I could think of was how I wanted to hug Ava one more time. How I wanted to wrap my arms around her and make sure she felt my love in my embrace.

"We'll come up with a game plan. We'll figure out how to make this the most comfortable situation for everyone involved."

"I'll do anything," she said. "I'll do anything to make this work."

"Okay. Good. Now…can I buy you a cinnamon muffin?"

After meeting with Claire, I headed back home to meet up with Ava and Gabriel. To my surprise, when I pulled up, I saw an archway beside the house with sparkling strings of lights all over it. Under said archway stood Gabriel who was smiling my way.

My heart began to beat faster as I realized what was happening.

I parked the car and climbed out. Each step I took in his direction felt like a step toward forever and always.

"What are you doing?" I nervously asked as I approached him.

He smiled his lazy smile and took my hand in his as I reached the arch. He kissed my palm before he spoke. "Did you know that when penguin males find their partner, they present them with a pebble? They search time and time again to find the perfect pebble to propose with. They first build a nest to make sure the foundation is good to start a family, and the final pebble the male brings is the one that ties him to his partner, making them mates for life. I searched for a long time to find the right one for you, with some help from a good friend," he said, gesturing toward Ava, who was smiling widely on the front porch.

When I turned back to face Gabriel, he was down on one knee. "Kierra, you are my penguin, and I want to build my nest with you. You're my everything. You've been the planet that I've been orbiting my whole life, even when my mind became foggy. My soul always knew you, and it called out your name every single day. You are everything I could ever dream of. An amazing woman, an amazing mother, an amazing partner, and an amazing best friend. I want you, and this, and us, for the rest of our days." He opened the ring box and I gasped at the beautiful diamond sitting in the box. "Marry me?"

I couldn't think of anything else to say except for an excited, "Yes."

I leaped into his arms and kissed him before he even had a chance to slide the ring onto my finger. He kissed me back and laughed as he tried to place the ring on.

"Yay!" Ava shouted, darting over to us to celebrate. She wrapped her arms around both of us and we all cried and hugged one another.

I couldn't believe it.

I couldn't believe that Gabriel and I had found our way back to each other again.

Out of all the wishes I'd ever wished, I was thankful that my wish for him came true.

EPILOGUE

Kierra

ONE YEAR LATER

Ava, Gabriel, and I sat outside our home, staring up at a huge tree in front of us. Stacks of lumber lay beside said tree, waiting for the build to take place for our future. A future tree house, that was. It wasn't just any tree house, though. It was a carbon copy of the one Gabriel's father built for him when he was a little boy. When his mother gave him those blueprints, I knew it was something we'd have to re-create on our property. I loved that Gabriel and Ava added a few of their own architectural ideas to the design, too.

As Gabriel sat on my left side, and Ava on my right, I held both of their hands in mine as we stared up at the sky, drunk in love with stars. I felt a burst of peace as the quietness of the night swept over us.

"He's kicking!" I said, nudging Ava in the side. She quickly turned toward me and placed her hands against my growing stomach. I was eight months pregnant and felt it through my whole body.

"Oh gosh. The dude sure has a lot of movement going on," she observed.

"Maybe he'll be a track star," Gabriel joked.

I went to laugh but a yawn came out instead.

Gabriel kissed my cheek. "Bedtime."

I agreed. "Bedtime."

He helped me stand and Ava headed off to her room for the night.

"I'm so tired," I whispered as Gabriel led me to our bedroom. "But so, so happy." My back hurt, but I was happy. Whenever I sat, I was uncomfortable, but I was happy. Whenever my sweet baby boy turned in my stomach, I was happy.

I had so much to be happy for. For Gabriel. For Ava. For my future baby boy, Elijah Gabriel Sinclair. Named after two of the best men I'd ever known.

After so many years of trials, I couldn't help but feel as if I was finally getting the one thing I thought I'd never receive—my own authentic happily ever after.

Gabriel pulled back the blankets on our bed, and after I climbed in, I collapsed into the pillows. I was beyond tired, and my feet were swollen and aching. Without me even stating that fact, Gabriel moved to the edge of the bed, took off my socks, and began massaging my feet.

I closed my eyes, feeling a level of bliss hit my soul and my sole as his thumbs circled the arch of my foot. "Thank you," I said, melting even more into my pillow.

"Always."

"How are you?" I whispered when he lay down beside me after the foot massage.

"Happy," he replied. "How are you?"

"Happy," I echoed. So, so happy. "Thank you for finding me again."

He kissed my forehead and pulled me in more, holding me so close that I was able to rest my head against his chest. "Thank you for staying this time."

As we fell asleep, I knew, come morning, I'd be just as happy as the night prior because I had everything I could ever want surrounding me day in and day out. I had laughter, I had peace, I had joy, and I had love.

This was it. This was ours. The good and the bad. The uphill battles and the downward slide. The easy days and the hard nights. We'd faced them all together, no matter what.

Gabriel Sinclair was mine, and I would always be his.

Therefore, I had no other choice but to stay by his side, to stay in his arms for the rest of forever. I was home.

Home.

I was finally home again, because of Gabriel Ayodele Sinclair.

My joy had come home.

ACKNOWLEDGMENTS

First and foremost, I'd like to thank all the women who surround me. Girlhood is everything to me, and without you all, I wouldn't have been able to create this story. Thank you for holding my hand during my dark days. You all are the loves of my life. I am nothing without women.

Secondly, I'd like to thank both of my agents, Flavia and Meire, for always helping me remember how to return to self in life and in my novels. Your leadership and guide mean the world to me.

Mary—my amazing editor at Casablanca—thank you for answering all my panicked emails about this story. I knew you could tell that this was a special one for me, so thank you for helping make it better. You are a phenomenal human being with such a gift when it comes to editing. It has been a privilege to work with you and your team.

Thank you to Sourcebooks Casablanca for giving me a platform to share Kierra and Gabriel's story. Thank you for making this so much bigger than me.

Lastly, I want to say thank you to the strong women—
which is all women. I want this to be your reminder that you
are remarkable. You are worthy of love and respect. You are
important. And if you are ever in a situation that scares you,
please know you can reach out for help to break free. Please
know that on the other side of getting help, there is a new
foundation, a blank canvas waiting for you to begin to build
again with your own blueprint.

It's never too late to start over.

You are worthy. You are strong. You are powerful.

Until next time,
—BCherry

ABOUT THE AUTHOR

Brittainy Cherry is an Amazon bestselling author who has always been in love with words. She graduated from Carroll University with a bachelor's degree in theater arts and a minor in creative writing. Brittainy lives in Milwaukee, Wisconsin, with her family. When she's not running a million errands and crafting stories, she's probably playing with her adorable pets.

Other novels by Brittainy Cherry include: *The Air He Breathes*, *Loving Mr. Daniels*, *Art & Soul*, and *The Space In Between*.

Website: bcherrybooks.com
Facebook: BrittainyCherryAuthor
Instagram: @bcherryauthor